TRUTH
IN THE NIGHT

MICHAEL McLAVERTY

POOLBEG

First published in 1952
by Jonathan Cape Ltd., London

Paperback edition published in 1986
by Poolbeg Press Ltd.,
Knocksedan House,
Swords, Co. Dublin, Ireland.

© Michael McLaverty 1952, 1986

ISBN 0 905169 72 7

The generous assistance of the Arts Council of
Northern Ireland in the publication of this book is
gratefully acknowledged.

To Dan Clarke

Cover design by Steven Hope
Printed by The Guernsey Press Co. Ltd.,
Guernsey, Channel Islands.

*Hast thy dark descending
and most art merciful then*

G.M. Hopkins

CHAPTER I

THE L-shaped row of houses above the concrete pier gathered its armful of morning sun, and on the scuffed grass in front of the doors lay a few geese as white as the gables of the houses and whiter even than the stone walls that curved across the flinty fields of the island. The geese were content in the sun and without rising to their feet they would nibble the grass that grew in reach of their necks or pausing would dab at their breasts, and the downy feathers lifting on the wind would come to rest in the crevices of walls or sailing higher would sway like flakes of snow and lighter than the breath of wind would alight on the backs of the waves that swelled to the grey sand of the shore.

A door opened and a dog rushed out, and shaking the hearth ashes from his hide he scratched at the earth to ease the night's stiffness from his limbs and leaped at the geese with a spiteful snarl. The geese struggled to their feet, and screeching and scolding they padded awkwardly over the rough road, their cries tearing across the water, the fields and the cliffs. Folding their wings they settled easily into the waves, calling now with subdued contentment as they felt the cold water wash the grit from their dry feet. They shook their tails, dipped their red beaks in the water and curved about on the out-going tide. The tide was going out fast: it was going out from the sand leaving shreds of froth like half-melted frost, it was going out clear and green over the tumbled masses of white rock, going out from the low shore at the back of the pier, and slithering through heaps of searods stripped like bone, and farther to the south it was withdrawing from the black cliffs, slipping over their gables of shadow, falling with a suck over the glossy boulders and hissing softly through the foliage of rooted wrack.

Above the cliff tops the sun cleaved through gaps in the hills, resting on the sheep, on the rabbits, and on the snails that were groping towards the shadow of stones or to clumps of grass that offered a store of cooler shade. On the loughs among the hills the sun also shone, and there amid the seclusion of the reeds the wild duck quelled the gabble of their young for they had heard the cantankerous cries of geese or the rattle of a cow's chain as it moved in the milking shed.

In a whitewashed house above one of the loughs Martin Gallagher had risen earlier than usual and having milked his cow he was now cleaning the steering wheel of a ship that he had wrought into an ornamental gate that led off the road to his house. He whistled as he worked, polishing the brass tips of the wheel and the brass boss, and with an oily rag wiping the eight spokes till they shone resin-red in the sun. He oiled the runners of the gate and on returning to the house drew out his horse and cart, and after he had rubbed black polish on the hooves of the horse he brushed them vigorously till they shone as bright as the shoes on his own feet. The previous evening he had repainted in white letters his name on the shaft of the cart and it was now dry and clean except for a midge that had wriggled itself to death on one of the letters. He picked it off with his finger-nail, and spreading a piece of clean sacking on the driving-board he was ready for the road. His dog heard the first rock of the wheel and came racing from the back of the house.

'What were you up to?' Martin said. 'I'll have to leave you behind,' and he turned and lifted a small board like the seat of a child's swing from a nail on the outside wall. The dog slunk away from him and he had to call twice before she came cringing back to him. He took the board with its short loop of rope and fastened it to her collar so that it swung loosely in front of her forepaws. 'We'll stop using the board when you stop worrying the sheep,' he said and patted her on the head to show that he wasn't vexed. She licked his hand, and when she hobbled away

8

from him he called her back and shortened the rope so that the board wouldn't strike her too roughly.

From the road he looked back, saw her lying down on the doorstep in the sun, and smiled at the way he had tamed her. He loved his house at this time of the morning with the two ash trees crouching their shoulders at the gable-end, and the smoke hunching above the blue slates and bundling off on the breast of the wind. His heart went out to it, and he did right, he told himself, to leave the city and come back to the island where he was reared. Although he was only thirty-six years of age he had had enough of wanderings. For some sixteen years he had laboured in the city and worked on a coal boat that sailed between Belfast and Whitehaven. He might still be on the coal boat but for the unexpected meanness of a friend who had stolen money from him while he slept in a lodging-house near the docks. It was that that had finally finished him with the city, and that morning when he awoke and discovered his loss he packed his belongings in a suit-case, drew his savings out of the bank, and returned to buy back the tumbled roof of a house that had belonged to his dead father, and with it five acres of land and a few hills for rearing sheep. At first the quiet of the place had unsettled him and he used to hurry from his lonely house of an evening and go to the pub in search of company he thought he'd never need. But in the pub the discontent of the young men who were bent on the city used to draw him into arguments that almost ended in a fight and he had to struggle with himself to beat down the urgency to flee once more to the city where life was not so confined as on the island. But always, when he had weighed the life of one against the other, he had discovered something to control him. There was honesty here, he told himself, honesty and truth: there was no call to lock the fowl-house of an evening or to rise early to tend the lobster-pots in case of mean thievery; there was no policeman here, and no need for one. Men did not hinder one another: they helped a neighbour with the ploughing, they would share their bulls, would help with a cow that was calving, sit up through the night with a mare in foal, or if your cow was dry they would ladle out milk to you without thought of payment. Time and again he had pondered these things as he sat his lone of an evening, and this morning as his cart knocked in the ruts of the road and the rope-reins hung slack in his hands he had reflected on them again with a burst of refreshing satisfaction.

He began to sing but seeing a net of flies dandaling above the ears of his horse he broke off the spray of an ash and tied it above her head. He jolted on, past lakes as blue as the sky and bluer than the sea that could be seen in the wedges of the hills. Overhead moved a solitary cloud and below on the land its shadow crawled, creeping over the cart, drawing its blind across the pane of a lake and rolling it up again till the water shone with the blueness of potato-spray. On approaching a hill he dismounted, threw the reins into the cart, and let the horse make her own time. At the top of the hill he saw below him the flat plain of the island, the geese in the fields, the sun-quiet houses, and the broad bay rippling in the wind. Around one house a knot of people stood on the white road and two carts were moving off. It was the Craigs leaving the island, and Martin hurried, hoping he'd be in time to carry a box or two for them on his way to the pier where he himself was to await the arrival of an orphan lad to help him with the farm.

At the back of the Craig's house he saw the old grandfather parading back and forth and paying no attention whatever to his little grandson who was shouting to him and throwing a painted ball in the air.

'So the day has come at last,' Martin hailed him and pulled up.

'It has! It has that!' the old man said, coming to the breast-high wall and resting his arms on it. 'They'll rue this day with every week that ends.'

Martin nodded in grave agreement.

'They're promising me the grand sights I'll see. They'll take me to the shipyards and they'll take me to see the tobacco made in factories. And they'll take me to see the fine churches and to see Dublin – they tell me. But there's one place they'll take me,' and his fist clawed one of the loose stones on the wall. 'They'll take me back here, in God's name, and they'll bury me with my own people. Some day soon you'll see a boat coming into the bay and a yellow coffin shining on her in the sun and on the plate of that coffin you'll see my name: Michael John Craig.'

'I wouldn't look at it like that. You'll settle down in it like many another islandman.'

'Not with my load of years! You need to give yourself to a place if you want peace out of it. I'll never do that! I've dug my grave in giving in to them. But it's done now and there's no going back on my word. The house is as bare now as the empty boat-house. There's all that's left,' and he swung his arm towards a sunny patch at the back of the house where there was a wooden box with a basin and a towel, and his razor on the window-sill above them. A white cat ran along the top of the wall and the old man fondled it, the cat rubbing her side against his watch-chain and pushing her head under his oxter. 'Will you take that cat, Martin? She'll run wild if nobody takes her. She's a great hunter.'

At that moment the little boy's ball flew over the wall and the horse shied and tumbled Martin into the cart. He scrambled to his feet and plucked at the reins, the wheels swerving and cutting into the gravel. The noise drew the boy's mother from the house but when she saw it was Martin Gallagher she looked at him coldly. She turned to her father and told him to hurry and tidy himself and brush the cat's hairs from his waistcoat.

'I'm tidy enough as it is,' he shouted, 'and if I'm not fit enough as I am you can go on without me. There's neighbours here who'd give me a corner to myself and ask nothing in return.'

'You've no right to torment us a morning like this,' the

daughter blazed at Martin. 'He was easy in his mind till you came along — you that can sit up high and mighty after making your pile in the city.'

'I made no pile,' Martin said quietly.

'You didn't buy your bit of land on the clippings of tin.'

'I bought it on hard-earned savings.'

'God increase it,' the old man said.

'Could I take a box or two down for you?' Martin said, trying to divert their talk.

'Everything's gone.'

'I could give the old man a lift.'

'He's coming with us. Drive off for God's sake,' she said with harsh impatience.

'What's that you said, Martin?' the old man asked and strained over the wall with a hand to his ear.

'Nothing, nothing,' the daughter spoke back and glared fiercely at Martin; and as Martin pulled off and the wheels crunched on the gravel he heard above the noise the old man barging and shouting at his daughter and saying that he'd not budge a foot from the land that bred him.

'It's a great pity I didn't trot past them and just bid the old man the time of day. I should have shown them I was in a hurry,' Martin said aloud to himself. But even that would have been wrong. It was better not to think of it. But he knew one thing that was certain: the old man would never be content, and in trying to change his life the daughter was changing her own and making a change for the worse. She'd never know peace of mind. There'd be nothing between them but strife and wrangling from dawn to dusk. The old man was right: 'You must give yourself!' Give yourself — that was the secret of life. Give yourself! Give yourself! He chugged at the reins and as the horse moved briskly down the hill to the pier its hoofs seemed to ring it out from the stones. From this day on he would give himself to the island, and when the lad would arrive to help him he'd do his best to make a decent home for him. He gazed seawards and saw the motor boat, far out, as black as a buoy. He drew the horse into the shade of the boat-house and sat down on the short grass overlooking the pier.

The day was fresh with clean sunshine and clipped shadows. Geese lay asleep on the warm sand, gulls stood on their own reflections on the thin lip of the tide, and in the bay a light breeze scrambled across the water with dabbles and scallops of light. There was the smell of tar from two men patching a boat, the salty fishsmell of rotting wrack, and on the point of the pier a bundle of boxes and trunks with their labels swinging in the wind. Below him among a cluster of nettles was an old can so eaten with rust you could have put your foot through it. He threw a stone at it and shivered the rust to tatters.

'So there you are! Clodding stones like a young fella,' a woman's voice broke above him.

He jerked to his feet and smiled with shy embarrassment at Vera Reilly who was holding her daughter by the hand.

'It's a wonder you didn't hail us a morning like that and give us a lift in instead of having us bursting our hearts and scalding the feet off ourselves.' She went on with an ironic smile, 'Indeed I saw you slipping past the door and not giving a look near us.'

'I didn't slip past the door. You can't expect a horse to go on its tiptoes.'

'I suppose Mary and myself would be too much of a weight for it,' she laughed and glanced at the horse in the shade of the boat-house. 'And look at it with its ash mantilla! It's a pity you didn't think of sticking its head in a veil. I never saw anyone so easy on a horse as yourself. When my poor husband was alive he used to say you'd rather pull the plough yourself.'

Mary was pushing back her wind-blown hair from her eyes and Martin smiled down at her.

'That wind's a bit of a tease,' he said.

'She doesn't comb her hair properly,' her mother said, and

13

taking a comb from her pocket she combed back her daughter's hair and tightly rearranged the clasp. 'Now run on and play yourself. We'll not be leaving till the post comes in.' Mary ran over to the pier, jumped into the air to catch a floating feather, missed it and jumped again, but the feather swung over the coping of the pier and settled out of reach on the slabby wrack. She took a ball from her pocket and began to play against the gable-end of the row of houses.

'She'll have somebody to play with in the Lower End if this lad of mine turns up this morning,' Martin said.

'A lad from an orphanage! Do you think I'll allow Mary to gallivant with somebody's . . . No, I'll not say the word — a lad that maybe never saw his own mother and doesn't know his own father. You'd no call to fetch him among decent people.'

'He may be better than most of us for all we know.'

'Keep him tethered to your own door if you think so. I'm sorry now I sold you that field at our side of the stream. My mind was distracted after Tom's death and I didn't know what I was doing. His people didn't like it when they heard what I'd done.'

'You can have it back,' he said.

'I don't want it back!' she answered, and her voice rose in spite of herself. 'I wouldn't have sold it to you if I wanted to keep it . . . You shouldn't aggravate me like this,' and she took out her handkerchief: 'I sold it to you because it was more useful to you than to me.' There was a trace of tears in her eye and he didn't know what to say to her or what to do. But at that moment the Craigs appeared on the high road leading to the pier.

'They're getting a good day for crossing,' he said.

'It's well for them to be leaving a place like this. Oh, only for the schoolmistress wanting to put Mary on for the teaching I wouldn't stay long here, I may tell you. It's their love for one another that keeps me in this dreary place.'

Martin's eyes were fastened on the black group of people that were moving slowly down the hill. The old man was in front, his grandson holding him by the hand, and behind came his daughter and son-in-law and a few neighbours with suit-cases. There was no sound of a voice from any of them, just the dull grit of their feet following their shadows on the dry road.

'If I were leaving I'd run!' said Vera. 'I'd expect nobody to give us a lift that morning. I wouldn't feel the rough stones under the shoes of my feet. I'd leave with my head held high and a smile on my face.' She suddenly caught him by the sleeve, 'What on earth made you come back here!'

His eyes never left the group that was slowly approaching.

'It's like a funeral,' she said, 'I feel I'd like to sing and cheer them along. And would you look at all the women moving out from the houses. Even the very dogs are quiet.' Mary came running from the back of the pier holding a fluttering ribbon of wrack above her head and her mother seized her by the arm and silenced her. The group moved down to the pier, where their feet grated on the gravel and their voices mumbled like a prayer. The little boy clutched his painted ball in one hand and held on to his granda by the other, but when the ball fell and bounced on the pier and rolled into the water his mother's voice could be heard shouting: 'Leave it be and hold on tight to your granda.'

The little boy clutching the wet ball was the first to go down the stone steps on to the boat; his granda, after shaking hands with all on the pier, went next and sat beside him at the stern. He lowered his head, fingered the loose skin on his neck where he had cut himself shaving, stared with a chilled emptiness at the dry boards at his feet and listened to the clop of water rising and falling among the slimy steps of the quay. The sail was unfurled and flapped above his head, and as the boat moved out he raised himself up and stood with his hat held against his breast. He looked at the women with their handkerchiefs in their hands and at the men who were silently waving their caps at him.

'Some day I'll be back among you,' they heard him say. 'Some day I'll be back among you, and that day, please God, will not be long.' He sat down and put his arm round his grandson, the boat lepping into the waves, the wrinkles in the canvas smoothing out in the wind.

'They shouldn't have dragged him away,' the women cried from the quay. 'He'll fret himself to death . . . It was cruel to take him . . . They'll rue this day . . . As sure as there is a God above they'll rue this cruel day . . . It's a pity he listened to her . . . Only for the grandson they couldn't have taken him . . . He loves that boy . . . He is his best company . . . He'll be back again never fear . . . He'll be back . . . He'll not be sitting up that day and clasping his grandson's hand . . . He'll be clasping his own and his rosary beads lapped round them . . . The men will carry him to his grave . . . He'll be at rest then and he'll be at peace amongst his own.'

The boat moved out quickly, the wind stripping her heels; and the forms of the people in the stern merged black in the distance and there was nothing to be seen only the tilt of the boat's sail and her black hulk bucking into the waves. Vera released her daughter's hand and allowed her to sit on the parapet of the pier. The people remained as they were, knotted together with the intimacy of a common sorrow, and when the motor boat came slowly in with her few passengers and her canvas bag of mail, Martin was the first to run forward to catch the mooring rope that was thrown on to the quay. His boy was on her, a thin lad with tightly drawn skin that was pinched with sea-sickness. Martin gripped his hand as he stepped ashore; his hand was icy cold and the lad smiled sickly around him and gazed at the people with a pained bewildered look.

'You'll be as right as rain when you've a cup of tea in you,' Martin said as he hurried him from the pier and hoisted him and his suit-case into the cart. He was pulling out from the side of the boat-house when he was aware that Vera Reilly had followed him.

'Do you want a lift home?' he asked her.

'No, we can walk — there'd be too much of a load on the horse . . . If there's a letter for you I'll bring it over myself.'

'There'll be no letter.'

'Well, maybe not . . . That's a fine boy you've got there,' she went on, looking up at the lad. 'He might be too fine for a windy place like this . . . You'll not hold him long I warrant you.'

To get away from her he chugged at the reins, the horse lurched forward and giving it a skelp with the rope they set off at a gallop. The boy smiled as he felt his feet jiddering on the floor-boards and he held on grimly to the seat for fear of falling. Presently the horse slowed down on a hill and the boy took a letter from his pocket and handed it to Martin. It was a letter from the orphanage and Martin learnt from it that the boy's name was James Rainey and that he was fifteen years of age; he read it aloud to himself and the boy heard for the first time that he was 'willing, honest and obedient', and that the nuns would appreciate a telegram to announce his safe arrival.

'Sit you here, James, with the horse and I'll be back in a minute,' and Martin swung over the side of the cart, cut across a field to the post-office and sent off the telegram and hurried back.

'Now,' says he, taking the reins again, 'we'll not be long hitting the road.' He questioned him about his journey and told him that he'd soon get used to the boats and the sea and that in no time at all he'd feel as much at home as a sheep on the hill or a wild duck in the lough.

Nearing the Craigs' house he saw the last smoke from the last fire struggling weakly from the chimney. He stopped and jumped down from the cart. The white cat was on the window sill but as he tried to catch her she fled from him and squeezed herself under the garden gate and hid among the dockens and nettles. There was a new padlock on the door, a thin bit of soap on the window sill, and through the bare pane he saw the

17

tracks of a brush on the floor and its sweepings smouldering among the ashes on the hearth. He got into the cart again, handed the reins to the lad and set off into the face of the sun. He was silent for a while as he thought of the old man and of the first signs of decay that would settle themselves on the empty house: the padlock would rust in the salty winds, the starlings poke holes in the thatch, and the square chimney loosen and decay like a blackened tooth. Nothing decays like an empty house, he had heard said, and nothing shows its reward like a well-cared one.

He sighed and patted the lad on the knee: 'Never fear, James, but we'll have the brave times together . . . What's mine is yours . . . I've a handy wee boat and some fine evening we'll give the fish a flake or two with the rods . . . I'm making a model yacht and the two of us will carry off the first prize in the lough some fine Sunday.'

'Have you a dog?'

'I have, Jamesy, but she's doing a bit of hard labour just now. She'd worry sheep if you didn't watch her and if she doesn't mend her ways we'll have to get rid of her and get a pup from the lighthouse.' He turned round on the seat and with his arm on the boy's shoulder he pointed out the lighthouse standing like a bandaged leg on top of the cliffs.

Martin began to whistle and James sat closer to him. They dipped into a hollow and turning a bend on the road the horse moved smartly for there in front of them was the house, standing clean and solid in the sun, the brass tips of the gate shining, and the dog with the board hanging from her neck, and her tail wagging with the slow rhythm of pleasurable recognition.

'We're home at last, Jamesy,' he said, 'and I'll not be long livening up the fire and boiling the kettle for the tea.' He took the board from the dog's neck and the dog whining with delight jumped up on him, raced among the hens, ran back again and sniffed at Jamesy's leg and followed them into the kitchen.

CHAPTER II

VERA, holding a letter for Martin in her hand, shoved her way through the crowd around the post-office, and as she drew near the quay where groups of women still lingered talking in low voices about the Craigs she swung past them with a silent nod, and as they ceased their talk she felt their eyes levelled at her and her young daughter. She hurriedly turned the corner of the row of houses and being immediately out of sight of the staring women she took her time, picking her steps on the white shingly road that edged the sea. She knew full well that the women would fault her for hurrying past them but she didn't care a groat what they'd say or what they wouldn't say. She did what was right and proper and what her own nature bade her do: for what would be the use, she told herself, in joining them and listening to their sighful lamentations over the Craigs and the mouthfuls of spite and grudgery they would hurl at the old man's daughter for wrenching him away from his own fireside and breaking up the old home. All that womanish talk would make her flinch in silence or maybe force her to blaze up in defence of what she felt in her heart was right. But anyway, she was sure, these island women gossiped differently among themselves than they did with her. She came among them thirteen years ago as a stranger from the mainland and a stranger among them she'd always remain. It was true she had married one of them, and although she had seldom gone to any church she became a Catholic to please him, and in their first year of married life had borne him a child. But even then they had never received her warmly, and to this day her own mother-in-law was as much a tangle to her as a bundle of hard twisted wrack you'd find high up on a summer's beach. Tom, when he was alive, had often told her it was her own fault for feeling

19

strange among his own people; and that she had imagined unfriendliness where none existed and that she was too proud to call into the island houses. 'Deed that was true! — as if she'd bow and scrape to them like somebody who had lost their shame and in losing that had lost their personal pride. Wasn't she glad that she lived in the lonely Lower End of the island, for it helped to cut her off and preserved her from having too many neighbourly callers. Her nearest neighbour was this Martin Gallagher who had unexpectedly returned to the island; and although she resented the first few months of his arrival with his endless hammerings at the roof and the sheds, and the sound of his melodeon in the evenings, yet the light in his window after Tom's death was, she must admit, in some way a comfort to her. But it was strange she could never understand why he returned and she could never discover what he did in his years away from it. Tom had told her that the years in the city hadn't changed him one bit. He was quiet and calm, and neither Tom nor herself could ever rouse him or get him to talk much about himself. But some day she'd loosen his tongue and find out why he left the city and why he came back to this rugged slab of loneliness. It was annoying to have a neighbour as dumb as an old horse and as cold and distant with you as any shy islander that had never left its four corners. And she had never known him to ask you a question twice — he'd never coax you to do anything against your will. If he asked you to take a lift in the cart and you refused — well, that was the end of it. He resembled no man she ever knew. But maybe he was different if you happened to meet him with the neighbours who were part of his own blood. To find out what he was thinking was like putting your fingers in a spider's web — it broke in your hands and left you nothing but emptiness.

'Mother, what are you thinking about?' her daughter broke in on her. 'You haven't spoke a word since we left the post-office.'

'I'm thinking of nothing, Mary. It's the heat of the day. Run down to the rocks and gather sea-flowers for yourself.'

And this letter — and she looked at the envelope in her hand after Mary had run down to the warm rocks.

'There'd be no letter!' he had said to her. It was true she had seldom seen the postman calling his way and it could all be that he had no relations living and had made no friends in all his years in the city and on the sea.

She glanced furtively around her and then at Mary bent over the tufts of sea-pinks that coloured the rocks. She held the envelope up to the sun and saw the shadowy fold of a letter and a blurred collection of words. She stretched the envelope tightly and peered at it for a few minutes, then once more she held it up between her and the sun, tantalized by the imposition of inky words. She scrutinized the postmark that circled the stamp but it, too, was a smudged, inky ring.

For all she knew, or anyone knew, he might be married and had separated from his wife. That'd be a nice neighbour for you! She halted on the road, feeling a hot flush on her cheeks and hearing nothing only the quickened pulse of her own blood. Once more she stared at the envelope, put her finger under the flap, but at that moment Mary came running up with a bunch of sea-pinks.

'What's their names, mother?' she asked.

'Sea flowers.'

'What kind of sea flowers?'

'I don't know. I wasn't born and bred here, and I'm not a walking encyclopaedia. Ask your teacher and she'll tell you. Run on in front and stop chattering, I'll overtake you at the mill.'

The sun reflected strongly from the limestone walls and its warm braids of heat swathed round her like a woollen scarf. She opened her coat and let it swing loosely to her step. She stowed the letter in her pocket and hurried after her daughter. Time and again she stumbled on the loose stony road, but at the

21

bay near the mill she sat on the short grass and took off her shoes, grateful now for the coolness that aired her smarting feet. Mary laid the sea-pinks on the grass but her mother seeing their stems shiny with sweat bade her hide them from the sun and go and paddle her feet in the pools. She looked around and then took off her own knitted stockings, and seeing the web of stitchmarks on her legs she smoothed them with her fingers and damned Martin Gallagher for not having the decency to wait and give them a lift home. She went down over the hot beachstones to join her daughter, and as she swirled her feet at the sandy edge her own mind swirled with the thought of how best to open the letter. She raised her head to the mill with its old wheel rusted by stillness, its solitary door closed, and a donkey standing in the shade cast by the walls. There was no one about. She could easily let the letter fall into the water, prize open the wet flap, and seal it up again. That would satisfy her, and she could tell him it fell out of her pocket when she was wading.

Mary was in front of her, giving a jump of gleeful fright to escape the incoming waves from rising over her knees. Her mother followed after her and without looking behind dropped the letter on the water. For a moment or two it lay floating, then a wave covered it and it slid and turned in the swaying movement of the water.

'Oh, Mary, the letter fell into the water,' she shouted, and allowed her daughter to see her lift it up and shake the drops from it. She carried it to the bank, poked her finger under the sodden flap but it tore, and her face reddened. She threw it from her and stared at it with a baffled expression of guilt and defeat. Her failure eased her. No, it wouldn't be right and proper to do the like. What possessed her even to think of doing that! She was a fool to carry the letter for him. It was to save the postman the journey in the heat of the day that made her do it — nothing else. She was too considerate, and in future she'd not be postman or message boy for anyone. And anyway when she came to think of it what did she care about Martin Gallagher. She was always independent and that's the way she'd remain until the day came when she and Mary could leave this place for ever.

The letter dried in the sun, became stiff and creased with the salt water. She called Mary to her and with a handkerchief dried her legs for her. She put her arm round her and squeezed her to her side.

'Mary, my little girl, work hard at school and be something worthwhile. It'd break my heart to think you'd be stuck in this sock of an island for all the days of your life. Did you see the Craigs today and young Timmy with his painted ball all going away. That's what I want you to do. Get away as soon as you can. You're twelve now and in a year or two you'll be made a monitress in the school and later you'll do your examination for the training college. Are you listening to me? And that'll be the day that you'll leave and I'll leave with you. Get away from this place. Won't you do that? Promise me you'll do that.'

'I will, mother. I'll go away. But why don't we go now like the Craigs?'

'Go now!' her mother almost shouted, and after a long pause added: 'We can't go now — that's all. You can't leave your teacher that's so kind to you.'

It had often occurred to her to leave after Tom's death but she always dismissed the thought, afraid to follow it to its confusing and indefinite conclusion when all was said and done. She couldn't go now, for she had no place to turn to. Her own father and mother with three grown-up children were still alive in the town across the bay but she was determined not to go back there to share their poverty and the stuffy congestion of the little kitchen. It was to escape from that life that she had married Tom. She had worked in a shop that overlooked the quay where the islanders moored their boats, and when Tom came in to her to buy tobacco they used to have a long chat together. Then one stormy evening Tom was forced to remain

23

over and as they wandered together about the cliffs above the town they saw across the eight miles of water the island lighthouse wheeling its powerful spokes of light through the sky. She would never have agreed to marry him only her mistress had given her her notice and she dreaded returning to the back of the town to the cheerless street where the water lay green in the cobbles outside and where there was nothing, she thought, but flies and a finch in a cage and old men and old women seated on chairs taking the sun. And then she was the eldest of the family and being the eldest she had to take care of the rest. She had married then and cut herself off from all attachments to the place, and even when she visited the mainland she never called to see them. No, she'd never go back to that life: far better to stay where she was and rot her heart with longing, than go back to that cramped place and sour and wither her life before its time.

'Mary,' she said, and squeezed her so fiercely that she left the imprint of her coat button on the child's cheek.

'Yes, mother?'

'Come now. The letter is dry.'

'Martin won't be vexed?'

'Vexed — I like that! In future he can fetch his own letters or sit on his heels till the postman brings them to him. Often when you want to do someone a good turn it turns out to be ill.'

'Let me bring it to him. He has sweets in a bowl and he always gives me some.'

'A big girl like you shouldn't be looking and begging for sweets. You've money of your own in the broken jug on the dresser.'

'But you told me to put it by for my Confirmation frock.'

'We'll see. Come on or you'll get a headache with that sun.'

They got up slowly and on turning their backs to the sea they reached the road that wound between the hills of the Lower

End. Here the heat drowsed in the windless hollows and the grasshoppers sizzled madly in the clumps of heather. Vera took off her coat and as she draped it over her arm she thought of the selfishness of Martin Gallagher·driving home in an almost empty cart and leaving them to foot it. Someday she'd let him know what she thought of him!

Here and there they gathered withered heather or charred whin bushes that had been burnt to allow fresh grass to elbow its way up for the sheep. A semi-blind man Mick Devlin came along pulling at his donkey which drew a slipe heaped with dried mountain sods. The slipe had no wheels, and the heels of its metal-covered shafts screeched on the stones, setting Vera's teeth on edge.

'Good day to you,' Mick shouted when their shadows crossed him. 'Come up to hell you! Divil the stop you'll get till you've the load at the gable-end. You'll excuse me, Missus, but I daren't stop. There's nothing he likes better than a good chat with somebody.'

Vera and Mary stood off the road, and Mary put her fingers in her ears till the donkey, with its hooves tinkling on the stones, had slid its load over the hill. Vera smiled to herself: he was doing more work than the donkey, and she recalled a day at the quay when the priest had reprimanded him for abusing a beast that had once carried Christ into Egypt and Mick had told him if Christ had been on his donkey He wouldn't be at the end of his journey yet.

They reached the path to Martin's house and pushed open the ornamental gate, its brass-tipped spokes warm to the touch. Outside the closed door were four new lobster pots with their freshly tarred ropes shining in the sun. Vera rapped twice before lifting the brass latch and entering the kitchen. Martin was placing an unpainted yacht in the deep ledge of the window and he turned round dusting the shavings from his jersey for he had been planing the hull. The cleanliness of his house struck her with an undefined envy as she glanced rapidly at the recently plastered walls, unpainted and unpapered, and the furniture raised up on little blocks of wood.

'I've a letter for you,' she said, 'and Mary there can tell you what happened.'

'Come here, girl,' he said, and Mary stood between his knees and he put his arm round her shoulder. 'Tell me the whole story.'

She told him how the letter had fallen into the sea and was covered by the waves. Vera handed it to him and he glanced at it and tossed it unconcernedly on the table and asked Mary to sing a song for him.

'Is your new boy in the room?' she asked.

'He's out with the dog but the dog won't follow him. Don't mind about him. Give us the "Castle of Dromore",' and he squeezed her gently, and sang the first line with her. Vera put her coat over a chair and went to a shelf at the side of the fireplace where Martin's books were arranged according to size and not to contents: the tall ones on the inside descending gradually to a small pocket dictionary on the outside. She saw books on Home Carpentry, Model Yacht Building, novels by Zane Grey and P. C. Wren; Conrad's *Typhoon*, *Nigger of the Narcissus*, and *The Shadow Line*, Melville's *Moby Dick*, novels by Jack London, and an edition of Thomas à Kempis's *Imitation of Christ* and poems of Robert Burns. She lifted a book and as she turned the pages her eyes glanced at Martin, at his blue jersey fitting tight to his body, his black uncombed hair, and the anchor tatooed to his right forearm. He was admiring Mary's green frock and counting the black windmills knitted into the skirt.

'The wind will blow you away some day,' he said to her.

'My granny knit that,' Mary said, holding in her hand a fistful of caramels.

'Your granny has plenty of time on her hands now that she has retired from teaching in the school,' Vera put in. 'And anyway I think the frock's too childish for a girl of your age.' She

26

pulled her blouse tightly in at the waist and lifted *The Shadow Line*. 'What kind of a book is this? It looks short.'

'It is short,' Martin said. 'It's a tale of the sea. There's no women in it.'

'What kind of an unnatural book would that be?'

He went over beside her and as his fingers tapped along the rows of books his shoulder touched hers; she did not withdraw but looked shyly at him.

'I don't believe I've one would suit you. But look through them yourself. That one, *Moby Dick*, has no women in it either,' and he went back to his chair.

'You've a strange collection, I must say,' she said with dry contempt, pulling over the cretonne curtain that draped the shelves.

'Come, Mary, and leave Mister Gallagher to his work.'

'I'm grateful to you for bringing the letter.'

'By all accounts you were in no great hurry to get it.'

There was a timid rap at the door and Jamesy came in. His eyes were bright with excitement and his pale face was flushed. He hung his head with embarrassment and moved towards Martin.

'These are our neighbours,' Martin said. 'Shake hands with them; they'll not take a bite out of you.'

'As I said before, it is cruel to bring a growing lad to a place like this. What is there here for anyone?'

'Dammit all, there's plenty here,' Martin said. 'I know what I'm talking about. Through that window at the front you can see the sun rise and in the evening through the back window you can see it set — A man that can have the sun all day for company should be a contented man. We have decent neighbours and a man can get more than enough to live on by the work of his own hands.'

'You talk like the exile's return. But wait till your hunkered at the fire for a whole winter and you'll wonder if the sun hasn't rolled out of the sky. That's all right for a travelled man like you, but that poor boy will want some more excitement than fishing for lobsters or hunting the raven. He'll rue it in a few years. The sun's shining and it's summer but the winters are dark and rough!'

'That's for him to say. I'll not hold him against his going. He hasn't come to a penal settlement.'

As he watched them go down the path he told Jamesy not to pay heed to what she was saying, but the lad only nodded his head, ruffling the dog's neck and touching its belly with his toe as it rolled on the floor. Vera came back again and asked for a few matches in case the fire would be dead out on her, and as he opened the matchbox she saw that the letter still lay untouched on the table. From the window he watched her swing through the gate and hurry off down the road. He turned and opened the letter. It was stiff and crinkled with the salt water and inside was a note from the orphanage and the boy's baptismal certificate. He saw the boy's name, his mother's name, the sponsor's name, and in the space for the father's name there was a stroke of a pen. The note said that the certificate would be needed when James would be going forward for Confirmation. Martin put it carefully in his pocket, and sitting down to light his pipe he asked Jamesy how long he had been in the orphanage and if he could remember his father and his mother.

'My mother used to call and bring me sweets but then she went away to work in England a long time ago and I haven't seen her since and I forget what she was like.'

'And did your father ever call to see you?'

'My mother told me he died when I was three months old.'

'You'll like this place, never fear,' Martin said. 'But if you ever want to leave you'll come and tell me straight. I don't want you to be fretting your soul away in a place you don't like. Don't heed what Vera Reilly says. You'll find she's a good neighbour for all her talk.'

He brought him out to the back of the house, and together they inspected the byre, the stable, and the two sheds for the fowl, and from where they stood they looked down into a hollow where a stream flowing into a lake marked the boundary between Martin's land and Vera's land. They saw her fine slated house tucked under the oxter of a hill, and as the smoke rose straight from the chimney they saw it reach the summit of the hill only to be met by a slight wind that shook it back into the hollow again. They walked over the hills, the dog running after rabbits and the sheep with their lambs bounding stiffly away to the rock-heads. High over the cliffs they watched two ravens wheel about in the sunny air, somersault and glide, shoot up and curve out towards the sea, then in again, colliding in the air, tumbling and twirling, the male flying for a while on its back and then righting itself to skim below the cliffs, its huge outspread shadow causing the sheep to bleat. This cliff and patch of sky they had won for themselves — and no gull or puffin or diminutive wren was to be seen.

'Someday we'll trap the pair of them and their whole family,' Martin said. 'That's if we're able. They're a crafty bird. My father used to say when he failed to catch them: "The wisdom of the raven is as wise as the wisdom of man!" They beat him, Jamesy, but they'll not beat us,' and he told how when he was a young lad he saw a live ewe with her eyes pecked out by the ravens and her two lambs hacked to pieces at her feet. 'That's the kind of thief a raven is. But I must say I haven't much to say against the behaviour of that pair. They've stolen a few ducks' eggs when they lay away among the rocks but that's all I know of.'

The dog looked up at the birds and barked, and when the ravens had flown off and settled on a hill about a quarter of a mile away she scraped at the ground with her forepaws and brushed against the prickly whin bushes, scratching her sides with them, whining with delight and eating blades of grass.

'When you see her carrying on like that it's a sure sign of rain,' Martin said. 'But a drop or two of rain will do good for there's not much growth in the potatoes or corn.'

They saw Vera come from her house with two buckets, pass down a path at the side of her field, and cross the stream by a plank bridge that led to the spring well.

'There's a job for you, Jamesy,' Martin smiled. 'Run down and fill the buckets for her.' The sleeves of her blouse were rolled back, and the sun shone on her bare arms and on the V at her neck.

'I don't think she'd let me,' Jamesy said, 'and anyhow I'd be afraid of her.'

Martin laughed: 'She doesn't mean the one half of what she says — women are all like that. Wait till you're here a while and she'll be wanting you to run to the shop for her messages. Indeed I wouldn't be surprised if she'd take you from me', he joked. 'Sure she has nobody to help her in the fields except young Mary.'

CHAPTER III

I F it were raining heavily in the mornings Vera roused Mary
at the usual time, for she realized that on wet mornings there
would be only a few children present in the school and the
mistress could then give Mary more of her time. And on wet
mornings she always accompanied her in case she would delay
unnecessarily on the road and arrive in a cold school as soaked
as a bundle of thrown-out clothes. She would put a raincoat over
her head, and Mary would stand under its tent-like folds and
with an arm round her mother's waist they would set off through
the driving rain. The mother took the windward side, holding
out a flap of the coat like a protecting wing, and the rain pitting
on it with remorseless fury afforded the child a mysterious sense
of forbidden comfort; and as they slapped along the road she
would listen to the rain pecking at the coat like a flock of birds
or she would glance now at her own feet, now at her mother's,
watching the grit gathering on the toes of their shoes only to be
washed off again by a stumbling fall of water from the coat. The
white stones on the road would be scoured as clean as new-laid
eggs, and the water running at the sides of the road would plait
itself like her own hair or in the gravelly places rib out like
the fronds of a fern. She loved these mornings, and pushing her
head out for a moment a rush of noise would whorl about her
ears like a shout and she would gaze through the fabric of rain at
the milky blur on the sea and the hills. Her head would be
tucked in again under the winged comfort, and by glancing sideways at the dripping walls of the road or feeling the stiff trudge
of their feet on a hill she would guess their progress and await
with reluctance the final lift of the coat, and feel the cold
surrounding air as a young nestling when its mother has flown
off. Inside the porch of the school the coat would be shaken and

31

hung on a peg and she would be told not to forget it on her way home, and then the two ribbons on her hair would be teased and smoothed and she would disappear through the door that led into the one-roomed school.

On leaving her Vera would call to see the child's grandmother who lived nearby. She hated these calls for at no time could she sit among Tom's people and feel her own mood spread out from her and merge with his own mother's or his sister Sarah's or with the sullen mood of his own brother Pat. She was always defensively withdrawn, and time and again she had to strengthen her patience to smother the quarrelsome feeling they aroused in her. Tom's people were kind to her but, if they were, it was for Mary's sake and not for hers. Weren't they tired of asking her to come up and live with them; and she was sure it wasn't out of any love for her that suggested that — it was her child, Tom's child, that they sought to win from her, and month after month she had to manœuvre against them by warning Mary to hurry home from school and not to be bothering her granny. It was true that they supplied her with butter, with meal, or with a bit of fresh meat if they happened to kill a lamb, but if they did she had never asked for these things and she could, if put to it, get along without this deep-meaning assistance.

This morning her mood was not of the friendliest: only yesterday she had occasion to chase that James Rainey fellow from the road where he was talking to Mary and distracting her from her work; and she knew, too, what answer would rise immediately to the lips of Tom's people if they heard of it: 'Let Mary stay here for a while and she'll grow away from him.' No, she wouldn't have that, and what's more she'd take her own way and her own time of getting rid of Martin Gallagher's nobody!

She climbed up the path to the Reilly's fine-slated house. She stepped into the porch, cleaned her feet on the mat, and opened the kitchen door and looked in.

'Are you not coming any farther?' the grandmother said from

her armchair at the side of the fire. 'Come on, Vera, and rest yourself till that shower slackens.'

Vera walked into the wide kitchen and sat on the sofa with her back to the window. The old woman with a black knitted scarf round her head was feeding the fire with withered heather that lay bundled at her feet. There was no sound in the house except for the blaze and flit of the heather and the rumbles of a pot hanging by a chain above the fire. The blaze reflected in the woman's eyes as she bent over, preoccupied with her task. Vera eyed her and waited for her to speak. She sensed something cold and unfriendly in the eyes that persistently turned to the blazing flitter of twigs. It discomfited her but whatever it was she was content to wait for its slow unravelling, and she sat erect, stiffening herself for what would come.

'The morning has turned out bad,' the old woman said. 'It was fresh and sunny when we were rising for Mass.'

'It's well for people who live within a stone's throw of the chapel.'

'It is,' the old woman said slowly, 'it is indeed,' and she lifted a bit of heather, wrenched off a bushy twig, and instead of shoving it under the pot she swept the grit from around her feet into the well of the hearth.

'God forgive us but we don't make enough use of that,' the old woman went on.

'Of what?' Vera said with mock innocence, and she crossed her legs, staring with exasperation at the old woman as she brushed and re-brushed the flagstones. 'Have you dropped a pin or something?' Vera added, and there was a certain peevishness in her voice that made it more of a challenge than a question.

'Within the shadow of the chapel, as you say. Indeed that's true, and we don't make enough use of that — God forgive us. You're right, Vera, we should be up and out on a fine morning, praying on our knees. They that live in the shadow of the chapel will have a hard judgment in the next world,' and she pushed

33

the twig under the pot, and in the blaze that followed, the wooden lid rose up and frothy water slavered down the sides and sizzled on the coals.

'Will I lift it off for you?' Vera said.

The old woman didn't answer her: 'It's only a few potatoes for the hens. It was Tom made that wooden lid. God be good to his kindly soul. He left many things behind him and when you come on them in odd places you think of him. It's a wholesome thing for a man to leave parts of his handiwork behind him. It makes you offer a prayer for his poor soul.'

The rumbling in the pot grew louder and a chilly sound of rain gravelled against the window. Vera folded her hands on her lap, unfolded them again, and turned the wedding ring on her finger. Before long she might know what was at the bottom of the old woman's mind. Why doesn't she speak out straight and say what she has to say without hanging her head and brushing at that infernal flagstone!

'Mary grows liker him every day that passes,' the old woman said.

'Many's a one thinks she's like me. She's working hard these evenings at her books.'

'A lot of good that'll do her — her legs are as thin as that potstick. If she hasn't her health she has nothing.'

That's queer talk for a woman that taught for over thirty years in the school herself, thought Vera, as the old woman stretched over to the fire, raised the handle of the lid and balanced it on the lip of the pot.

'Many another man would have left a nail sticking out of that lid. But Tom didn't do that. He made a handle — a good smooth handle to fit the biggest hand. Tom was always thoughtful. He was always thinking of others and seldom gave thought to himself.'

'That's true.'

'It's a pity there's not more like him in this patch of country.

34

He was too good for this world. God takes the good away young. Poor Tom!'

A wet brightness swept into the kitchen and for the first time the old woman's gaze rested on Vera, and Vera flinched from the deep look of puzzled sorrow that confronted her.

She stood up and turned round to the window: 'I think I'll hit the road again. The rain's over and the sun is struggling out.'

'What's your hurry? Rest yourself till Sarah and Pat come in from the fields. They'll not be long now.'

But, as if she hadn't heard her, Vera moved to the door and the old woman grasping the arms of the chair hoisted herself to her feet, and joined her in the porch where they stood looking down over the road to the wet fields and the sea with its heaving load of sunlight. There was a sound of a river tumbling over stones, and from the drenched bushes that hung over it a wren was singing, flinging out its song in one breath, and then without a pause winding it up and unreeling it once more. The old woman looked towards the chapel with its granite walls polished with rain.

'There were only a few people out at Mass this morning, Vera.'

'You couldn't blame them. Isn't it enough for anyone who lives far afield to go on a Sunday.'

'You don't know what day is this?' the old woman said, looking straight at Vera. Vera didn't answer her, nor could she collect her thoughts before that steady soul-reading gaze.

'It's the twenty-first day of June — now you know?' and the old woman rested her hand on Vera's shoulder. 'How did you forget, daughter? And it was a morning like this two years ago that he died — wet and fresh and the sun struggling free.'

Vera's face reddened. To please the old woman she should have cried but her tears would be insincere and she would not shed them. At least she'd be honest with herself, for to be dis-

35

honest in sorrow was the greatest dishonesty of all. She felt no anger with herself. It was that James Rainey, she was sure, who caused her forgetfulness — thinking how she could get rid of him and his company, all for Mary's sake.

'There's many a way of remembering Tom than by hurrying to Mass on his anniversary,' she excused herself. 'He wouldn't have wanted me to do that and bring out the child in the wet or leave her in the house alone. Tom had sensible thought for everyone when he was alive and I'm sure he has the same consideration for us now that he's dead.'

The old woman still kept a hand on her shoulder, and Vera felt the hard fingers press on her soft flesh.

'Listen to me, child,' the old woman said, 'I heard Pat say that if the day holds good he'd go down to mould your potatoes. You'll not say anything to him, Vera; not say that you forgot about Tom's anniversary. He would take it ill, so he would. You and Pat are the ones that miss him most. Pat and Tom grew up together and it would bruise his heart if you tell him you let the anniversary slip away from you unnoticed.'

'Sure I could get Martin Gallagher to mould them for me. He has plenty of loose time on his hands since he got that strap from the orphanage.'

The old woman raised her hand from Vera's shoulder and went on as if she hadn't noticed the strangeness in these words.

'Pat will be down today for sure. That sun will hold its strength and Mary can get a sail down with him in the cart when he's going. Like a good girl say nothing to Pat that would hurt him.'

Vera didn't answer her. She knew her own mind and she knew full well what she'd say if Pat steered the talk to Tom's anniversary.

'Goodbye, I must be off now,' she said and walked abruptly out of the porch. On reaching the road she knew it would please the old woman if she turned towards the chapel but she didn't do it. She halted, her back to the house, stretched out her hand as if feeling for spits of rain, and then quickly and smartly she turned left while behind her in the porch she was conscious of the old eyes upon her, condemning her, puzzled and defeated by this strange and perverse behaviour. There would be tears of sorrow, of anger, of bewilderment forming in the eyes now, and once inside in the quiet of the house she would go on her knees and pray that this stony heart would be changed to one of living flesh.

The old woman would never understand her, she was sure of that. She had acted truly and it wasn't pride or anger at being caught with such a bad memory that forced her to do what wouldn't please—it was her own honest nature that bade her do it. She didn't give a snap of her fingers for the whole batch of them—and even if they were kind to her she knew the deep plan that was behind that! It was Mary they wanted — Mary who was the living image of their own flesh and blood!

How often had she pleaded with Tom to leave the island and how often had he put her off by saying that a complete wrench like that would kill his mother. And now he was two years dead and his mother as supple and as smart as a mountainy goat, and ready always to offer advice and would, if she could, mould other people's ways of living to her own. 'But they'll not change mine,' Vera said aloud to herself, 'they might as well try to change the tides in the sea or dig a hole in the surface of the water!'

Wasn't it well Tom had the good sense to leave her the bit of farm in the hollow, for in having that she had the right end of the rope. In ways she was like an old bush harried by the winds, pulled this way and that, and not allowed to grow up in its own way and its own time. Day after day she felt herself being bent and twisted into island ways — ways that she, in her deepest heart, despised. They were striving to win the child from her, and this lapse in her memory of Tom would strengthen and quicken their strides to do that. But they'd fail — where you have honest determination, there you've courage and strength.

Within an hour or so a scene would take place in that kitchen she had just left. She saw it all: Pat and Sarah would come back from the fields and find their mother with a handkerchief squeezed in her fist and her rosary beads on her lap. There'd be a sharp silence for a minute as Pat and Sarah would take off their wet coats, shake them at the door and drape them over the backs of chairs near the fire.

'You're strange this morning, mother. What ails you?'

'A great deal ails me — to think that a daughter-in-law of mine could be so heartless.' Weightily and pinchingly the words would drop from her, one by one; and she would unfold in the dreary silence that it wasn't sickness that had kept Vera from coming out to Mass on Tom's anniversary. 'It was her bad memory — she forgot. She forgot! She told me so to my very face — as brazen as you like.'

'Forgot! How could she ever forget our Tom!'

The words would swing slowly again, as slowly and surely as the pendulum of a clock, and each word, each gesture, each movement that she had presented to the old woman would be relived and acted for them. And then silence again as Pat or Sarah would stare out of the window.

'She's not fit, mother, to look after Tom's child. We'll have to do something about that. I always knew Tom was wrong to marry a stranger. And to think he even left her that patch of land in the hollow.'

'It's God's will, Pat. We can pray for her.'

'And bide our time.'

'She'd marry again if she'd get the chance — that's my opinion of her, mother. She'd marry Martin Gallagher if I'm not mistaken.'

As Vera reflected on these things, an impassioned urgency leapt out from her in a reckless laugh and she found herself clenching her fists in her resolve not to budge one bit from the attitude she had taken. They would all bend to her ways before she would ever think of yielding to theirs. In a few years' time she would be able to show them what she thought of the farm in the hollow and what she thought of this lump of rocky desolation where there was nothing free and fresh but the swooping of the winds and the burl of the tide. She knew one thing: Mary would stand by her mother and stand by her books and her schooling — those things would free her, and in freeing her would free her own mother! But she must be careful not to let her get too friendly with that James Rainey fellow. Martin was all right in his own way, only he needed a piece of manly sense and not be giving so much of his time to his melodeon and to the craze of building and sailing model yachts. The priest had little else to occupy his mind when he organized that sport — it's only a sport for children and not for grown-up men. Indeed, over the head of them, they'd let the land go to the seeding whins and to the bracken. Hadn't she often seen Tom labouring at yachts when it would have suited him better to be labouring in the fields.

The sun came out strong, and the road in front of her began to dry. A light breeze flung the raindrops from the drooping ears of corn, and from the bean fields there came to her a heavy sweetish smell. There was no doubt about it now — the day would grow out fine. Pat would be down in the afternoon and she'd better call at the shop and get a loaf or two of bread. She wasn't going to bake bread on the griddle a warm day like that. Not if the bishop himself were coming would she stand over a hot fire and sweat the face off herself watching bread. And if Pat doesn't like shop-bread let him, in future, bring his own bread with him in a can.

She came out of the shop with two loaves of bread wrapped up in a newspaper. And what would be wrong, she thought, in asking Martin Gallagher to run the plough up a few drills for

39

her. He wouldn't expect payment — many a day she had given him eggs when his own hens weren't laying.

In the hollow near the house Martin's dog barked at her from the hill and she saw James Rainey come to the door and go inside again: 'It's nobody,' he'd say, 'it's just Vera Reilly coming back after leaving Mary at the school.'

Yes, nobody! She supposed that's how she was named between them. Nobody! With her toe she pushed open the gate that led to her house, and flinging down a bundle of faggots that she had gathered she left the loaves on the window sill and searched in her pocket for the key of the door. She couldn't find it and she scanned the ground at her feet and the path to the gate until she suddenly realized that she had left it in the raincoat that was now hanging in the draughty porch of the school. She vainly tried the latch and went round to the back where one of the windows was propped open with an old boot-brush. She lifted out the brush and let the window fall down. 'I can't get in,' she said aloud to herself, 'and I can't stay out here till the end of schooltime. And there's one thing certain, I'm not going to drag myself back there and face the old woman again.' To halt the making of an abrupt decision she withdrew to her patch of garden and sat on a seat under the tremulous shade of a few wind-bent poplars.

Here she was at rest, at rest from the inquisitive questionings of the old woman and from the thought of the key that was lying in the damp pocket of the old raincoat. With her hands on her lap, her black shiny hair parted in the middle, her pale face and long lashes, she looked like a convalescent exhausted by the sun. Where she sat she was sheltered from any wind from the sea, and around her was the silence of the garden, the sun warming the loose stone walls and the vegetable beds marked off by alternate white stones and black. Two ropes from a child's swing hung from one branch of an ash and near it were stone slabs holding pieces of broken mirror, bits of delph and withered flowers — Mary's playground; and as she gazed dreamily around it she thought it was a pity she hadn't had more children, even one or two more. But that like many another thing had been denied her — and it wasn't her fault. And it was strange, when she came to think of it, that a fine bodied man like Martin Gallagher hadn't married and he so fond of children — look at the affection he has for Mary and the affection he has for that unknown scrap of an orphan, James Rainey. There's surely something strange in his nature, some twist or blemish that has made him the lonely man he is. She herself was alone with a loneliness dried of a man's love, a loneliness wrenched with regret, a loneliness that could never be satisfied with a lonely life like his.

She lifted a lump of clay from the seat and crumbled it with her fingers, and breathing the damp odour from the languorous folds of the drying soil she crushed back the dark thwartings of her nature, reclined against the wooden back of the seat, and looked at the slow rise and fall of her breast. It was here she had often come to nurse Mary when she was a baby and often on these occasions Tom had come and sat near her, usually sand-papering a board, filling the air with a sweet smell of wood, covering the earth at their feet with a dust like scattered meal, content that she was content, and Mary nuzzling loudly at her breast. 'That was the only happy year I had in this place,' she said, and drove it instantly from her mind, watching now the swallows streel across the garden and cling with outstretched wings on the sunny gable where they had their nest. A robin alighted on the swing but as she turned to look at it it flew off, setting the swing in gentle motion.

'This won't do,' she sighed to herself. She had to make the dinner and the beds; she had to feed the fowl and have everything ready if Pat should come on his errand.

She got up, and without coming to any decision she went over to Martin's and found him seated outside on an empty sack putting tarred rope on some new lobster creels. She told him what had happened and he suggested that he would send Jamesy up to the school or he himself go on the bicycle. She waved that aside by telling him that one of the windows was open.

'We'll go over so,' he said, wiped his tarry hands with a rag and shouted to Jamesy that he was needed to go through one of Vera's windows.

Jamesy came out of the house with the dog and ran ahead of them down by the back and over the stream where he cart-wheeled in the field at the other side.

'He's as fresh and as active as an eel,' Martin said, laughing at his antics.

'He acts like somebody not right in the head if you ask me,' Vera said, for at that moment Jamesy was walking on his hands, and when they reached the door he was sitting up on one of the window sills, the dog beside him with her pink tongue hanging out.

Martin raised up the unfastened window and Jamesy bounded through it but he was so rash that his trousers ripped and caught in a nail. Martin had to stretch in to release him, and as Vera now held up the window she noticed with a blush of shame the unmade bed with the clothes turned back and the two night-dresses lying in a nest of folds.

'I'm thankful to you, Martin,' she said when the door was opened.

'You needn't thank me. It's Jamesy did it all,' he said, nodding to Jamesy who was fingering the long rip in his trousers and gazing at a rigged yacht on top of the dresser.

'That's the best boat in the island,' Martin said.

'Could she beat your new one?' he said, hiding the rip in his trousers and closing his coat which had only one button.

'I'm sure she could, and maybe beat her by half the length of the lough,' Martin said, and observing the uncomfortable look on Jamesy's face he added: 'Turn round till we see the length of the rip.' But Jamesy backed to the door and ran off with the dog bounding after him, and instead of passing through the gate he ran round by the back.

Martin and Vera stood at the door, Martin laughing at the disappearing figure, seeing from where he stood the bare thigh as he scrambled up the hill to the house.

'He's mad about that dog and she's mad about him,' he said.

Vera noted the affectionate ring in his voice and she wondered how any man could feel so strongly about a boy whose blood was not his blood. It was unnatural, she told herself, and it could not last — not last like her love for Mary which had warmth, the hidden natural stream of her own life.

'I'd have made him do what you told him,' she said.

'He's shy because of you.'

'He needn't be shy of me. He means as little to me as the stones in that wall. I've my own child — but you wouldn't know what that means.'

'Mary's a fine girl.'

'Her father's two years dead to this very day.'

'God be good to his kindly soul! If Tom had lived we'd have been great friends. We were planning to work at the lobsters together that spring he took bad. We lost a good man in losing him. I loved to see him with a plane or a chisel in his hand. And look at his fields — well-drained and fenced and tailored. Your whole place is a credit to him.'

'If he were alive now, that field of potatoes wouldn't be crying out for somebody to mould them. Pat, I may say, is thinking about starting on it today.'

'And what kind of a neighbour does he think I am? Does he think it'd be any trouble to me to yoke up the horse for a few drills? I'll gladly do it if the soil dries up by the afternoon. You needn't put that journey on Pat.'

'I didn't ask him I may tell you. It was his mother told me he'd be down.'

'I'll give him a nice surprise. I'll tackle the horse and give her a bit of exercise. And anyway it'll be a lesson for Jamesy — he'll have to learn sometime.'

She said nothing: she'd let things take their course, for if it'd please him to do that job for her, she wasn't the one to baulk him.

'You can depend on me, Vera,' he said as he strode off. He looked up at the sky and added: 'We'll be round in a couple of hours.'

CHAPTER IV

SHE watched him go down the path, and lifting the loaves off the window sill she went in and left the door open to the bright sun. The fire was almost dead, and without taking off her coat she tenderly piled up a few fresh coals and twigs around the smouldering ash and at the first hurrying stream of smoke she went into the room and arranged her hair at the mirror. The damp morning air had curled her hair above her ears and she smiled at the fresh brightness it gave her. She wasn't faded-looking for a woman turned thirty-three, a woman out in all weathers that would leather any face, and she hadn't, she was sure, the distraught and beaten look of a woman whose husband was two years in his grave. Two years! The time had galloped past. It seemed only a short while ago that she had attended Tom, night and day, in this very room. It was true that she had had his mother to help her, his sister Sarah and his brother Pat. They had taken turns at sitting up at night, for his illness had dragged, dragged beyond her endurance and what surprised her most was the feeling she had had on the day he died. It wasn't sorrow she had felt but relief. Relief from the neighbours who were never done stepping into the kitchen at all hours of the day and night; relief from the priest who was on the doorstep every morning after he had said Mass, relief from the drone of prayers and from the restless movements of the old woman.

And it was strange that only for the old woman she would have forgotten to dwell on these things on this very day. She had something more to occupy her mind, she consoled herself, than these disturbing memories. She sought release from them, not by looking back but by looking forward — it was the future she permitted to control and to nourish her mind. What was past

45

was past and that was the end of it! Why should she languish in a past that afforded her such scant happiness or anchor herself with a load of painful regrets that would age her before her time. No, she always believed in looking forward and it was that attitude she knew, that marked her off from Tom's people and made her aware of her strangeness to them and they to her. She was of different stock and the dear knows how she had ever allowed herself to marry and live among them for so long. Hadn't Tom promised her time and again that he'd leave the island but she realized now that he had as much notion of leaving as the reedy lough out there in the lap of the hills. If he had lived he'd have remained here like a limpit to a rock. If only he had quarrelled with her, struck her, she believed she'd have left him and taken Mary with her. But Tom wasn't the man for quarrelling: he was too thin and delicate, too soft and quiet in his manner. You couldn't anger him, and yet he was as deep as a draw-well, and she felt she never knew him, and it was that unfathomable darkness in his character that caused her lack of desperate love for him.

On the day of his death she had shed few tears and even when she had caught the eyes of his mother upon her she struggled successfully to strangle any signs of grief that might have arisen in spite of herself. It was the assault of their unspoken minds that made her proud, and it was the fact that in his moments of delirium he had never cried out her name but the name of their child, the names of his sister and brother, and the cry, 'Mother, mother!' that was seldom away from his lips. If he loved her it would have rushed from the depths of his heart at a time when his mind was loose and drifting free. And then the way he clutched the crucifix, the despairing look in his eyes — she would never forget that! Why should a man who was so honest and kind in word and deed face death with such limp weakness. And the priest had given comfort to her, tried to console her as if she were in sore need of consolation: 'Vera

46

Reilly it's the end on this earth of a good man. His soul is now at peace with his Maker. For weeks I have attended him and no one has impressed me more with such simple faith and love as your husband. May God give you grace to bear this great blow He has sent you,' he had put his hand on her shoulder as he said this — 'Our Blessed Lady, if you put yourself in Her hands, the Mother of Sorrows, will not cease to guide you and your little child. Have faith in the will of God and remember we are not the measure of all things.' She could always hear these words, distinct in their gentleness, and see the shaking of his hands as he rolled up his purple stole, and the unshed tears in his eyes as he moved past the young men who knelt on one knee on their caps near the door. They were all struck with grief and she felt that each of them, in his own island way, knew her husband better than she did herself.

She, herself, was never one to affect something she didn't feel and there were times, especially at the graveside, when noticing their accusing eyes upon her and feeling entangled in their web of thick hostility that she asked herself what did she not do that she should have done, and what on earth would these silent people have her do. To these questions there came no answer and because there came no answer she ceased to question herself about what was right and what was wrong, and with that ceasing there came the drag of days to mark out her life: days of harvest with its work in the fields, days of winter with its sharp gaps of loneliness, spring with its laboured fields, summer with its sun, and winter again . . . And now she had seen another spring pass and had entered a summer full of growing. How many more would pass before she could find release from this airy cage where herself and Mary were held captive like sea-gulls with clipped wings. Even the sea-birds, the ravens and the swallows leave it — enjoy it for a while and then go. She never enjoyed it and she'd take care not to allow Mary to give her heart to it.

47

She sighed as she finished the making of the beds and taking a brush and dust pan she brushed the room and emptied the dust and fluff at the open window. She looked out and saw that the potato tops were drying but that in the lower end of the field the soil was black from the morning's rain. But the sun was strong and it may dry out by the afternoon. Already the wooden sides of the hen-sheds were dry except for an odd damp patch near the bottom. 'Mm,' she spoke to herself, 'if the old woman were here now she'd be praising that well-made shed and pointing out the well-made gates and the fine home-made presses in this room. But why should a man get praised for doing all that was his part as husband and farmer to do. That's what I'd like to know. These people are too ready with their praise of one another. When all is said and done I'd have to admit that Martin Gallagher has as well a kept house as my own — and he has no woman to help him. I listen far too much to that old woman but someday I'll blaze out at her.'

She came into the kitchen, got food ready for the hens, and was preparing dinner for herself and Mary when she saw clouds pushing the sun from the hollow and a few drops of rain streak silver on the window. In a few minutes large drops of rain as white as hailstones were spilling into the hollow and the sight and sound of them gladdened her for she knew that Pat wouldn't arrive to mould the potatoes. With her elbows resting on the table she watched the heavy burst of rain and saw troughs of water stretch out in the lower end of the potato field, and satisfied now that her afternoon would not be interrupted she drew out her sewing-machine from the wall and began to hem a light summer frock she was making for Mary. She worked rapidly, and when she had finished and was stowing the frock at the bottom of a chest so that Mary wouldn't come across it before it was complete with its buttons and belt she found an old snapshot of Tom. It had been taken by a visitor a few summers ago: Tom was standing with his arms folded, his thin face staring at the ground where lay his model yacht and the silver cup it had won. He was smiling, that pained smile of his, and a peak of sun-shadow under the cap on his head.

But she did not linger over any of these things; she saw the small patch she had deftly made on the mainsail where it had been rust-stained and torn. She remembered making that patch on the sewing-machine and how he had stood over her watching the speedy jump of the needle and how he wouldn't allow her to double stitch it in case it would stiffen the mainsail and produce some inferior alteration in its strength for sailing. Even when she suggested making a new sail for him he wouldn't allow her as he thought there was something in the fabric of the original cloth that was uncanny. And so against her will she had patched it with a piece of red cloth and that had pleased him: 'Red for luck,' he had said. 'From now on she'll be called the boat with the red patch in the corner of her sail.'

She looked at the photograph again and wished that it had been coloured so that the red patch would have stood out clearly against the white sail and not appear, as it did, like a dirty smudge. She put the photograph back again at the bottom of the press and took the yacht down from the top of the dresser. It was covered with dust and cobwebs and she wiped it with a cloth for she supposed that Pat would be entering it for the next big race in the lough. That would start another litany of praise that she would have to listen to: how Tom made that boat, how he had gouged it and planed it till you could see the glow of a candle through its sides, how every man in the island had copied its shape and how none of them could beat her. 'Some day it'll be beaten,' she said to herself as she tapped her knuckles against the hollow-sounding hull, 'and it wouldn't surprise me if a fine workman like Martin Gallagher built one that had the beating of it.'

At three o'clock she went out to meet Mary, and when she saw her coming with the raincoat over her arm she hoped she hadn't dropped the key. The coat was the first thing she took from her, and as her fingers groped in the pocket and found the key she smiled and told Mary how she had been locked out.

At dinner she asked what she had learnt today at school and Mary recited for her *Four Ducks on a Pond*:

> Four ducks on a pond,
> A grass-bank beyond,
> A blue sky of spring,
> White clouds on the wing;
> What a little thing
> To remember for years —
> To remember with tears!

'I don't know what anybody would want to cry for on remembering that,' her mother said. 'It's like something your granny would weep over or maybe old Craig when he's walking about the streets in the city. Can your teacher not give you something to look forward to instead of these things that look back?'

'I'll tell her what you said.'

'You'll tell her no such thing. She'll give you your answer some fine day. She'll say "Is it your mother or me that's preparing you for your examination?" You must be careful, Mary, and not repeat everything your mother happens to say.'

'All right, I'll not . . . Can I go to the lough with Martin Gallagher this evening? Jamesy Rainey told me yesterday that he's going to sail his new yacht today.'

'You'll do nothing of the kind. You're becoming a regular tomboy. You'll play about your own doors and in your own garden and on your own swing.'

'Tomorrow's Friday — could I stay at granny's until Sunday?'

'So there you are! You don't care if your mother is left alone. After all there's three people in your granny's house.'

'But you said you'd let me stay week-ends with them in the

long summer evenings when the swallows come, and they're here long ago.'

'You've too many wants for a girl of your age — a girl that's supposed to spend time at her books.'

Mary became silent, and when they had the dishes washed Martin Gallagher came to the door and Jamesy stood outside with a yacht in his arms. He told her that the rain had made the ground too sticky for moulding but that he'd start on it first thing in the morning. Vera knew there was something else on his mind by the way he hung about the door but she was determined not to help him to unfold it. She'd ask no questions.

He looked at Mary: 'I'm going down to try out the new yacht,' he said. 'Mary could come with us if she likes.'

'We might stroll up the hill later on and watch,' Vera said, brushing a few crumbs off the table onto her hand.

He looked up at Tom's yacht on top of the dresser and then at Vera. 'If you'd lend us Tom's yacht for a while you'd see a bit of a race,' he said. 'I know my own couldn't touch her for speed but there'd be more sport to see the two on the lough together.'

She stood on a chair and as she lifted down the yacht she noticed with quick disappointment that he kept his eyes on the boat and not on her, and then as he and Jamesy hurried off they didn't stop once to look back at the house.

'Well I'll let you go today,' she said to Mary, 'because I can't bear to see you sitting there with a pout on you that'd stop a clock! But I'm going with you.'

About fifteen minutes later they set off down the road to the lough. Martin, standing on top of a hill, saw them and waved to them to hurry, and Mary ran from her mother and joined him, seeing the two boats with their square mainsails and jibs, her father's in front with the red patch glowing vividly across the silver width of water. She clapped her hands and shouted to her mother to hurry, and when Vera reached them out of breath she put her hand on Martin's shoulder to rest herself.

'Not another boat on the island could touch her,' Martin said excitedly. 'She'll blind them all on Sunday. To look at them out there together you'd think they were twins. I needn't tell you that I copied Tom's faithfully but there's something in his that has the gift of sailing. Look at the way she grips the wind in her sail and my own pig-headed fellow cutting away from it as if he were afraid of it.'

At every gust Martin's would lean over and gain ground but with the weakening of the wind she would sit up with a jerk, hesitate for a moment with her sail flittering, and then catching the remnants of the breeze she would tag off again with a cumbrous uncertain movement. Tom's took its fill of every breeze, never spilling a taste of it, and moving steadily forward with uncanny purpose. The boats reached the top of the lough and Martin cupped his hands to his mouth and shouted to Jamesy, to hold them until he got round. Vera lay back in the heather, soothed by the warm mossy smell from the water, the larks singing in the sky, and the continual churr-churr of the grasshoppers. Resting on her elbow she idly watched the two yachts as Martin released them with their mainsails full out, driving now before the wind. They seemed to hug together for a while and then Tom's went in front, heading straight down the lough as if following a charted course.

'You've seen the two of them sailing into the wind and sailing before it,' Martin said as he climbed up and sat beside them in the heather. 'What do you think of them?'

'I think you're a foolish man to get so worked-up. Look at the way your hands are trembling,' Vera said as she took one of his hands and held it firmly. 'I'll keep it steady for you,' she laughed.

'You're only joking me,' he said. 'I don't mind when Tom's beats mine — she's the best boat I've ever seen with a sail on her.

She'll beat them all on Sunday if Pat enters her. He didn't mention it — did he?'

'He didn't but he's as crazy about it as the rest of you,' she smiled. 'Indeed there's little work being done when this madness catches the hold of you.'

'God knows it's a short enough season and we'll labour and fish enough that'll do us.'

When she was on her way back with him along the road she told Mary to hurry on in front for she didn't want her to linger behind with Jamesy who was now standing at the water's edge and flinging sticks into the water for the dog.

'Anytime you like you can have the boat,' she said, 'and you needn't be afraid of asking for it. Indeed you could keep it for that matter. It's no use to Mary and it's only gathering dust on top of the dresser.'

He looked at her with shocked surprise wondering if she really meant what she said.

'No,' he said, 'I couldn't take it. Even if I hadn't a stick or a chisel to build one of my own, I wouldn't take it. Tom's lovely boat! No, no, you'd only regret it someday when you'd notice there was a vacancy somewhere about your kitchen.'

She said nothing more; she knew what he was thinking — knew by the sombre smile that spread across his face that Tom was more of a fretful memory for him than he was for her. But she'd hold her peace — why should she reveal the charred waste of coldness that lay at that moment on her heart. Martin was different from her and she was a stranger with a stranger's blood.

He didn't mention the boat again and when they parted he looked steadily at her for a few moments: 'First thing in the morning I'll be over to mould that field for you. Mary could leave word with Pat on her way to school.'

CHAPTER V

THE following morning after Mary had gone to school without any message about the field for Uncle Pat, Vera was taking a dish-cloth from a bush outside the door when she noticed on top of Martin's hill that he was yoking up the horse and cart. She tried to deceive herself that he might be going to the quay for a bag of cement, and she stood irresolute, smoothing out the stiff creases in the well-aired cloth, but on seeing the cart move off she withdrew quickly and closed the door behind her. In a few minutes she heard the wheels rock on the road, then she heard them stop, and move with hollow smoothness on the earthy track that led to the potato field. The thought of Pat's probable arrival in an hour's time swiped across her mind and she rested her hands on the table and strove to halt the impulsive force that would send her out to Martin and ask him to leave off. But that would be fear, she counselled herself, and what crime had she done that she should fear anyone. What claim had anyone on her and, above all, what claim had Pat on her.

She poured the water over the breakfast dishes in the basin, and to deflect her mind from what she'd have to say to Pat she wiped and polished each dish with studied concentration and when she had finished she went into the room and saw from the small window in the gable-end that Martin had already done two drills and was now allowing Jamesy to take the plough. For a while she watched his slow patience with the lad as he struggled awkwardly to keep the plough from burying itself too deep in the soft soil, and she wondered, once again, why a man so fond of children hadn't married or, if he had married, why had he left his wife? Next year she'd let that field to him and then she'd be under no obligation to Pat or anyone else. Indeed it was foolish for a woman to hold land that needs to be laboured. It was as much as she could do to look after the fowl and the cow without worrying herself over work that needs a man's hand. Today, maybe, when Pat would arrive they could come to some decision in that direction.

She came from the room and busied herself with tasks inside the house, guarding herself from going outside, moving about with unnecessary stealthiness, and time and again opening the front door quietly and listening for the sound of a cart on the road. At last she heard one, and in a short time saw Pat arrive and above the wings of his cart the shining blades of his mould-ing-plough. From the edge of the window she saw him loop the reins to the gatepost and lean on the loose-stone wall that overlooked the potato field. She lifted the brush and was sweep-ing the already swept floor when he raised the latch and stepped into the kitchen.

'I see you've got Martin to mould,' he said, without sitting down.

'He didn't start, surely?' she tried to say with playful surprise and hurried to the open door and pretended to see him for the first time. 'Well, he's a glutton for work I must say,' she said sprightly, and began to explain without pausing for an interrup-tion how Martin had said he'd run the plough over the drills when she had remarked that the potatoes need it badly: ' "I'll give Pat a surprise" were the very words he said to me, and he even abused me for daring to take you from your own work.'

'It's none of his damned business to interfere with what con-cerns us. Let him attend to his own place and he'll have his hands full. You should have sent me word and saved me the journey of carting the plough and wasting the good morning on me.'

'How did I know he was serious? It was yesterday he men-tioned it when he came over to ask for that yacht there to sail against his own.'

Pat sat down. The yacht lay against the wall and he lifted it and rested it on his lap, toying with the boom of the mainsail.

'It's not yesterday I'm talking about,' he said, and his fingers tapped the varnished deck. 'It's this morning I'm talking about. You'd loads of time to send me word and loads of people to carry it. You could have sent it with Mary or with James Rainey when you saw them turn the horse into the field.'

'To tell you the truth,' she lied brazenly, 'I didn't know they were in the field until you stepped on to that floor.'

'You've become hard of hearing all of a sudden,' he said, looking up at her as she sat on a corner of the table with her arms folded.

'I suppose you don't believe me!'

'It's hard, Vera, to expect me to believe you. There's so little stir down here that I'd expect the pair of you to hear every wheel that'd turn on the road, every foot that'd fall, and every dog that'd bark.'

'I hope you'll not throw his kindness back in his face!'

'I'm going to bridle my tongue — that's what I'm going to do. But I'll say again that he should not concern himself with our business.'

She always disliked this coupling of her name with theirs and had hoped that after Tom's death his people would have been more distant with her, and that with the passing of time the two houses would have grown independent of one another. That wasn't to be. They endeavoured to come closer to her as if she was in constant need of them, and week after week would send butter home with Mary; and each spring Pat saw to the sowing of her corn and the sowing of the potatoes. But all these kindnesses caused her much resentment and no pleasure, and realizing now that they were cautious inroads cutting across her own way of life she decided that now was the time to put an end to it.

'I don't think I'll bother next year in having any of the land tilled,' she said.

'It's no bother to me,' Pat said. 'What vexes me is that when you told him I was going to mould it should have been enough for him. I'll go out and have a word with him.'

'Leave him alone and let him finish. I think he took it in hand so as to give his new boy some experience.'

'He can give him all the experience he likes on his own land and not on ours.'

There it was again, she thought, 'ours', 'ours', she'd soon show him what 'ours' meant only she didn't want to make a scene.

'And what was he wanting the yacht for? Was that for experience for the race on Sunday?'

'I told you it was to try out against his own,' she said, throwing a cloth on the table and rattling down on it a few cups and saucers.

'Did he tell you how the boats fared?'

'He had no call to tell me. I saw them myself racing up and down the lough, and Martin said after it that there wasn't a boat in the whole island fit to beat Tom's. His own would have a chance if Tom's was out of it,' she said and poked the fire under the kettle. She must keep moving, she told herself, to control her anger.

'You can tell him from me that Tom's won't be out of it. We'll enter her on Sunday. Let him put some of his travelling experiences into the making of a yacht and it'll suit him better than stirring up trouble among us.'

'You don't want to understand,' she said. 'If Martin thought the moulding of a few drills would breed trouble he'd not have moved a foot in that field — I'm sure of that.'

'I'm glad you've some thought for somebody,' he said, and strode towards the door. 'He has already made you part with one of the fields. Take care or he'll grab the others.'

In her anger she made a step forward but drew back and

folded her arms: his mother had told him about her forgetfulness over the anniversary, she was sure of that, and it was that that had irked him more than the moulding of a few drills.

'Come back here,' she said firmly. 'Tell me what you mean by "having thought for somebody".'

He turned at the door to face her. She approached him with a hard stare in her eyes that suddenly cowed him. 'Nothing,' he said; and at that moment the latch was lifted and Martin Gallagher came in.

'You've put a right wholesome journey on me this morning,' Pat said. 'I didn't know Vera had asked you to mould or I wouldn't have budged from my own fields.'

'She didn't ask me. I done it on my own bat to help a neighbour,' Martin said, pretending not to notice the edge on Pat's voice. 'Dammit all, you'd do the same yourself without being asked.'

'I've laboured that land out there since my brother's death — this time two years ago. I've still the strength and time to do it without taking any man away from his own work.'

'It was no trouble to me to give a hand,' he said. They were silent for a moment and Martin recalled the day the Craigs were leaving and how the daughter had flown at him with the same unnecessary wrath, and he felt there was something wrong when a man's kindness led him into trouble at every turn — he had come back to the island but the island hadn't come back to him, the people had changed or else he himself had changed without knowing it. 'Vera was to send you word,' he said.

'That would have saved me the trouble if she had. But I don't think her memory's fresh these days — it's apt to go stale in the warm weather.'

'It's done now and I'm sure done to my satisfaction,' Vera said, ignoring the insolent irony in his words. 'Sit in to the table and I'll make a drop of tea for the lot of you.'

'I've worn out the morning already and I'm not going to wear out the whole day by sitting on my backside drinking tea,' Pat said.

'We'll not force a man against his will,' she said, turning her back on him as she poured water into the teapot. 'It's here if you want it — you needn't tell the whole island that I sent you away without a bite in your mouth.'

He didn't answer her. He opened the door and shut it behind him. But outside he noticed the seat of a child's stool chopped up for kindling and the ravaged sight of what was once a bit of Tom's work maddened him and he kicked at the pile of wood and sent it flying across the street. He walked up the path towards his horse but half way up he turned back and entered the kitchen again.

'I'll be down to race Tom's boat on Sunday,' he almost shouted in spite of himself.

'I can tell you there's nothing will whip her,' Martin said from the table.

'They've all tried to beat her,' Pat went on in a voice that gathered anger. 'They've built big boats and broad boats and they've rigged them with sails as big as bed-sheets. But they've failed — every damned fleet of them!' He sat down on a chair near the fire and Vera handed him a mug of tea and a slice of bread for there was something in his mood that frightened her and crippled her tongue. Martin, too, was aware of it and he sipped his tea without enjoyment and glanced occasionally at the hearthstone where the mug of tea and the bread balanced on its mouth lay untouched.

'My brother Tom, God rest him, could make a boat,' Pat said, staring at the yacht against the wall. 'He could make more than a small boat. Look around you at this house! The chest, the stools, and that press with the diamond windows — that's all his work. It could stare you in the face day after day and you'd never tire of running your hand over the smooth timbers and praising the man that made it.'

'Where did he learn it?' Martin said gently. 'There was no carpenter here in my day except Alex, the miller.'

'Learn it! It all came out of his own head — out of his own learning. It was a gift of God's since he wasn't the size of that lad of yours out in the field. He was always making things and writing off to Glasgow and London for books and plans and tools. It was a gift — I tell you. But no one appreciated him. They'll talk about his yacht but I suppose if the wood-worm crumbled it to meal tomorrow they'd cease talking about him.'

Vera, quenching the anger that was burning in her throat, stared at him with a clipped bitterness and he got up and brushed past her to the china-press. He turned the key and opened the two wings of the door: 'Look at that for fine work. Every tiny screw, every hook, every shelf tells you the man he was. He wasn't appreciated. He put his heart and soul into everything he turned his hand to.' He lifted up the lid of the chest of tools but on seeing specks of rust on the saw and on the chisels he let the lid fall with a snap.

'God!' he said, 'that anybody could be so heartless. Rusted, rusted, and nobody caring a seagull's curse! Is there nobody living that gives a thought for the people that are gone? That a man could leave behind him a well-made box or even a stool for a child to sit on and the next you hear of it is that it's kindling for the fire!'

'What are you driving at?' Vera, at last, said to him. 'A man that's thirty years of age should be able to speak clearly what's in his mind and not be parading round the floor like a half-demented bull!'

'Half-demented! Wouldn't it drive any man mad who had a heart for Tom's things to see them so ill-treated. I'm his brother but anyone would cry out at the crime done to the work of Tom's hands. There's no respect and no reverence for him and he only two years in his grave.'

'What crime are you talking about?' Vera asked, getting up from the table.

'Sit down the two of you,' Martin said, 'and don't be raising your voices over nothing.'

'Look at the stool outside,' Pat went on. 'It's hagged and ripped up for the fire and you with roots of heather as thick as seawrack at your doorstep!'

'A cinder charred one of the legs of it and it was a danger for any child to sit on it. There's no man about the house to mend what's broken!'

'There's a man not far off could mould a few potatoes. From all accounts he could fix the leg of a child's stool if he was asked.'

'He wasn't asked to mould the field!' and she turned to Martin for support.

'I done it to help a neighbour,' Martin said, 'but if I knew I was going to cause strife in a family I can tell you I'd have held my hand.'

'Maybe you'll sail the yacht to help a neighbour. Maybe you will . . . On Sunday she'll sail but I'm the man that'll sail her!'

'We'll all be glad to see her in the race and we'll all be glad to see the best boat win,' Martin said calmly.

'The best boat'll win — never fear! And that boat was made by my brother Tom.'

'She's a clinker!' Martin said, half-amused now by Pat's anger, and at the same time careful not to cross him. He stole a glance at Vera, standing with her arms folded. Was she, too, baffled by this man's anger, he wondered, or was he himself becoming a stranger among his own people?

'I'll leave you,' Pat shouted. 'It's clear by your silences that I'm not wanted here.'

They said nothing as he went out and banged the door.

CHAPTER VI

WITHOUT glancing back at the house Pat jumped into the cart and set off; his shoulders drooped and the rope-reins hung loose between his knees: 'Tom, my boy, you married wrong when you married a stranger from that mainland town beyond — a town that rears selfish, grudging, penny-loving people! Two years you're dead and you're nothing to her now — not even the rag of a memory. Her blood's as cold as the waters in a wintry lough.'

His hands closed on the reins and suddenly he struck out at the horse and it broke into a gallop, sending the stones flying over the sides of the road. The horse arrived home in a sweat and he loosed it out of the shafts and let it stray around the yard. He came into the house and without greeting his mother where she sat in her usual chair by the fire he drank a cup of cold water from the crock and wiped his mouth with his sleeve.

'You're back early, Pat,' she said.

'I am. She employed Martin Gallagher and by the time I arrived on my fool's journey he had the job half done.'

He strode about the kitchen and pulled out drawers and lifted up old magazines and papers that lay on the window-ledge, his mother eyeing him with bewildered curiosity.

'In the name of God what are you searching for?' she said to him.

'Searching for! I'm searching for nothing!' and he pulled himself together jerkily. 'I suppose he thinks he'll win the race on Sunday.'

'Who thinks?'

'Martin Gallagher! He'll not win this race. I'll win it for Tom's sake if for nothing else. Tom's memory will not be easily forgotten, I may tell you.'

'Whatever you do, Pat, do nothing till you calm yourself.

Anger and strife have broken many a home. Do you think a load of spite and grudgery would add to Tom's memory?'

'Wouldn't it anger a living saint to think that Tom's two years in his grave and his wife forgot to go out to Mass on his second anniversary? Forgot! Forgot!'

'Mother of God! Why did I ever tell you that? I blame myself for putting you in this state. Sit down and quieten yourself. Whatever she is she's Tom's wife and Mary's his daughter.'

'What made him marry that one?'

'We can't answer these things. We're all in God's Hands. For all we know, Tom could have got a worse wife — and you wouldn't need to travel far for that.'

'Not if he had combed the four corners of Ireland could he fall in with worse. She had no respect for his soul and I wonder what respect she had for him when he was alive. For all we know she might have broken his heart. At his death she shed few tears and we thought she was choking her grief.'

'Tom had nothing for her only the good word always.'

'That was his nature. He could have been suffering a living hell for all we know or ever will know.'

'Don't be bitter, Pat. Rid your mind of those things. It would have bruised Tom's heart to hear you talk like that about the mother of his child. Whatever we do we've Mary to think of.'

'I wish we could win her away from her.'

'It's a bad thing for anyone to come between mother and child. When God gave her that child he meant her to rear her. All we can do is to help her to do that.'

'She doesn't want us. She's turning the child away from this very door and she fills her head with hatred for the island and all things in it. She never speaks to her about her father, and in front of the child she breaks and hacks what her father made with his own two hands. Today I saw a stool she had splintered for kindling the fire.'

63

'A stool! No man would be foolish enough to rouse himself to anger over a bit of a stool.'

'You're standing up for her but I'll not heed you. I'll change her step. You yourself had nothing good to say of her when she forgot the anniversary.'

'I was angry then like you are now, and in anger you see no truth and you judge when you shouldn't judge. God forgive me. When I see the twists and knots of your own temper I feel I misjudged her. We can all make mistakes. The way of good is always the hard way but it is the hard way we turn our backs on. In the evil mood you are now in you'll do harm — not only to Vera but to Mary and to the memory of your brother. A stubborn gate will swing to the easy touch but if you force it you'll wrench it past all mending.'

'She'll marry again.'

The old woman pulled her shawl tightly round her shoulders and tapped the floor with her toe: 'I wouldn't fault her if she did. Often when I stand at that door and see the handful of school children scampering home I see the island dying out. In my young days I taught in that school when it was so crammed with children that their voices drowned the noise of the river below. But now it's as quiet as the church. Vera's still young enough to have children and if she'd marry again I'm not the one would throw blame at her. I'm telling you that this place will soon be only a nesting place for wild seabirds. All your people will be lying in that grave at the shore and a time will come when nothing will move in it but the long grass and a wren singing on a fallen headstone.'

'It would be a crime and an insult to us if she married again.'

She poked the fire and after a long pause continued: 'What do you know of what's a crime and what's not? What do you know of the temptations that a girl like her might house in her mind? For God's sake will you leave her alone and not be meddling and cross-graining your nature with these streaks

64

of malice that may drive her into bad ways. If you were married you might talk with a gentler tongue.'

'She'll marry Martin Gallagher and you'll live to see Tom's house and land slipping away from us.'

'Land! That land belonged to your father and he was only too willing to give it to Tom when he wanted to strike out for himself and build a home. I wish you had done the same. One grandchild — and that a girl — is cold consolation for me that reared you all. "May they both see their children's children unto the third and fourth generation." Aye, aye, I haven't seen much of them and I don't think I'll see many more.'

'If she marries him we'll not only lose the land but we'll lose Mary. Do you see now what would happen?' he said with quiet triumph.

For a few minutes she didn't answer him. She looked into the fire and lowered the scarf from round her head. She raised her eyes and looked at him sadly: 'The land is slipping away from over the whole island because there's not enough hands to stub out the groping whins and the damp bracken. If marrying would make Martin stay on the island, then maybe I'd be glad.'

'Maybe you would but I'll not be! You're getting soft with the years.'

'When you're my age you'll look at things in a different way. You'll yearn and pray to be left a little longer in this world so that you can do some of the good you should have done. When you draw near the grave you want to live differently — in the only way that matters: the forgiving way.'

'There's no sense left in your head when you'd sit up and see what was ours passing to the stranger.'

'Martin Gallagher's no stranger! I taught him in the school when he wasn't the size of that table.'

'He's as big a stranger as Vera. Sixteen years in a city would change any man. As long as I've breath in my body I'll see he'll not grab what was ours.'

65

Once more he rummaged about the drawers and the pile of papers on the window-ledge. He tramped on the dog's paw as it lay under the sofa, and when it leaped to its feet with a whine he made a kick at it and it fled in terror to the back of the old woman's chair.

'In God's name, son,' she pleaded with him, 'will you pluck this bitterness from your mind?'

'I can't! I can't do it I tell you. I looked at her today and I hated the living sight of her.'

'You're souring the very soul out of yourself. Didn't I see your father's leg cut by the swipe of a scythe from an angered man? Didn't I see your father lying in that room, and the doctor and the nurse struggling to stave off gangrene, and didn't I see the man that slashed him broken in spirit after your father's death?' She poked the fire and smoothed the dog's head with her hand. 'It was wrong for me to tell you about Vera's forgetfulness. I did wrong to tell you! In God's name will you throw it behind you and don't go forward with this hardness lining your face like a rock and you a young man! If she has proud and strange ways your ill-will will not change her.'

'And who'll change her?'

' "God writes straight with crooked lines" — did you ever hear that?'

'I heard it from you but could never understand it.'

'The longer you live you'll understand it or maybe you'll be brought to understand it when you're sitting happed up like a bundle of clothes and you an old man with nothing but the fire all day for company. Maybe you'll be able to look back and see in all the twists and hollows of life that there was a straight purpose in it all.'

'I don't understand you. I'm going out!'

'Pat, come here to me. Promise me one thing: you'll not go near the lough on Sunday!'

'Is this the next epistle? Well, I'm going to the lough on

Sunday and that's the end of that story!' he shouted, his lips wet with spittle. 'And I'll bring home the prize — not for my sake but for Tom's. I'll not be the first to bring you the news. You'll see them passing on the road on bicycles and you can hail them and they'll shout up to you: "Tom's won it again!" They'll not say "Vera's" or "Pat's" — they'll say "Tom's". For one day at least I'll make his name ring on the lips of the people. All round her Vera will hear them shouting: "Tom's has it again! There's no one alive could match Tom Reilly in making a model yacht." When she hears that it'll tear the stony heart out of her if she has one to tear. She'll have good cause to think of him then. And what's more I'll make sure she doesn't stay away from the lough on Sunday. I'll call for her in the cart and drive her down in style.'

'How can we judge that she doesn't think of Tom? What do we know of what goes on in a person's mind? There's many a one can look kind in action and be a very devil in his thoughts.'

'Would you listen to what you're after saying?' he said, and he turned his back to her and looked out of the window 'Don't you know rightly that if she thought of him she'd have been the first to cross the chapel door on his anniversary?' He spun round again and shouted: 'She forgot him! She forgot him as you'd forget last week's rain!'

Sarah came in. Her mother and Pat were silent. She looked from one to the other trying to lift the dropped stitch of their quarrel.

'What's all the shouting about, Pat?' she said. 'You could hear you at the foot of the brae with your voice as loud as an auctioneer's.'

'She doesn't want me to go to the lough on Sunday. She thinks there'd be a fight.'

'There's no sense in men's heads if they'd fight over boats that's only fit for amusing children. I wouldn't walk the length of myself to see them.'

'Nobody's asking you,' Pat said sharply.

'You've the poor horse outside in a fine bath of sweat, let me tell you. Galloping over the roads with the sun mad with heat and everybody shading their eyes to look after you.'

'There's more than the sun going mad,' the old woman put in. 'Your brother, there, is burning himself up with a madness, and he doesn't know what he's doing. The fields won't get much good out of him till after Sunday. If he'd listen to me he'd put it out of his head and let them sail boats from dawn till sunset and not bat an eyelid to see them.'

'I'm going on Sunday I tell you, and neither Martin Gallagher nor Vera Reilly nor anyone else will stand in my way. I warrant you I'll wreck their plans the way they wrecked this fine morning on me!'

The old woman sighed, a sigh of exhaustion. She had said all she had to say and she'd now hold her tongue for fear she'd nourish his growing anger; before long it might blaze itself out in its own flame.

'If I'm not here when Mary's getting out of school,' Sarah said quietly, 'will some of you get her the fresh butter I left for her? I put a few prints in the can to harden and the can's standing in the stream outside.'

'I'll not fetch it for her,' Pat said. 'Let Martin Gallagher plunge the churn-handle for her mother. He's useful in other ways and I'm sure he could do that.'

'When Tom was alive,' the old woman said, 'it was the custom to give them butter. We're not going to break that off and have his child eating dry bread. Vera has only the one cow.'

'You can do whatever you like,' he said. 'I'll waste no more of this day listening to the pair of you. I'm going out now to thin the turnip field.'

The dog, lying at the old woman's feet, jumped up when he opened the door and went out with him.

CHAPTER VII

WHEN he had gone out and Sarah after him the old woman was left alone. She sighed and closed her eyes, and when Mary came out of school she found her saying her beads by the fire. In her hand Mary carried a glass jam-jar filled with black mould from which grew a chestnut shoot bearing a few leaves. She told her grandmother how the teacher had got a chestnut seed from the mainland, planted it in the jar, and how month after month it lay on the sunny window ledge of the school until the leaves grew up and topped the mouth of the jar. 'I'm taking it home now to plant in the garden and when it grows up it'll be the first chestnut tree in the whole island.'

Her grandmother put her arm round her: 'Your father, God rest him, would have loved that. Many a tree he tried to grow — poplar and ash but never a chestnut. A tree has a hard struggle against the salty winds and you'll have to plant it where there's shelter and where it can take its fill of the sun.' She got up from the chair and while she was pouring out a cup of sweet milk and buttering bread for her she told her to fetch the can from the stream and get a big cabbage leaf from the garden.

The can was ice-cold from the flowing water and the old woman prodded the butter with her finger: 'It's well seasoned now, Mary, but you'll need to mind and carry it on the shady side of you on the way home.' She lifted out the three circular prints of butter: on the face of one was the print of a cow's head with horns, on another an acorn, and on the third a shamrock leaf. She tore the cabbage leaf into four pieces and put one below each print, and then saying out aloud: 'In the name of the Father, and of the Son, and of the Holy Ghost,' she sprinkled salt on top of the last bit of leaf and fastened on the lid.

'Don't dally on the road, Mary, like a good girl and don't

69

forget to call tomorrow and tell me where you plant the chest-nut.' She stooped and kissed her on each cheek and Mary hurried out.

She looked back a few times to see her granny wave to her from the door and she waved back in reply until a turn in the road swung her out of view. She held the can in her shadow and the trembling chestnut leaves in the sun. Passing the little shop on the road she heard the door-bell ring and saw James Rainey come out backwards with a canvas bag of groceries on his back. She hurried past but on turning round to see where he was she noticed he was eating sweets and she slackened her pace so that he would overtake her. He drew near her and she heard the rustle of a paper bag.

'Here,' he said, 'there's a couple of caramels that'll keep you chewing.'

She rested her can and jam-jar on the road and after peeling the paper off the caramels she licked the paper and put the two sweets into her mouth at once and set off with him at her side. He asked her what she was doing with that thing in the jam-pot and she told him, pausing now and again to chew and swallow, that it would grow into a chestnut tree and be the first chestnut tree that was ever heard of in the whole island.

'But you couldn't get a tree to grow out of a jam-pot.'

She laughed at him: 'I'll break the glass with a stone before I plant it. And you can come over some day and see where it's growing.' She swallowed audibly and looked at him with sly entreaty. He lifted out another caramel from his pocket, took the paper off it, and put it in her mouth. She smiled back at him with her lips closed.

'Wouldn't it be a great thing to be said about me that I was the one who planted the first chestnut tree on the island?'

'I suppose it would,' he answered, looking at the leaves nodding in the jar, 'but who'll be here to tell everybody that you were the one who planted the first chestnut tree?'

70

'Won't you be here?'

'I might be dead tomorrow.'

'But supposing you didn't die and were spared for a long while, and suppose that I was a teacher in a school wouldn't you tell people I planted the chestnut tree if you saw them looking at it or picking up the chestnuts in the autumn?'

'But I mightn't be here.'

'Are you going to leave Martin Gallagher and go back home again?'

'I've no home to go back to.'

'You've no home to go back to? But sure everybody has a home.'

'Well, I haven't. I came out of an orphanage.'

'Then you're father and mother's dead.'

'My father's dead but my mother's in England.'

'Does she write to you?'

'No, I don't know where she lives.'

She began to laugh: 'You don't know where your mother lives — that's very funny. Then how do you know she's in England when she might be in Scotland?'

'The nuns told me she was in England.'

'Then she must be in England if the nuns told you she was in England. But why didn't they tell you what place she was in England?'

'I don't know.'

'Did you ever see your mother?' she said, laughing. He was confused and disconcerted by her laughs, and for a few minutes he didn't reply to her. She asked him again, and with desperate bravery he resolved to tell her lies as he drew from his memory a few people who visited the orphanage at Christmas and whose presence remained for him an unexplained but pleasurable mystery.

'If you want to know I did see her hundreds of times at Christmas.'

'What was she like?'

'She was a tall woman and she had a fur coat with scent on it and her lips were red and she had shining rings on her fingers and the man that brought her in her motor car carried out boxes and boxes of sweets and toys and apples and loaded them on the big shining table that was like a pool of brown water.'

'Then your mother's a lady?' she said with respectful astonishment.

He nodded his head, not turning to look at her, and then as they reached the top of the hill where they could see the blue loughs lying in the laps of the hills of the Lower End, Jamesy lifted the canvas bag from his shoulder and sat down to rest on a bank by the roadside. Mary would have rested with him to hear more about the grand lady with the rings but at that moment she saw her mother standing out in the middle of the road and beckoning to her with threatening impatience.

'There's my mother, I must run,' she said to Jamesy, and as she approached her mother she noticed that she was cross.

'I called at my granny's,' Mary explained before her mother had time to question her.

'Wasn't that James Rainey I saw at the top of the hill? What made you come home with him? He's not the class of company I want you to keep.'

'I didn't know.'

'Well, you know now and let that be the end of it . . . What's that trash you have in the jam-pot?'

'It's a chestnut tree.'

'A chestnut tree! It looks more like a couple of sick leaves to me.'

'I'm going to plant it in the garden where the hens won't tear it up with their feet. And some day we'll be able to sit under it when the sun's hot.'

Her mother laughed scornfully: 'It'd take a dozen years or

more to grow a decent size and by that time you'll be far from here.'

'It'll be like a tent: a green tent in the daytime and a black tent at night,' Mary went on, following the run of her own mind.

They entered the house and Mary left the can and jar on the table, struggled out of the straps of her schoolbag and took a big spoon from the table-drawer. She went out into the garden and after digging a hole with the spoon she placed the jam-jar on its side and broke it with a stone. She put the plant gently in the hole, crumbled mould around it with her fingers, and scooped back the dug soil and pressed it firmly with her toe. She stood back admiring its five leaves and the scroll of shadow they made with the sun, and in imagination saw the full-grown tree with its spiky chestnuts and herself resting against the trunk with her own children around her.

She sat at the table to take her dinner and her mother questioned her about her Uncle Pat and if he was going to the race on Sunday.

'I saw no one only granny,' Mary answered her and relapsed into silence.

'You shouldn't be calling there every day. They'll not want you.'

Mary said nothing, and time and again her mother would tell her to take her dinner and not let it go cold, and then she would rap the table with her knuckles to draw her away from her dreamy abstractions. She asked her about Jamesy Rainey and what they had to say to one another along the road, and Mary told her with bright eagerness that his mother was a great lady with rings on her fingers and that she lived in England and sent him loads of parcels at Christmas.

'She's no lady!' her mother answered sharply. 'Put that wild notion out of your head, and don't talk about her again. Keep to your own side of the road and don't be gallivanting about with a fellow like that. A lady, indeed! You lady yourself at

73

your books and it'll suit you better than listening to the silly stories of a poor orphan that maybe never saw his mother in his life.'

'Never saw his own mother?' Mary said with surprise and looked up at her mother for further explanation.

'Tell me what you learnt today,' her mother said, and lifted the dishes to escape from the look of astonished curiosity that knitted her daughter's face.

'And why could he not see his mother?' Mary asked again.

'I don't know how he couldn't see his own mother. Go and learn your lessons for school and stop chattering about James Rainey. He means nothing to you and he means nothing to me. Let him keep to his own side of the stream and give over talking about him!'

In silence Mary did her homework in arithmetic, read through an act in *The Merchant of Venice*, wrote out and learnt a page of spellings, and then took her ball to play outside. With an old teapot she watered the chestnut, had a few turns on the swing that hung from the poplar, watched the swallows at their nest under the apex of the gable and on hearing Martin's dog bark she ran up the hill at the back of the house and looked across the hollow seeing Martin and Jamesy with their fishing rods and the dog scampering ahead of them. They went out through the ornamental gate, hopped over a tumbled gap in a stone wall, and disappeared over a hill leaving a strong silence to hover above the hollow. Her mother coming out to lift the washing spread out on the bushes also watched them, hearing the cheerful whistling of Martin and seeing the smoke from his pipe hanging like gun-puffs in his wake. She felt the stiff airy freshness of the clothes, picked a green caterpillar off one of Mary's frocks and stamped her foot on it.

'Could I go fishing some evening with Martin?' Mary asked her, coming down from the hill.

'You could not! They'll not be back till long after dark and

74

by that time you'll be in your second sleep. What kind of a notion is that to take? Did James Rainey tell you to ask?'

'He never spoke about fishing.'

'What put it in your head then?'

'I don't know; it just came into it.'

'Then let it run out of it just as quickly.' In silence Mary gathered up some of the clothes, putting them to her cheek to smell and feel their strange fresh coldness. They went into the house and her mother spread a blanket on the table, lifted a smoothing-iron from the hob and began to smooth the clothes, Mary sitting in the light from the window and knitting a glove.

Her needles moved stiffly as she counted the stitches in a loud whisper. The smoothing-iron thumped on the table or gave a slight hiss when drops of water were sprinkled on the wrinkled clothes. The burnt smell soothed Mary's discontent as she followed in her mind Martin's boat rising on the swell, the lines plucking stiffly, and the fish pounding the boards with their tails. If her father were alive he'd have brought her out on a nice night like that, wrapping her up as he used to do with his heavy muffler and tying a sou'wester well over her ears.

She stood up and looked out at the daylight shrinking from the sky and a few shadows crouching in the crevices of the hills. Her mother called her to lay the table for the tea; and as she did so, humming softly to herself she thought once more of the boat, and at the back of her mind saw the dog sitting up in the bow and answering the bark of a dog hidden somewhere in the darkness of the land.

Before going to bed she went out to the front of the house to see the lighthouse beams cleaving long wedges through the sky, their silent powerful sweeps widening her stretch of earth and filling her with the mystery of the night: its coolness that you could almost touch, its rock-shadows that were like a herd of sleeping cattle, a wing-rush of birds that you could not see, and stars that were as bright as the stars of Bethlehem. She

75

counted the flashes of light: one — two — three — four: four
flashes of long light and then darkness until they once more
wheeled round in her direction. She saw them flash on the brass
boss of Martin's ornamental gate on the hill and she wondered
if the light would warm the gate as it swept past with its great
golden brush. She tiptoed away from the door to where she
could see the beams cut through the ropes of her garden-swing
and strike the gable where the swallows built their nest. Would
the light make the swallows blink their eyes, she wondered, or
would they turn their backs on it or crouch below the lip of
the nest where they wouldn't see it. She leaned her cheek against
the patch of gable where it was warmed from the fire inside but
heard nothing as she listened intently for a cheep of sound that
would tell her that the birds were there. She stood quietly,
transfixed with a secret joy for she saw the starlight shine on the
broken jam-jar in the garden, saw it shine on the deep wrinkles
that spiralled down the ropes of the swing, and in imagination
saw the chestnut tree spread its branches until its leaves sheltered
the swallows from the tormenting glare of the lighthouse and
shook its leafy pattern on the white gable.

Her mother called her to go to bed and when she was in bed
and the door open to the lamplight in the kitchen her mother
folded up the smoothed clothes and was preparing to add some
stitches to Mary's glove when there was a step outside on the
gravel and Martin knocking at the door.

'I brought you a few fish,' he said. 'We got a good haul.'

'You'll not sit down for a while?' Vera said.

'The lad's waiting for me in the house,' he answered standing
on the floor, his oilskin confettied with fish scales.

'There's some big fellows there you could salt for the winter,'
he said as he helped her to put them into a small tub.

'The winter! Don't talk to me about the winter — every
season is winter for me in a place where there's no life. Before
long you'll find the same truth. Wait till you've a few beasts to

sell and wait till you try to land them at the other side where the sand is piling up round the quay and nobody gives a straw whether it's dredged or whether it's not. You'll know then the hardships that face everyone that tries to make an honest living here.'

'If we fought for a deeper quay we'd get it!'

'Fight! Who would fight here?—nobody! They'd grumble but they're not the kind to get together and make their voices heard.'

He laughed: 'You've a bit of spirit in you anyway. And for all your talk against the place I feel you love it.'

'Love it! I hate the living sight of it!' she said, the heavy emphasis on each word making Mary stir in her sleep.

'We've wakened her,' he whispered, 'I'd better go.'

'What's your hurry? She'll drop over in a minute or two,' and she tiptoed to the open door, patted her daughter on the head, and standing sideways at the mirror gave a quick comb to her hair and fixed her blouse tighter at the waist.

He was bent over the yacht against the wall when she came into the kitchen again.

'I suppose you'll be for the dance after tomorrow's race?' she said as she lifted her knitting and sat under the lamp where the light fell on her parted hair.

'I'll take a turn there for an hour or two. There's nothing I like better than to hear a good song or a good bit of fiddling. You'll be there yourself?'

'Indeed I'll not,' and she nodded towards the bedroom door. 'How could I go and leave Mary?'

'She could stay at her granny's for the night.'

'I'd like that! Not after Pat's performance in this kitchen! The cheek of him coming into my house and opening presses that don't belong to him! And what's more: he wouldn't race the yacht tomorrow if yours wasn't in it. He would not. He wouldn't budge a foot from his Sunday hillside if I know anything.'

'He'll forget all about his row over the moulding when Tom's yacht streels home ahead of the others. He'll be standing me a drink then.'

'I'd like to see your own or somebody else's win for a change. There's not the same interest if the same boat always takes the prize.'

'If Pat heard you he'd whirl a few more times round the kitchen,' he said with a pleasant smile. 'I'll go now, for James will be wondering what's keeping me.'

'You have him spoiled I'm thinking. You're too kind and little thanks you'll get for it in the long run.'

Suddenly there was a scramble on the gravel and a loud hammering at the door.

'In the name of God what'd that be?' she said with a start. 'Open the door, Martin, I'd be afraid.'

He flung open the door wide and Jamesy stood before him, the colour of death.

'I heard something padding in your room and I ran out.'

Martin put his arm round his shoulder: 'I know what it is: the window's open and the cat has hopped in. The same thing frightened the life out of myself one night,' he added with a laugh. 'Give him a sip of water, Vera, and we'll leave you in peace.'

She held the door wide open to give them light down the path and as she watched them she saw the light shine on the backs of their hands and on Martin's oilskin, and when they reached the gate she shouted, 'Good night,' and then heard Martin whistling loudly to dispel the boy's fear.

She lifted her needles but they moved listlessly, and time and again she rested her hands on her lap as she thought of Pat's anger and then of Martin's kindness: the one assailing her and drawing her erect, the other bending towards her with a slow unexpectedness that filled her with a warm confident pleasure. She sighed and rolled up her knitting, and stooping over to sweep the hearth she came upon the pieces of broken stool that were warming for the morning's kindling. As she lifted the yacht to sweep behind it her hand stroked the red-painted hull: 'I'd love to burn it and give him something to rage about in earnest!' she said to herself. She put it down roughly against the wall, and then as she was putting her knitting into the chest she suddenly halted, crossed to the door and bolted it. Coming back to the fire her hands trembled as she drew out a steel needle and plunged it into the red heart of the fire. She stood erect, waiting without a move, her hands clenched by her sides. The needle grew red hot at its tip, and wrapping a cloth round her hand she drew it out and taking the boat on her lap she pointed the needle at the hull near the fin. There was a hiss, a spurt of solid smoke, and a smell of burnt wood that smarted her eyes. At the other side of the fin she pierced the wood again, leaving two holes like the nostrils of a goose on the red-painted hull. She prized off a lump of clay from her working-boots below the table and smeared it over the two holes, and as she put back the yacht its mast-head rattled against the wall from the shaking of her hands.

'Let him rage now! He'll have something to fume about tomorrow when she fills up and sinks to the bottom of the lough. He'll have less call then to come into this house and parade around it as if he were lord and master.'

CHAPTER VIII

FROM the window where she sat with Mary after their Sunday dinner they saw the loops of cloud-shadow crawl over the hills, and in the sky, gaps and channels of blue that widened in front of the climbing sun. Then the first cart with its white-rigged yachts passed on the road to the lough, then people on foot, and lastly lightkeepers, in their linen-covered caps, went by on bicycles. At any moment Pat's cart would halt outside the open gate. Vera rose slowly from the table and gathered the dishes. She wouldn't go to the lough today; in all truth she'd say that she had a headache but that Mary could go with him and enjoy herself.

As she stood at the far table bent over the dishes Mary went to the open door watching the people on the road, and now and again calling over her shoulder to her mother, telling her to hurry or they'd be late. But her mother, concentrated and abstracted, didn't seem to hear her, and when Mary scampered away from the door and rushed back again shouting that Uncle Pat was here her mother remained silent, and when he stepped into the kitchen, holding Mary by the hand, she was still engaged at the few dishes.

'Come on the pair of you in the cart,' he said jauntily. 'We haven't a great load of time on our hands and we'll need to hurry.'

'I've a few things to tidy up. Mary can go ahead with you. I've a splitting headache and I think I'll lie down for a while.'

'Come on,' he said, gathering the yacht under his arm. 'The air and the excitement will lift it for you. We can't leave you behind on a day like this,' he went on, with feigned concern.

She arranged the dishes on the dresser and wiped the table.

'Hurry, mother,' Mary said.

'Hurry now,' Pat enjoined, taking his watch from his pocket,

'I'm behind time as it is and I want to give her a stretch across the lough before the race starts. They'll all be well-trimmed for that wind before I arrive.'

'In a minute,' she said, going into her room.

She must delay him, she thought, and sat on the edge of the bed to control the agitation that fumbled all her movements. She could hear the impatient grit of his feet on the kitchen floor and she could hear him telling Mary that she'd see her father's yacht come home first.

'Hurry, Vera, for God's sake,' he shouted in to her. 'We can't delay a minute longer.'

'I'm coming . . . They'll not start without you.'

She came from the room, her eyes avoiding his as he hurried out in front of her, and by the time she reached the gate he and Mary were already in the cart. She put her toe on the felloe of the wheel and he took her hand and hoisted her up.

'Hold the yacht on your lap,' he said, as he sent the horse forward at a gallop. Their feet dizzed on the floorboards and the brass rings on the mast rattled and glinted in the sun . . . A long bamboo rod for turning the boat projected over the tail-board of the cart and looking at it she asked him who was going to partner him in the sailing of it.

'I'm sailing her all on my own. I'll run from one side of the lough to the other and turn her off as she nears the shore.'

They jolted on in silence but each knew what was uppermost in the other's mind. When Tom was alive it was he who saw her off from the starting point and it was Pat, on these occasions, who partnered him, standing up to his knees in the water near the opposite bank, the long pole poised like a fishing-rod to turn the yacht off on her next tack.

'You should get somebody to help you,' she said.

'I don't need anyone. I'll sail her without help and it will add to the honour of winning — Tom would like that.'

Her sober concern loosened his cooped up anger: it could all

81

be that he misjudged her and that the moulding of a few drills was what any neighbour would have done out of clean friendliness and that the chopping up of a stool was, as his mother said, nothing to row or rage over.

'We're getting a good day, Vera,' he said, feeling the dregs of his hatred thinning away from him. 'God be merciful to Tom — I wish he were with me.' She didn't speak and as he turned to look at her he saw her patting down the collar of her blouse with her fingers.

'Get up!' he shouted at the horse, and when they had come in sight of the lough and into the mouth of the wind he felt again a lean rush of excitement and with it a bitter determination that strengthened him. Groups of people were lying on the hills, men were standing in groups near the edge of the lough, and two yachts were coming ashore, their tackle geared to the temper of the winds.

He drew up and before he had climbed down with his yacht some men were shouting to him to line up. He deliberately took his time, feeling irked that his boat wouldn't get a reach or two before the commencement of the race. He joined the cluster of men. They were collecting the entrance fee, others taking bets, and children running in and out of the groups shouting aloud the names of some of the boats: *Shooting Star*, *Mystical Rose*, *St. Anne*, *St. Patrick's Pride*, and Tom's boat *Whin Blossom*.

'*Whin Blossom* will win,' a little boy shouted and whirled a stick above his head. 'The boat with the red patch will win again.'

'Line up, men,' the starter was saying.

'There's a damned great flurry on you today,' Pat addressed no one in particular.

'That wind might fall away before long,' someone answered him.

'There's a good scud of it out there at the moment. Would you not wait till I give my boat a skelp across the narrow channel?' Pat asked.

No one answered him. 'You can all get ready now,' the starter ordered, and youths in brown dungarees and with long poles over their shoulders disentangled themselves from the group, stubbed out their cigarettes on the heels of their boots and made off to the opposite side, a narrow channel about ten perches in width. The lough was shaped like a map of England, the starting point at Southampton. They agreed to a three-course race; one beat up the length of the lough against the wind, one down before the wind, and one reach up again. A boat that could sail well into the wind could reach the head of the lough in three tacks, and for this purpose Pat stooped low over his yacht, drew in the mainsail and tightened the two jibs.

Martin Gallagher took his place beside him: 'Good luck, Pat,' he said, 'and may the best boat win.'

'The best boat always wins!' Pat said and he stood back and allowed the other boats to set off before placing his own in the water. He had done right: three boats ran foul of one another a short distance from the shore, and as they hugged and butted one another, hopelessly entangling themselves in a directionless clump, people shouted and waved their hands in despair. Then suddenly a youth snatching up a long pole rushed into the water up to his neck and shouting with excitement he released the boats and they set off freely after the others. Pat didn't stop to look at them. He set off with his long pole and before he had reached the opposite side his boat was lying ashore. He turned her off quickly and as she headed out for the long stretch across the full width of the lough she was lying about sixth but going more to windward than the others. Martin's with her two brown jibs was skimming out ahead of the line, and Jamesy who had turned her off was smiling with confidence and relief at not having blundered.

Pat, with a heavy sense of powerless rage, heard the people shout at him from the hill to get a helper: 'You're not giving Tom's a fair chance!' they were saying; and as he ran, encum-

83

bered by the long pole, he struggled out of his coat and waistcoat and threw them on the bank. He shot a hurried glance at the pack of boats; there were about six striding ahead of the others, his own lying fourth.

'Tom's is doing nicely,' a man shouted to him as Pat stumbled over the rocky path at the lough's edge. His breath scorched his throat and his black hair wet with sweat hung over his forehead. He overtook Martin Gallagher.

'Mine's doing well,' Martin said proudly.

'And why shouldn't she — and you out all morning clipping her to the wind. Them that live next door to the lough should be handicapped — that's what I'd do if I had my way.'

The boats were now bearing into the full trough of the wind, every mouthful tightening the sails and flinging strings of foam across the face of the water. Martin's was in the lead but two others were hanging at her tail with not a hand's breadth between them. Four men with poles were plunging up to their knees at the water's edge and as Pat ran past them he saw Martin's was the first to be turned. Once again his own had reached the shore before him and when he noticed that Martin was eyeing him he turned her out with unnecessary slowness and smiled as she headed dead-on for the two heaps of stones that marked the end of the first lap.

'She doesn't need anyone's help only my own,' he said to himself as he saw her hold her course with uncanny accuracy. 'She's like a trained dog. She knows what's asked of her.'

Three boats arrived at the first mark together, and a couple of yards behind them came Tom's. None of the four men spoke. They rushed into the shallow water, their hands and feet scrambling around their boats. Mainsails were loosened to the full; jibs folded, spinnakers attached to the masts and flat pieces of lead clipped to the stern; and as the four boats, looking now like Chinese junks, hurtled down in front of the wind the onlookers on the hills rose up to watch them. Mary, sitting with her mother, got up and wrung her hands: 'My father's is winning! Get up, mother, till you see better.'

'Calm yourself like a good girl,' her mother said.

'It's running away from them. Get up, mother! Look at the red patch! Come on!' and she pulled at her arm till she arose and stood limply beside her.

Martin and Pat with their long poles over their shoulders were hurrying towards them on their way back to the foot of the lough. Their eyes were fastened on the clump of boats and by the time they had reached the top of the hill Martin saw that Tom's was five or six yards ahead of the others.

'Tom's has it again,' he said.

'There's another lap,' Pat answered slowly, trying to conceal his deep confident pleasure.

They reached Vera and Mary. Pat smiled to them and stood resting for a moment on the pole. His boat seemed to lag as if some under-surface force was holding her. He saw the others gain slowly, and then his two hands gripped the wet pole when the stern of his boat hung heavily and a wave broke over it. A gust struck her and she struggled up and shouldered the water from her deck, dipped her bow, and plunged and bucked to throw off the burden of clinging water. The other boats drew abreast, hung close to her for a moment, and then cut freely past her.

'Tom's is sinking!' someone shouted, and a crowd ran down from the hill to the edge of the lough. Nothing was seen of her except the mainsails above the water and her swinging boom catching the tops of the waves. Once more she lifted to a burst of wind and tilted the water from her deck.

'She's filling up! She's going to sink!' A squall struck her and as her red hull gleamed wet for a moment Pat flung the pole from him and running down the hill made a gap in the people at the shore and dived into the water. He swam with bent head; his trousers filled up like sacks of coal and his shirt bellied out and then collapsed like a fallen parachute. He raised his head when a belated yacht struck him but his powerful sweeps swept it behind him and his boots snapped the mast and kicked her with a hollow sound. Once more he raised his head and as he did so he saw his own boat slowly disappear with her red patch below the water. He reached the spot and stood for a moment treading the water. He breathed deeply and dived, and in a few seconds he emerged, his hands twined with long green weeds, his black hair covering his eyes. He tossed back his hair and dived again, and when he rose once more with a net of weeds about his head the people shouted and waved to him to come in.

'Let it go, Pat! Let it go to hell! The weeds are as strong as a net. Come on in!'

Mary was crying and her mother gripped her hand so firmly that it hurt her. She looked at the bobbing head in the water and then turned away: 'God!' she said. 'What have I done?'

Pat slowly headed to the shore and his tired arms rose and fell heavily. Two men took off their boots and shirts, and standing in their trousers at the edge of the lough they waited till he'd sign to them for help. He lay on his back, and with his eyes bulged with terror he glanced sideways to mark his progress.

'Will you make it, Pat?' the two men shouted at him. He didn't answer them as he turned on his front again, and lowering his head he thrashed the water in a last rush of powerful energy and didn't look up until he felt the stones under his hands. He struggled to his feet and scrambled up the bank, his shirt hanging loose over one bare shoulder and the hair on his chest lying flat like the quills of a bird. His mouth hung open, his breath gulched in his throat, and as water streamed from him and slithered into the lough he stared at the calm wedge he had swept on the wrinkled surface.

'She's gone,' he said, 'and the man that made her's gone! There never was a boat like her and there never will be.' The people stood around him and no one spoke as he stripped the water from each sleeve and eyed the broken patch of water that was now merging with the huddled surface. They began to speak to him, advising him to go home or he'd get his death.

'She's sinking now in the mud and no one knows what happened to her,' he said.

'She had it won!' they all agreed.

'She had, she had,' he said. 'Tom knew how to make a boat.'

'There's no one left could equal him.'

He turned and climbed up the hill, the water squelching and hissing through the brass eyelets of his boots. Vera approached with his coat and waistcoat, and without looking at her he took them and draped them over his arm.

'Was Martin the last to handle her?' he asked.

'I think he was,' she faltered.

'You think he was! You know he was! He done something to her I'll warrant you.'

'He wouldn't! It's not in his nature.'

'You'd stand up for him even if he did.'

'He wouldn't tamper with it.'

He shook his head spitefully, and as he walked away she followed after him, beseeching him to come up to the house and dry himself.

'You can stay on and watch the brown-jibbed one take the prize. That'll be something to delight you! That'll be something to remember!'

She cast a look of tight scorn at him and turned away without speaking.

He threw his clothes into the cart and neither glancing to right nor left, sent the horse home at a gallop, and Sarah, who had been up at the chapel arranging flowers on the altar, met him as he turned into the yard.

'You must be powerful hot,' she said, noticing him without coat or waistcoat. 'Have you the first prize?'

He didn't answer her as he jumped out of the cart and began

untackling the horse. She drew nearer on seeing the damp-twisted folds in his trousers and the shirt transparent with wetness.

'Did you fall in or what?' and there was a touch of humorous mockery in her voice that angered him.

'I dived in if you want to know. The boat's sunk!'

'If you'd listened to my mother's advice you wouldn't have stirred a foot near the lough. She's lying down now and you best slip into the room and don't let her see you in that state. I never heard the like — diving into the lough to save a boat. A man thirty years of age making himself a laughing-stock for all sightseers!'

'Don't stand there like a statue of curiosity! Lend a hand here!'

She was afraid to go near him and he let the shafts fall to the ground and wrenched the bits from the horse's mouth.

'That temper of yours will be the undoing of you,' she said.

'It'll be the undoing of you if you don't get out of my sight!'

She went into the house and without making a noise that would disturb her mother she prepared a meal for him. He entered his room and in a few minutes flung his sop of wet clothes on to the kitchen floor. She gathered them up quickly and steeped them in a bucket, and when he came from the room tightening his braces she implored him, in God's name, not to mention anything to his mother. He sat at the table in silence, and then after drinking the hot tea he told her what had happened: how the boat was winning when it suddenly struck dead, plucked at the water like an anchored vessel and sank like a stone as he swam out to her.

'It was misfortunate! But you can't expect to win all the time. Anyway whose boat won the day?' she said with quiet interest.

'I didn't wait. But by all accounts it'd be Martin Gallagher's. And what's more I think he did something to Tom's. She didn't sink without good cause.'

'You're a man without much sense. You can't bear to lose.'

'And do you imagine I'm thinking about myself? It's our brother Tom I think of,' he said, looking round at her from the table.

'You think it was but it wasn't,' she said. 'You went out of this house divided between hurting Vera and honouring Tom — you can't deny that! And let me tell you an unsettled mind has as much sense in it as a tangled string.'

'You talk like your mother!'

'Tom! God be good to Tom but he'd be the first to shake the man's hand that beat him.'

'That's if he was beaten fair and square!'

'Maybe it struck a stone. Didn't I often hear you say she was as thin as a sheet of notepaper.'

'She struck a stone in the middle of the lough! It must have been a floating stone! There was a stiff wire from the tip of the bowsprit to the edge of the fin to prevent that. If you ask me she had as many holes stitched in her as there is in the edge of a postage stamp. That's what I believe!'

'Her seams may have opened in the hot sun — did that ever occur to you?'

'It might if she hadn't come from the hands of Tom. Tom wasn't the man to pick a bit of timber with a bad grain or a bit with a cluster of measely knots. He knew the feel of good timber as I know the feel of a good horse.'

The old woman came from her room, fastening her shawl about her shoulders.

'Well, Pat, did you win?' she said, going to her armchair at the corner of the fire.

'I did not!' he said, rising up from the table.

'Something told me you wouldn't. You were in no frame of mind going out to win any race.'

'I'd no luck.'

'There's no such a thing as luck. The eye of God is over everything we do.'

'I can't listen to that talk. I'm going out to the hill and Sarah can give you the whole story if she likes.'

'Come here, son. I don't want to vex you. I told you nothing comes from bad temper — nothing only a restlessness that grits the blood.'

'You're always preaching at me and you have Sarah nearly as bad as yourself. Will you leave me alone and let me be in peace?'

'I want to see you at peace and I want to give you the advice that'll bring you peace.'

'I don't want it. I'll get peace in my own way.'

'And at your own price — and that price will be a hard one.'

'I'm going out of this,' he said, and he took his pipe from the window-ledge and slammed the door behind him.

CHAPTER IX

H E climbed the hill at the back of the house and resting his back against a cushion of heather he gazed down at the deserted white road that stretched and hid itself among the hills of the Lower End. There was nothing to be seen except the geese asleep in the warm fields, the houses sitting on their own shadows, and the cows lying in the shady side of the loose-stone walls. He smoked his pipe and waited for the first flash of a bicycle on the road.

The wind had fallen away and he knew that the race was surely over and he wondered what had happened to detain those who had no yacht to sail. He got up stiffly and was ready to set off down the road when he heard the hollow sound of feet in the hall near the school, and saw whorls of dust come out through the open door. Inside, two girls were sweeping the floor, their voices loud and laughing in the empty hall, and on seeing him they asked him if he would lift down the overhanging lamps and fill them with oil.

'Did you hear who won the race?' he asked them as he stood on the step-ladder and lifted one of the lamps.

'I'm sure we're bothered about who won the race It's a good dance we want. Isn't that right, Josie?' said one of the girls.

'Tonight I'll give the pair of you the dance of your lives,' he said, smiling down at them.

'That's a bargain . . . No going back on your word. And you'll give us a song, too, as good measure.'

'A song and a tight dance I'll give you.'

'Then it's going to be the dance of the year by all accounts . . . I hear we'll have three melodeon players. Martin Gallagher has promised to come, and there's a fiddler from Belfast on holidays and he's coming too.'

The two girls joined hands, did a fantastic step or two on the floor, bowed to their upright brushes and swung them round, laughing loudly, but as their feet dragged and gripped on the rough boards they tossed the brushes from them in disgust and produced candles from their coats hanging behind the door. They pared the grease off them with a knife till the floor was covered with tiny flakes, and when Pat helped them to ground the grease into the boards with his heavy boots they laughed and said they could have done nothing at all without a man to help them.

'Oh, Josie,' said one, stretching out her arms and twirling round on the floor, 'you could break your neck on it if you weren't careful.'

Pat grabbed her round the waist and as he swung her round her hair flew round with her and her screams broke in a glitter of delight against the bare walls.

'You're the very divil, this day, Pat Reilly,' she said as he let her go and she flopped down on the bench out of breath.

'Are you drunk or what's the matter with you?' the other girl said.

'Divil the drunk!' he said, catching her and swinging her up and down the hall till she cried out for mercy.

'Oh, dear, we're flat!' they said as they put their hair-clips in their mouth and combed back their hair.

They swept up the empty cigarette packets and spent matches from around the threshold, turned the key in the door and went off with their brushes into the schoolhouse.

'Don't forget your promise,' they shouted back as he leant against the wall of the road waiting for someone to bring him the news of the race.

'Leave it to me,' he said, leaning over the wall and spitting into the heap of dust they had swept out of the hall. In a few minutes a lightkeeper came up on his bicycle and Pat hailed him, and on hearing that Martin's yacht had taken the first prize he kept silent about his own for fear he would display any sign of ill-will in front of a stranger.

'She's a good boat,' he said.

'She's modelled on Tom's, I believe,' said the lightkeeper.

'She's a fine little boat,' Pat said again. 'If Tom's hadn't sunk it'd been a tight race.'

'It would have been a one boat race — that's everybody's opinion that was there,' said the lightkeeper, mounting his bicycle.

'I don't know about that,' Pat said, smiling weakly.

'You're a good sport to take the loss so easily,' the light-keeper shouted over his shoulder as he cycled off.

'Take the loss so easily,' Pat said to himself as he went up to the house. And that evening as he was taking his tea it came into his mind again with a curious persistence to which he gave no heed. Through the open door he could hear the boys and girls laughing as they passed by on their way to the hall, and he could see the sky stippled with stars and the rising moon shaking its concertina folds on the sea. His mother was seated at the fire, getting ready for bed, the kitten sparring at the pom-poms on her slippers. He got up to shave when his mother went into her room.

'Are you not going to the dance?' he said to Sarah, 'Jimmy Neil will be down from the Upper End and he'll wonder if you're not there.'

'She wouldn't sleep till we came in again.'

'Couldn't you come for an hour or two.'

'I may look in at the door to hear the fiddler or a song — that's all.'

'I suppose yourself and Jimmy will have a quiet chat on that sofa.'

'We might,' she said laughing.

'Maybe the two of you have it all arranged. There's something afoot or you wouldn't have washed your face at this time of the night.'

He went in to see his mother. She was in bed, the clothes rolled round her like an arctic explorer.

'Is Sarah going with you?' she asked.

'She doesn't want to.'

'She'll have to go. If she doesn't go when she's young she'll regret it later on when she's old. She can't let her youth be tethered and chafed by an old woman. Tell her if she doesn't go I'll rise up and go down myself for an hour or two. Take her with you for I don't need her here.'

He called Sarah and she came in. Her mother sat up and smiled at her: 'You'll have to go and enjoy yourself, girl. You can't disappoint Jimmy.'

'He'll come up here when he misses me.'

'Get on your frock and none of your nonsense. You don't think I'd upset the lamp and burn the house down?'

'Will you promise to stay in bed if I go?'

'I came to bed to sleep and not to get out of it.'

'And listen, Pat, if there's any drink going . . .'

'I'll keep you a drop,' he finished it for her.

'If there's any drink going you'll not join in it — you know it doesn't agree with you.'

'If there's any drink going they'll carry it inside them where nobody'll share it.'

She squeezed his hand and looked at him with careful scrutiny but he avoided her gaze and straightened the quilt on the bed. She was going to say something else to him but changed her mind and said: 'I hope you'll oblige them with a song or two if you're asked.'

'I'll do that all right. Good night now.'

There was a crowd hanging round the door of the hall when he arrived, and inside a girl was singing. He waited till she was finished and couples were dancing before he paid his two shillings and sat in the corner at the back with Sarah. His hands drooped loosely between his knees and his eyes ranged slowly round the four walls of the hall. The floor was in great order, shining like the varnished seats in the chapel. It shook under the feet of the dancers, under the hobnailed boots of the men and under the light rhythmic tap and lift of the women's shoes. There was a cool swirl from their skirts, the human smell of sweat, the quivering oil-lamps sending shadows across the floor or tilting them on the walls, the loud breathing of men and the light breathing of the girls, and enfolding all was the music from two melodeons and the hurrying fiddle. The dance came to a halt and the dancers slowly dispersed to their seats or hung in groups round the door. A song was called for, and a young visiting priest sang 'Deep in Canadian Woods we met', standing erect and plucking the lapels of his coat in time to the refrain: 'We'll toast old Ireland, dear old Ireland, Ireland boys, hurrah!' and when he had finished they clapped and drummed on the floor with their feet until he arose again and with a sly exaggerated wistfulness sang:

> I know where I'm goin',
> And I know who's goin' with me,
> I know who I love
> But the dear knows who I'll marry!
>
> I have stockings of silk,
> Shoes of fine green leather,
> Combs to buckle my hair,
> And a ring for every finger.
>
> Some say he's black,
> But I say he's bonny,
> The fairest of them all
> My handsome winsome Johnny. . . .

They cheered him, and when the next dance was announced everyone was in such good form that there was an immediate

95

rush across the floor for partners, Jimmy Neil took Sarah but Pat sat on, his eyes fixed on Martin Gallagher who had lifted his melodeon and was laughing at the fiddler tucking a handkerchief under his chin where the fiddle rested. He's in fine fettle, Pat said to himself, and why shouldn't he be with the prize money in his pocket and the best yacht in the country at the bottom of the lough? But I'm not finished with him yet. He sat forward, and as the dancers parted he stared fixedly at Martin, a sour resentment stirring impatiently in his blood at every flourish of Martin's head as he shook his melodeon.

The next dance was a quadrille and on seeing Martin rise for it Pat put his pipe in his pocket, took one of the girls he had promised to dance with, and joined Martin's set. The girl was speaking to him of the crowd and the gaiety but he paid no attention to what she was saying. He lowered his head, tapped loudly at the floor, waiting for the beat, and then gave a whoop and went forward with his partner.

'She had the race won,' Martin said, but Pat didn't answer him, and Martin smiled then at the accusing cornered look he cast at him. Martin swung his partner with great alacrity, and as the girls encouraged him he shrugged his shoulders with emphatic joviality and now and again gave a whoop to emphasize his excitement. His boyish abandonment enraged Pat and he yearned to shout something insulting at him. He waited and shouldered him and as Martin stumbled the girls laughed, thinking that Pat, too, had broken the rope of his dour despondency and was riding free to the mood of the dance. The dance came to an end and instead of going to his place beside Jamesy, Martin walked slowly out through the door to slake his thirst at the stream below the hall. The night was still and the air swung cold under his arm-pits. A reflection of a star wriggled like an eel in the dark pool and as he bent down to cup his hands he could hear the water slipping over the stones and the drum of his own blood pressing at his forehead. The cold water chilled his teeth and he had to wait a moment before drinking again. This time he knelt and after drinking dabbed his forehead with his handkerchief. He stood up and heard the shuffle of feet behind him. It was Pat Reilly.

'It's a grand night,' Martin said, slowly wiping his hands.

'It's grand for some people,' Pat said with a tenseness that startled Martin.

'I suppose it's the race you're thinking about?'

'You supposed rightly this time ... You've nothing to say about it?'

'I have said it before and I say it again — the best boat's at the bottom of the lough.'

'You had something to do in the sinking of her!' Pat shouted, and a group of men round the door of the hall stopped their conversation and turned their faces towards the stream.

'I don't understand you,' Martin said calmly.

'You don't want to understand me — she didn't sink without good cause.'

'She filled up, I suppose.'

'Did she ship much water the day you took the lend of her?'

Martin pondered for a moment and recalled that when he had shaken his own boat the water slapped inside it like the belly of a horse but when he had shaken Tom's there was no sound except the seed-rattle of chips of wood.

'It's taking you a hell of a long time to answer! Was she dry?'

'She was,' Martin said.

'Why then did she sink on me?'

'That's a mystery for us all.'

'It's no mystery! You drilled a few holes in it!'

'We'll talk about it when your mind is easier,' Martin said and walked away from him. But Pat gripped him by the arm and halted him in his stride against the gable of the hall.

'My brother that's dead made that boat and you crippled her. Deny it!' he shouted and shook his fist in Martin's face.

97

'I made a copy of it — that was all,' Martin said, without cowering from the flourishing fist.

'You're a damned treacherous liar! You punctured it.'

'I wouldn't listen to you,' Martin said and attempted to walk away from him.

Pat gripped his arm tighter: 'Why didn't you bring Vera to the dance and celebrate in proper style? You've already grabbed one field — grab his wife now and you've got them all.'

'Let go that arm!' Martin said gravely. 'Let it go I tell you!' and seeing the flash of Pat's teeth as he curled back his lips he made a sudden twist and wrenched himself free. Pat unbalanced and fell on the road. He rose and rushed at Martin but Martin seized him by the lapels of the coat and held him close to him, their breaths hot on one another's cheek.

'I'll choke the lies out of you and choke sense into you!' Martin said as he quickly twisted the lapels together, raised him off his feet, and flung him into the hedge at the side of the road. The group of men moved down from the door as Pat struggled to his feet and raced at Martin who stood at the gable end with his fists raised. He swung at Martin but Martin swerved to the side and Pat's fist crashed into the gable, and the men gathered round them and held them apart.

'I haven't finished with him yet!' Pat said as he felt the bulging pain numbing his right hand. Martin buttoned his coat and went back to the hall and taking his melodeon from Jamesy he sat down and played as if nothing had happened. He saw Pat Reilly come in and sit down at the back, his right hand in his pocket, and later when Pat was asked to oblige the company with a song he stood up and sang 'The Flowing Bowl', the crowd laughing at him as he awkwardly stirred an imaginary bowl of punch with his left hand:

> No nor anyone it may control
> Keep me from my flowing bowl.
> When I'm single, single I'm free,
> Love, love, love will never conquer me.

He ended in a challenging shriek that rocked the hall with laughter and made his sister Sarah blush with repressed embarrassment, thinking he was drunk and was making a fool of himself.

It was an hour off dawn when the dance broke up and Martin and Jamesy left the hall. As they neared home, Vera, who was lying awake, heard them pass on the road and Martin playing on his melodeon. His dog barked from the hill and she saw through the bare window the comforting light spring up in his house. She hadn't slept. All night long the dance she had missed troubled her mind. She had even gone to the top of the hill behind the house, foolishly thinking that from there she would have heard the sound of the dancers or the sound of the music wading towards her on the smooth waves of air. But she had heard nothing only the gravel trickling at her feet and the startled rabbits drumming into their hollow burrows. She had gazed at the tiny lights in the cottages among the hills, at the long-striding beams of the lighthouse confidently sweeping the velvet sky and felt a sense of entrapped loneliness and isolation. She felt she should have gone, for she had an unquiet feeling that Pat in his anger would challenge Martin about the sinking of the yacht, and if she had gone she could have remained close to him and held him apart with unexpressed warning. But it was Mary, and nothing else, she had told herself, that had forced her to sacrifice the enjoyment the dance would have afforded her. She had come down then from the hill and peeped into the lighted room, and satisfied that Mary was deep asleep she had dragged herself out again into the freedom of the fields and sat down in her loneliness near a clump of bracken that lounged on its tumble of shadow. In her mind she had followed the dancers, heard the pound of their feet beating in time to the insistent pulse of her own heart and saw herself on the floor with Martin beside her, his strong arm round her waist, their shadows on the wall breaking, interlocking and meeting again — a rhythm of blurred shadows, of moving bodies, and of breaths warm and moist with the swift pattern of the dance. She had closed her eyes from the lassitude that had stolen over her. She had stood up then and gazed at the beauty of the night, at the thin cloud tearing across the moon, sending its creeping shadow over the breast of the hill, sliding into the valley that opened out like a flower, and then slowly withdrawing to leave the valley at rest and asleep in its own timid light. She had shaken her head and called to God to drive away the feelings that her thoughts had roused, and then standing stiff with resolution she had heard the wild duck in the lake and their moving feet flinging bangles of moonlight among the reeds. On her way back to the house she had heard a commotion in the fowl-shed and entering had struck a match and saw a captured rat rattling against the wired sides of the trap. She had lifted the trap by the handle and carrying it to the shallow edge of the lake sank it with the aid of a heavy stone. That was a job for a man, she had often told herself, and often wished that she had finished with it. But no, not even the sinking of the trap had delivered her, for in the morning she would have to come out and dig a hole to bury the drowned carcass; rebait the trap and allow the disgusting round of days to begin again. She had come back from the lake with her hands behind her back and wearily turned out the lamp in the kitchen and wearily got into bed.

She hadn't slept and she was wide awake now as she saw Martin's light leave his kitchen and reappear in his room, and she felt that he would sleep, sleep soundly, unaware of the thoughts she had herded through the long night. She put her arm round her daughter and drew her towards her, and listening now to her own breathing and to the breathing of her daughter she at last fell asleep.

CHAPTER X

AFTER days of making hay in the fields the men who lived nearest the pub would retire there of an evening to lift the dryness of their tongues with draughts of cool porter; and there they usually discussed the fishing, the crops, the price of cattle on the mainland, the diseases of fowl and the best feeding for putting a hard shell on the eggs, the uncanny behaviour of rats, and the importance of having a well-fed bull. But their chief talk now was centred on last week's race and on the mysterious quarrel that had risen out of it at the dance. No one rightly knew the reason for it but each risked a suggestion, and when Martin appeared among them they tackled him only to be countered with a dry smile or a silent wave of dismissal.

'How the hell do I know what it was for! Pat took some notion in his head after the sousing he gave himself in the lough. That's all I know about it.'

'He has a nice football of a fist, the nurse was saying. And to see him raking hay with his left hand is a sight to take the pain out of your eye.'

'Maybe he thinks you've an eye for Vera.'

'I wouldn't blame anyone for that,' an old man said with a smile. 'She's a woman in fine fettle with the stride of a thoroughbred. If I was younger I'd have two eyes for her and not one. What do you think, Martin?'

'I don't think anything in that line,' Martin smiled.

'Man, if I was living near her I'd have slipped the ring on her a year ago. She's still as fresh as the day she came here to marry Tom Reilly,' another put in.

'And with the right man in the saddle you wouldn't have to import orphans to help on the land,' the old man said.

'She hates the place,' Martin said, for some reason enjoying the banter in spite of himself.

'There's only one way to content her,' they laughed. 'Aye, there's only one way,' they all agreed, smoking and spitting on the concrete floor.

'A few extra children would shorten the wandering rope.'

'You're all damned smart at the talking,' Martin said with a quick glance at the unmarried men. 'You talk, but in the end you all settle down with your cat and dog.'

'You wouldn't want us to trespass in the Lower End.'

'You can trespass as much as you like and at any hour you like. I'm not the marrying sort,' Martin said.

'But she is!'

'And think of the lordly way Pat Reilly would handshake that news,' the old man said again. 'He'd give you a couple of heifers . . . Upon my word he'd dredge the lough and give you the yacht to stick up on the dresser.'

'He needn't mention yachts to me. I know where I'd tell him to stick it,' Martin answered.

They laughed till their faces were as red as the labels on the Red Heart stout.

'Sailing Vera is the best sail for you! And the safest!' they shouted after him when he left early for home because Jamesy was afraid when darkness fell.

The following Sunday at Mass the priest announced the date for Confirmation, and on their way out Martin told Jamesy they'd have to cross to the mainland for a new suit. Ahead of them on the road he saw Vera and he slackened his pace, and though Jamesy peppered him with questions about the colour of the suit he only answered him with scant and listless attention. His eyes were fixed on Vera and this concentrated staring impelled her to turn round and she waited till he reached her, Jamesy lagging shyly behind.

Together they passed the straggling scatter of cottages, and

102

women, just home from Mass, peered at them from the edge of the windows, and each thought the same thing: that it would be as well for Martin to have a wife but not a crabbed handful like that Vera Reilly, a girl that no man could mould into softness, or if he could then the same man could squeeze juice out of a stone.

Vera was aware of the lifting edge of the curtains and she walked upright, saying scarce a word till they reached the Craigs' empty cottage where they saw the thatch rotted to the colour of a dried sack and the cat sunning itself on the window and suddenly taking fright at their presence and scrambling up the wall and disappear through a hole in the roof.

'The Craigs will be doing well now, if I know anything,' she said. 'The old man will know he did what was right. You're the only one, Martin, who ran foul to what was natural.'

'I don't regret my return and I don't try to forget what I am and what I own. I am content and I don't live with the misery of hope. Jamesy is like a son to me and tomorrow I'm going across with him to rig him out for his Confirmation day.'

'Mary and myself are going on the same mission. She's away to ask Sarah to do sponsor for her. Indeed, it wasn't my choice but then there's nobody else I could ask except the teacher, and it was she who told Mary to first ask Sarah.'

'The teacher's wiser than me — she's not going to gather trouble around her the way I did.'

'Aye, that was a nice hand you gave Pat from what I heard. Wasn't there a fight between you? — Mary heard talk of it at school.'

'It was only a squabble. He blamed me for sinking Tom's yacht. He thinks I holed her. I've a good mind to cart a boat to the lake and spend a few days dredging for her.'

'He'll forget about it now that the harvest is ripening. She'd be bedded in six feet of mud by this time.'

'I hate to live with spite. The other day himself and Sarah passed me on the road and they didn't as much as bid me the time of day.'

103

'I told Pat to his very face that you'd be the last to meddle with it. And anyway the yacht was mine and I'm not holding spite. She's gone and I've no shred of sorrow after her.'

The sun blazed down on them and their feet dragged and slowed up on the road. Their shoulders touched, separated, and touched again with the softness of new clothes. The air, heavy with waves of heat, pressed against them, swelling sweetly from the clumps of perspiring bracken, moist and warm from the unsunned streams, and hot and dry from the parched stones on the road. The heat shadows wriggled like eels above the rocks, and in the lakes where the screeching swallows dipped their wings, nests of rings widened across the surface trembling the reeds and buckling the reflections of the hills.

Vera looked behind, then took off her hat, opened her coat and loosened her hair with the comb: 'That heat's like an oven,' she said, 'and I'm not going to be tortured with it any longer. You've a bit of freedom here and no eyes spying on you or caring whether you're hatless or in your bare feet.' She sighed loudly with the heat, aware of no one except Jamesy panting behind them like a faithful dog. At each side of the road rabbits lay like balls of dry clay and they could see their sides heaving and the red glow in their ears against the sun. 'They're a pest,' she said, stopping to look at them and give Jamesy a chance to pass on ahead. But he stopped when they stopped and amused himself by throwing stones at the coots in the lakes.

'I'd love to be a little girl again just to lie in that clump of bracken out of the sun,' she said, halting again on the road. She sighed audibly: 'I don't think I'll go any farther. I'll sit here in the sun and wait for Mary,' and she sat down, her two hands spread at each side of her on the grass, her head uplifted and her fine teeth smiling up at him. She eased off one shoe with the aid of the other and as she lifted them and placed them neatly beside her she was aware of the smell of hot leather.

'I wouldn't be surprised if you'd start and make a daisy chain,'

Martin said, standing beside her and waiting for Jamesy to come up to him.

She laughed and flung a fistful of grass at his feet: 'Even the very grass is warm,' she said, and she put her toe on a smooth stone to feel the heat burn through her stocking. She picked it up and held it out to him: 'You could fry an egg on it — it's so hot,' she said, moistening her lips with her tongue.

'You could dry corn on it if the harvest were cut,' he said, and tossing the stone into the bracken two rabbits bounded out and over the hill. Jamesy drew up and as Martin was walking off with him, his arm on the boy's shoulder, he stopped suddenly and told her that they'd be going early in the morning with sheep and a few lobsters but there'd be plenty of room for herself and Mary in the boat if they cared to come. She smiled but did not answer and he didn't ask her again. If she cared to come she'd be welcome, he thought, but if she doesn't she can walk to the quay and get a seat in one of the other boats that would be going.

Jamesy handed him a card that the teacher had given him after Mass: there were different spaces on it — one for the boy's name, his date and place of Baptism, one for his father's name, his mother's name, Confirmation name, and sponsor's name.

'You've to fill it in,' said Jamesy, 'and I mustn't forget to bring it with me on Confirmation day.'

Martin knew he would be able to fill in all the spaces except one, and in that space for the father's name there'd be the stroke of a pen.

'We'll not forget it,' Martin said, putting it in his pocket, 'I'll take charge of it and hand it to the priest. And I'll do sponsor for you on that day.'

They went into the house and as Jamesy washed the potatoes for the dinner, Martin lifted down the side of smoked bacon from the ceiling, sharpened his knife on the doorstep, cut five thick slices and left them in readiness on a plate with a few peeled onions. He spread a cloth on the table, rattled down the knives and forks, a jug of fresh buttermilk, mustard and salt, and a plate of home-made wheaten bread and fresh butter. Waiting for the potatoes to boil he took out *Moby Dick* which he was reading for the second time, and after the dinner, because it was Sunday, they wandered leisurely about the fields inspecting the sheep and the young heifers. Later they went down to the shore, bailed out the big boat, and oiled the little engine in readiness for the morning.

In the morning they awoke when the dawn was reddening the hearth above the hills and as they dressed they could see through the window the grass wet with dew, a white net of it spread on the headstrong whins, large drops hanging on the leaves of the ash tree, and a thin mist tearing apart above the lake. Martin tied a crate of eggs to a small wooden sleigh he had made for carrying mountain sods and together they pulled it by the rope down the slope where the boat lay lifting its heels on the incoming tide. The sheep huddled together were almost hidden in their own mist and as the dog rounded them into a shelter of four posts with a roof of thatched reeds their bleatings echoed along the silence of the cliffs disturbing the resting birds and sending them with a flitter of feet into the quiet water. They tied up four of the sheep by their legs and gripping their moist fleece carried them down to the boat and laid them on the floor boards on a bed of straw and bracken. On returning to the house to take their breakfast Martin saw Vera and Mary setting off on the road to the quay without looking back.

'We'll have the boat to ourselves,' he said to Jamesy. 'Hurry now and tidy yourself.'

They washed in a basin placed on an upturned crock outside the door, polished their boots, left out feed for the fowl and set off for the shore again leaving the dog behind them with the board hanging from her neck. They lifted in three boxes of lobsters moored below the water, ran up the sail to catch the stray fists of wind, and started the engine. His geese swam hysterically away from them and he flung an old bailing tin at them to increase their annoyance: 'Tame geese turning wild! If I could get my hands on them I'd sell every damned one of them. There's one thing, Jamesy, you'll taste on your Confirmation day and that'll be roast goose. I'll take the shotgun down some evening and ambush the devil out of the whole squad of them.'

They turned the point and saw two other island boats far away to the west: 'Vera will be sorry now she didn't come with us — we'll be in half an hour before them.'

A mist perched on top of the mountain behind the mainland town was lifting with the sun as Martin's boat drew alongside the rough stone pier. A man with a wheel-barrow lifted the lobsters and the crate of eggs, and throwing a sack over the wet boxes he rumbled up the quay, the water dripping in a zig-zag track on the dry stones.

Martin didn't wait for the arrival of the other island boats. He hurried the four sheep up to the big Square of the town where the fair was already in full swing and having sold the lot he bought new clothes and boots for Jamesy, and after getting him a neat hair cut and a good dinner he gave him the parcels and a few shillings and told him to be at the quay not later than four o'clock.

Jamesy, free now for a couple of hours, wandered from one stall to another, watching a man selling delph or breaking a saucer and mending it while-you-wait with his holdfast glue at only sixpence a tube. He bought a tube and then later bought a mouth-organ, and as he was backing away from the stall and running his fingers over the smooth metal fastenings of the mouth-organ he felt a tap on the shoulder and turned to see a red-haired boy whom he had known in the orphanage. The boys ears were smooth and large, his nose was freckled like a turkey's egg and Jamesy recognized him at once. He was older than Jamesy, a lad about sixteen who had left about two years ago.

'What are you doing here, Rainey?' he asked with a proprietorial air.

'I'm over for the day.'

'Over from where?'

'The island.'

'God above!' red-head laughed, lit a cigarette, and asked Jamesy if he smoked.

'No, I haven't started yet. The man I'm with told me to start on the pipe.'

'The pipe — a smoke from a pipe would kill you stone dead. Take a pull of that cigarette and buy yourself a packet before you go back to your island.'

Jamesy took a pull but the smoke swarmed down his throat in a smarting mass and made him cough till his eyes watered and the stalls swung before him in a blur of rainbow colours. His companion laughed, took him gently by the arm, and entering an ice-cream shop they sat in a snug at the back and ordered two bottles of lemonade and two buns. Red-head drank and ate and smoked, and leaning forward with studied conspiracy asked what was in the parcels. Jamesy told him, and red-head tore a hole in one of the parcels and fingered the material of the suit.

'It's long trousers,' Jamesy said bravely.

'It's the twin brother of the suit my boss bought me last week,' said red-head, and he leaned back against the partition with his thumbs in his waistcoat and recounted how his boss had also bought him a new bicycle with silver wheels for sporting himself on a Sunday. 'Look here,' he said, and leaning forward with a hand to the side of his mouth he told Jamesy how he could get him fixed up in a fine fat farm near the town. 'Now, listen, you can't go anywhere on an island unless you were a seagull with a bloody good pair of wings. No pictures, no places to ride on your bike, and no fellows to chum about with. It's worse than the orphanage.' He tapped the back of Jamesy's hand and whispered: 'Have you got a girl?' Jamesy looked round at the empty shop and told him he was in love with a girl who was going to be a schoolteacher.

'A schoolteacher!' red-head shouted and Jamesy blushed. 'A schoolteacher — heavens above! Hold up your head, clean your boots, take your hands out of your pockets, sweep up the floor and bar the door! No, a schoolteacher's no flaming use for a fellow like you. We'll have another lemonade and a couple of buns,' and he lifted the glass ash-tray and knocked on the small table. 'I could get you a bike dirt cheap, and I'll fork down ten good bob on it if you take the place I'll get you. Will you come?'

'But I couldn't go now.'

'And what's keeping you back?'

'I didn't tell him.'

'There's no call to tell him. The farmer I know would put a few shillings in your pocket before you'd lift a spade.'

Red-head took a gulp from the bottle of lemonade, lit another cigarette and rattled on about the bike. After a minute he blew out some smoke when he saw Jamesy staring at his mouth with innocent surprise.

'That's what you call "the trick". You'll never be a smoker till you're able to do it.' He inhaled once more, opening his mouth wide to show that the smoke had disappeared, and then after a long pause blew it out with leisurely satisfaction.

'Now put your hand on my chest and watch the smoke coming out of my ears,' he said, and as Jamesy followed his instructions and was watching the ears with keen curiosity red-head furtively put the lighted end of the cigarette to the back of Jamesy's hand. Jamesy jumped and a bottle rolled off the table and broke in pieces on the floor.

The shopkeeper ran out to them shouting she'd have to be paid for the broken bottle and Jamesy, confused with fear, gave her a half-crown and she took all payments out of it and handed him back the change.

'She's an oul bitch,' red-head said while she was turning away.

She stopped abruptly: 'What's that you said?'

'I said our dog had the itch,' red-head answered coolly.

'I've a good mind to draw the back of my hand across your lug, you wart you! Get out of this!'

'We'll not come back here again,' red-head said, and going to the door he put his hand on Jamesy's shoulder and told him he was a decent fellow for standing him that treat. 'But it's nothing to the feed I'll give you when you come to this side.'

Outside the sky was now covered with a dark crawl of angry cloud, the cattle in the Square were huddling together, and the farmers were looking skywards and slapping their ash plants against their legs. Red-head, seeing his boss yoking up the horse and cart, lifted an empty cigarette box from the street, slit it open with his thumb and wrote his address on it: 'When you want to leave write to me and I'll fix you up,' he said, and tapping Jamesy on the shoulder he stuffed something into his pocket: 'That'll pay you for the broken bottle,' and he ran off with haste, in and out by the canvas-covered stalls till Jamesy lost sight of him.

Jamesy pulled out from his pocket the glass ash-tray, stuffed it back again quickly and with a glance of terror at the shop he ran towards the quay. The clock in a church tower struck the hour of half-three, thunder rolled behind the hills of the town, and large drops of rain speckled the pavement and rattled on his parcels. The tops of the trees that lined the road were swishing darkly though he felt no wind; and then suddenly in a mad pelt of fury the rain loosened out like gravel from the clouds, broke in smoking fragments on the road and struck tiny mitres in the puddles around the choked-up drains. Martin, sheltering in the side doorway of an hotel, called out to him as he passed and they stood together out of the rain looking out at a suddenly deserted tennis court with its roller polished with rain.

'It's beginning to slacken, Jamesy, and we'll have to go,' Martin said, and taking the parcels he put them under his oilskin and told him to run on in front and shelter in the boat under the sail.

At the quay the islanders, soaked and pressed against the wall for a scrap of shelter, stared with patient silence at the slippery stones at their feet and at their open boats with their wet seats like shelves of shining glass.

'It's a disgrace and a shame!' Vera said bitterly to Martin as he stood among them for a moment. 'Why isn't there something done? — even a roof of tin would keep us all dry till that drunken lightkeeper would come and let us get on our journey.'

'We can't leave him behind,' Sarah said.

'I would leave him and I wouldn't think twice about it. He was told to be here at three and now it's long after four. I've a cow to be milked and there's poor Mary foundered and famished. Why don't you fight for a shelter?' she said, flinging out her hands in supplication. 'Why don't we march through the town shouting and singing: "We want a shelter! We want justice! We want a new pier!" What's a government for, I ask you?'

'For delivering forms and envelopes,' someone said drily.

'No one would thole this only a people like you with more patience than spirit. If I were a man I'd do something, I may tell you!'

No one spoke with her or against her. The day had begun miserably for her and it was ending miserably. For some perverse reason she had refused Martin's offer of a seat in his boat and as her own drew in at the quay she had seen the Upper End men try to land a heifer and part of the tail peeling off in one of the islander's hands. The sight of the animal with its tail stripped red to the bone had maddened and sickened her.

Later herself and Sarah had argued over the buying of Mary's Confirmation frock: Sarah had wanted it white and she had wanted it light blue, and in the end Sarah with much dissatisfaction allowed her to have her way. They had quarrelled, too, when Sarah had suggested that she should go and visit her own father and mother.

'No, I'll not!' Vera had answered her snappily.

'Not that I should interfere but you should — it's your duty,' Sarah had held on, using the words her own mother had advised her to use.

'I know what's my duty and what's not. I'm not going to listen to outside dictation from you, Sarah!'

'Very well, it's none of my business, Vera, but you know in your heart and soul that you should go to see your father and mother and let them see Mary.'

'If it's none of your business then why do you harp on it.'

Hardly speaking a word to one another they had moved around the town then, their suppressed anger infecting Mary who began to plead for sweets and chocolate, her mother refusing to buy them and staring with annoyance at Sarah who had stepped into the shop to get them.

'I'll soon not be able to rear my own child,' she had said but Sarah made no answer, and as they were setting off for the quay one of Vera's brothers had stopped her; and the sight of him with his shirt fastened with a safety pin, his face unshaven and his hair sticking out through a hole in his cap had repulsed her and as he besought her to call up at the house her anger had increased and she gave him a shilling and fled.

Standing now on the quay with the water gathering in a pool at her feet she saw Martin step into the boat and stow his parcels in the bow. With a shudder she thought of her unmilked cow and remembered the pain in her own swollen breasts when Mary as a baby was off her feed. She winced from that searing recollection, gathered in her shoulders with an instinctive protectiveness and squeezed Mary's hand. If Martin doesn't ask us to go with him, she said bitterly in her own mind, I'll let him know what I think of him. He started the engine, climbed out of the boat, and came slowly towards them. She felt all her limbs loosen with the ease and relief of surrender.

'I'm going now,' he said, 'the three of you better come with me for God knows how long you'll be kept here in that rain. You can shelter under the sail.'

'Thank you, Martin,' Vera said and he took Mary by the hand. 'Come on, Sarah.'

'No,' said Sarah, 'I'll go in the boat I came on. I'd have to walk in that rain from the Lower End.'

'That rain's easing off,' Vera said. 'Come on and don't keep us hanging about here any longer.'

'I'll not put foot or finger in his boat. He struck Pat at the dance and he holed the little yacht on him.'

Martin putting on the wooden lid that boxed in the engine was listening to them and he heard Vera say with bitter hardness: 'I holed it! You can tell that to Pat. I'm the one who did it and not Martin.'

He took her hand as she stepped into the boat. He had taken down the mast, and the rain was pecking on the sail under which Mary was sheltering, and as she made room for her mother she smiled with comforting release. In a few minutes they were moving out into a sea stubbled with rain that fell stiff as wire, and through its falling mesh they saw the islanders move to the point of the quay and stare after them without movement or even a spirited wave of a hand. Jamesy was at the tiller, a piece of canvas round his shoulders. Martin was standing upright beside the engine with tadpoles of rain wriggling down his oilskin and lying in greasy blobs at his feet. Vera and Mary were sitting near the bow with the brown sail shawled and tucked round them. She looked out at Martin from her warm cave of snug seclusion. He could see her face and her eyes glittering in the brown reflection from the canvas, and as she cast upon him glances of relief, of thankfulness, and of a pained mildness he felt confused with a calm disquiet that forced him to look seawards.

113

The boat lifted on the easy swell, the boards at his feet throbbed above the shaft of the propeller, and the rain in the water sizzled like a thousand grasshoppers. He could think of nothing only what she had said to Sarah at the quay; she holed it, she holed it. The rain glossed his cheeks and he shook the drops from the peak of his cap and motioned with his head to Jamesy to keep her more to the right. Under the lintel of mist that lay evenly over the island a soft budding radiance was flowering forth.

'It's going to lift,' he said. 'We might have a dry landing after all.'

Vera smiled out at him, opened her coat, and dried her neck with her handkerchief. Martin winked at Mary: 'I'm sure you've something nice in your parcels. You and Jamesy are going to be great swells on Confirmation day.' Jamesy fidgeted uncomfortably, stole a glance at Mary, and fumbled in the torn lining of his pocket for his mouth-organ. He picked bits of fluff out of the square holes and ran his lips up and down the scale. The sun shone out slowly, elbowing its way through the mist and gradually clearing for itself a wide and deep space of sky.

'Give it to me for a minute, like a good fellow,' said Martin, and though it was years since he had played he took the mouth-organ in his two fists, and moved it tentatively across his lips. He played for them, 'The Minstrel Boy', 'The Castle of Dromore', 'Oft in the Stilly Night', and ended it with a jig and a reel which he repeated till he felt a dizziness in his head. He swiped the spits out of it on to the boards, cleaned it on his sleeve, and handed it back to Jamesy. The sun had dispersed the mists and as it blazed freely down on the boat vapour rose from the damp sail and the wet seats.

'That's a day I'll not forget in a hurry,' Vera said, standing up and shaking her coat and smoothing out with her hand its damp wrinkles.

Ahead lay the island, its green hills wet and fresh in the sun, the brown cliffs fissured with shadow, and a family of ravens careering in the air like scraps of burnt paper.

The tide was out at the little port, and he shut off the engine and took the tiller as they moved over the oily surface. His sheep moved like maggots on the bulge of the hills and his geese lying at rest on the shore rose up and ran with outstretched wings into the water. The boat grated on the stones and Jamesy jumped into the water up to his knees and held the bow.

'I'll have to carry you,' Martin said and he took Mary in his arms and carried her and her parcels to the shore.

He put his arms tightly round Vera and she smiled up into his face.

'Why did you say to Sarah you holed the yacht?'

'I'd have said anything, Martin, to get away. I wanted to fight with somebody.'

He stumbled in the water and she clung to him with mock fear, her breath warm against his cheek.

'I'm too heavy, Martin.'

'Not a bit!' and reaching the shore he ran past Mary, through the wet grass and wetter bracken until he reached the path that led up to the road.

'Martin, you're great!' she said, and she closed her eyes as he stooped over and kissed her firmly.

He put her down on the path and returning to the boat he began to moor it with Jamesy's help, and on hearing a shout of greeting he raised his head and saw Vera and Mary waving from the loop on the hills. He waved back and stood watching them as they stopped and waved again before disappearing on to the road.

CHAPTER XI

ON the eve of the bishop's expected arrival yellow and white bunting was got ready to decorate the boats that were to escort him in state to the pier, but that night a storm hardened in the west, the island was cut off from the mainland and Confirmation postponed. The bishop's storm they called it, and for four full days it blew; the waves broke far out from the shore, and streeching and slavering in a white mass over the crabbed rocks, they filled the salty winds with a boom of thunder that continued throughout the days and the nights. Each morning as Martin stood at the gable end under the streaming leaves of the ash trees he saw the wind plunge its arms into the reeds of the lake and bend and twist them like a harvester, announcing in its melancholy rustle that the summer was at its end. His field of corn under the hill was beaten flat as if a few cattle had lain in it or as if it had been combed in all directions by a mad gleaner. Across the stream the withering potato tops shook out their warm heavy smell and tempered the chill breath of the winds. The flat stones at his feet were scoured clean, and the ash-seeds torn from the branches before their time were swirled under the scraggy bushes where his bit of washing dried stiff as a board in the salted winds.

With Jamesy to help him they dug heathery sods on the haunches of the hills, cut bracken for bedding, and at the edges of the lakes mowed down reeds that would thatch the stacks of corn at harvest time. And then when the wind had spent itself and the exhausted sea breathed and lapped like a cow after calving, piles of sea-rods were tossed on the beach, and they went down each morning over the slithering wrack and raked them into heaps, preparing for the short days of late autumn when they would cart them to rot and nourish the fields.

One Sunday, at Mass, the day for Confirmation was again announced and Martin hurried home, took his shotgun and ambushed one of his geese before it had time to race into the shelter of the sea. He hung it up for a few days and then plucked and cleaned it, and cut away the layers of yellow fat and stored them in a jam jar for use against sprains. He bought stout for himself and lemonade for Jamesy, preparing a feast as his own parents had done on his Confirmation day.

'You'll have cause to remember tomorrow all right,' he said to Jamesy as the lad scrubbed his legs and feet in a bucket near the fire, and, stripped to the waist, washed himself till his face shone like a polished apple. All that Martin's mother had done for him he rehearsed again, drawing it from his memory, keeping alive the custom of the island and making it a day for Jamesy to remember. He spread out the boy's new suit for him on the bench, pinned a Sacred Heart badge to the lapel of the coat, put a new prayer book in the pocket, and hung up the clean shirt near the fire in preparation for the morning. But when he was tidying up the boy's old clothes the weight of one pocket attracted him and he shook it till it jingled like a tambourine.

'You've some weighty valuables there, I'd say,' he smiled, and Jamesy taking it from him, rummaged in the pocket with the torn lining and drew forth a broken penknife, a bare spool, screw nails, loops of wire, a magnifying glass, and lastly the ash-tray which he handed royally to Martin.

'That's a present for you,' he said.

'That's a useful article — where'd you find that?'

'I bought it the day we were across for the suit.'

'Is that so,' Martin said dubiously, turning the glass ash-tray in his hand and reading the advertisement for Gold Flake cigarettes which branded the boy's lie.

'You didn't buy it,' he said slowly, 'I'm sure of that. Tell the truth — where'd you pick it up?'

For a moment Jamesy didn't speak. Under the light from the oil lamp the look of disappointment on Martin's face collapsed his venturesome lie and he swallowed the spittle in his throat.

'Did you steal it?' Martin said.

'I didn't steal it.'

'You bought a mouth-organ when you were over — what else?'

'Nothing, only lemonade and buns.'

'You bought them in the ice-cream shop at the Square?'

Jamesy nodded.

'When you're across again you can leave it back and we'll say no more about it,' Martin said and put the ash-tray on the mantelpiece beside the clock. He strode over to the table and in silence began plastering the goose with dripping.

'I didn't steal it,' Jamesy said, 'I didn't steal it.'

'Say no more about it,' Martin said. 'It was taken from the ice-cream shop and you can leave it back where you got it.'

Jamesy sat with the damp towel steaming in his hand, his mind torn by loyalty to his orphanage friend and Martin's estrangement. He stood up and got ready for bed.

'I didn't steal it,' he said again.

'Then who stole it if you didn't? It didn't jump into your pocket.'

Jamesy told him, but when Martin tried to question him about his friend and where he worked Jamesy's hesitation once more disconcerted Martin and deepened his former suspicion.

'Go on to your bed and sleep it off like a good lad,' Martin said. 'I'll help you sneak it back when we're over again.'

When the bedroom door was closed he drew out the Confirmation card, filled in the necessary details with ink, and put a stroke of the pen in the space reserved for the boy's father's name. But in the morning he noticed the distraught look on Jamesy's face and he tried to dispel it by making jokes about the goose. He was rendering suet in a big pot at the side of the fire and when the blue smoke was rising from it he carried the goose over on a plate and as he slid it into the pot he chanted: 'Who killed the goose? I killed the goose with my shot and gun — I killed the goose. Who'll pick its bones? We'll pick its bones, be its flesh as hard as stones, we'll pick its bones . . . Now, Jamesy, we are ready for the road. Head high and shoulders back like an old soldier.'

'Have you the card?'

'The officer in charge has the card. It's safe and sound in here, so never you fear,' and he tapped the breast-pocket of his coat as they marched along the sunweary road. Vera and Mary must have set out long ago, for there was no smoke rising from their chimney and the gate beside the road was closed. They met no one except Mick Devlin with his donkey and slipe on the ridge of a hill, and near the mill Alex, the miller, widening and deepening the stream that led from a lake to the sluice trap above the wheel. He was standing knee-deep in water, and at each side of him were mounds of red clay plastered and smoothed by the smack of his spade. He called out to Martin and asked him for a match or two. 'You've plenty of time,' he said to them, 'I don't think he has gone in yet.' He lit his pipe, eyeing Jamesy over the bowl. 'And who's that stranger you have with you?' he said, surveying Jamesy's new clothes with puzzled wonder. 'It's not Jamesy Rainey, is it? I declare to sod I didn't know one bit of him. He's like the crowned prince of Ballyjeuraslum, if I'm any judge. You can tell his lordship, like a good fella, that he can begin the ceremony without waiting on me — I'll not take offence. My London tailors, by royal appointment, made my trousers too short and I had to send the whole damned suit back to them. I've another suit below at the mill but I'm damned if the swallows didn't build a nest in every pocket of it — that's the way I'm thwarted and disappointed at every turn. I'll not keep you back any longer. Say a prayer for me, lad, won't ye?'

Descending to the flat plain of the island they saw no one in the fields or around the houses, and no one about the quay except the moored boats nudging each other and shaking their bunting above the incoming tide.

Both wings of the chapel door were open to the sunlight and the fresh air, and inside as Martin and Jamesy tiptoed to their places they were aware of the smell of new clothes and a stiff unaccustomed silence. Jamesy eyed the white altar and the small lighted candle at the right that was wrestling with a sleeve of sunlight that stretched through a side window. He looked at the mitre on the altar, the vestments arranged beside it, and at the vacant chair below the tabernacle; but he had no time to look at more for the bishop now ascended the altar, and after vesting himself sat on the chair while a priest placed the mitre on him and handed him his crozier. He spoke quietly, looking now to his right at the row of girls in white, and now to his left at the six boys with their clean faces and dark clothes. He impressed upon them the importance of the sacrament they were about to receive and then standing he prayed with his hands stretched in front of him while the congregation sang 'Come Holy Ghost'.

A boy beside Jamesy was bending his Confirmation card back and forth, putting the edge of it to his mouth, and staring round him with a look of dulled curiosity.

'Give me my card now,' Jamesy whispered but Martin ignored him, looking steadily in front with a dissimulated expression of intense devotion, and when the priest beckoned them to come forward to the altar rails it was Martin who handed up the card, and when they were back in their seats again and the little girls going forward with their hands joined and their new shoes squeaking, Jamesy out of sullenness kept his head lowered and refused to obey his inclination to look up at Mary, and out of the same stubbornness, when the bishop was in the pulpit and asking them to refrain from intoxicating drink till they were twenty-five years of age, Jamesy only mumbled the words of the pledge despite Martin's nudging him to speak out boldly. They got up from their knees then and sat down as the bishop cleared his throat in readiness to say a few words to them.

'This morning, my dear children, the Holy Ghost, the third person of the Blessed Trinity, has come into your souls, refreshing it with his seven gifts. The Holy Ghost is the comforter, represented often in the form of a dove, the messenger of peace. His gifts are given to you freely to enable you to withstand the pains and trials of this world and the snares of sin that would entice you away from Him. We will reach true wisdom and understanding if in all our struggles and sicknesses and disappointments we learn to say from our hearts: "It's God's will." Christ has shown us the way to Him; it is not an easy way; it is a rough way, the way of the Cross, but that is not the end — there is the resurrection of the body and eternal glory and happiness for those who try to serve Him here on this perishable earth. He has told us not to be afraid, that His Grace is sufficient for us, and that He will remain with us all days, even to the end of the world. These are words of hope but they are words we must often think over, striving always to co-operate with His Grace by keeping His commandments and doing good works. We must be like soldiers, soldiers of Christ, always on our guard and doing our duty with courage and obedience, fighting God's battle which is our own — not with arms but by prayer and the sacraments and right living: love and friendship, truth on our lips and justice in our hearts. . . .

'But the Holy Ghost will not remain with us, giving us His gifts, unless we ourselves become givers. We can't always be receiving: we must give, and the gift we can give is the precious gift of our ownselves. To do this we must become lovers — lovers of God and lovers of our neighbours who are our true spiritual brothers. The more we love and pray the more we show our love for God and realize the purpose of our lives. We go to God, the Father, through the Son with minds enlightened by the Holy Ghost whom, my dear children, we may compare to the sun that makes all things grow and ripen in the way they should. . . .

'Christ, as you know from your bible stories, loved the fields and man's work in the fields. He loved the flowers and hills and lakes, but then how much more must he love Man who was made in His own image. Your little island is a beautiful place but it is as nothing when compared to Man, and so your love for one another must always come before your love of place. That love is shown in friendship, forgiveness, and — from the depths of your heart — well-wishing. Jesus Christ died for us all and gained for each one of us the right to eternal salvation. Live each day in His presence, taking what it has of joy and sorrow. Be not troubled or over anxious. "Consider the lilies of the fields neither do they work nor sow yet Solomon in all his glory was not arrayed like one of these." Yes, God watches over nature and over the seasons. We labour in the fields and He directs. We are all in His hands — remember that always. Your life matters to God so don't live it carelessly like an animal in the field. And since Christ lived in Mary, His Holy Mother, we should pray daily to Her and ask her help in showing us what Christ expects of each of us. . . .

'Pray for guidance in all your undertakings — won't you do that? Do not always be thinking of yourself — pray for your parents who have taken care of you and who have gone to such trouble and expense to provide you with these grand clothes you have worn today. Always pray with fervour and try to live in love — a love that gives without hope of reward. . . .'

Martin was glad when the short sermon was ended: Jamesy's twisting and fidgeting on the seat had embarrassed him, and time and again he had to whisper to him to sit at peace, and it was only when they were outside again in the sunshine and he saw the schoolteacher there with her camera that he felt relief. She gathered the boys in a group and took a photo of them, and then after taking one of the girls she drew Mary aside and then called the grandmother over to be photographed with her. Vera and Sarah were watching them, and after Vera had run forward to make an adjustment to Mary's veil Sarah kept telling her mother to smile and to stay steady but the old woman kept moving her head, her eye fastened on Martin Gallagher who was standing among a group of men near the gate. She didn't want him to get away without speaking to him for it was with that intention that she had left the house that morning. She was determined to show him that she thought well of him in spite of what Sarah and Pat dinned at her ear every time his name was mentioned; she had heard of Vera's outburst on the mainland quay and she realized, better than Sarah and Pat, what it had all meant and that if Vera and Martin were in love she wasn't going to wish them ill: Vera was still too young to have her married life pushed behind her as an unsatisfied memory.

'That'll be a lovely picture I must say,' Sarah said sharply to her when the camera had clicked. Her mother didn't answer her but pushed past and joined Martin and Jamesy who were moving away from the gate. She shook hands with Jamesy and congratulated him, and turning to Martin she said brightly that he was getting more and more like his own father every day. 'Looking at the back of your head in the chapel,' she went on, 'it made me think of him and it made me think of your own Confirmation day. Tom and yourself were together, and do you remember that your father and mother and yourself came up to our house after it? Do you remember that?'

'I do,' he said, 'I remember it rightly.'

'And poor Tom spilt his tea over your new suit. Do you remember that?'

'I don't remember that part of it.'

'Well, I do. I was mortified and your mother kept saying that it was the suit's first baptism but it wouldn't be its last for you'd have the sun and wind through it inside a month. Oh,

Martin, I remember that day well and I mightn't have remembered it only for Tom spilling the tea.'

They stood below the house, the people passing by on the road, the old woman looking out for Pat and annoyed to see that he was still leaning against the boundary wall of the chapel.

'Tom and you got on well together. Poor Pat isn't like him at all — he's too hasty tempered but at heart he's good. Indeed when I heard of the row there was over the loss of the little yacht I blamed him so I did.'

'I'd have been in as bad a fix if she had been mine. I had nothing to do with sinking her — you know that, Mrs. Reilly.'

'Sure I know that well! It's Pat's stupid temper I'm faulting. She sank and no one sank her. And what Vera said to Sarah was all nonsense! I want you to forget it.'

She saw Vera and Sarah and Mary approach slowly and Pat standing in the same place, smoking his pipe. He didn't intend to come up — she was sure of that.

'Would you not step into the house for a minute or two? I'm sure Jamesy could take a drink of lemonade.'

'Some other time. We've a goose at the side of the fire and it might be burnt to a cinder by the time we get back.'

'A goose! You're going to celebrate in Christmas style.'

He laughed, fidgeting to get away, and Vera coming forward smiled at him, speaking with her eyes what she couldn't tell him with her tongue. Sarah stood back, holding a black kid glove in her hand and slapping it against her coat, while Mary stood beside her pushing back her veil and trying to attract Jamesy who was staring at the ground and kicking at the pebbles with his toe.

'I'm trying to get them to come in for a little refreshment,' the mother said to Sarah.

'Why can't you leave them alone, mother?' Sarah said. 'I'm sure they have their own plans made, and you can see that the boy, there, is dying with fright.'

Martin gave a forced laugh: 'You'd need a horse and a chain

to drag him up. Isn't that right, Jamesy?' and as they moved off he saw Pat slouch forward from his resting place.

Approaching the house Martin noticed that the dog was not out on the hill, and with a start he remembered that he hadn't slung the board from her neck. He put his fingers to his mouth and whistled and when the echoes had died away over the hills a wild duck struggled up from the reeds in the lake. He whistled again, waited for a few moments and hurried into the house.

He gave the goose a turn and stirred up the fire.

'It's doing nicely, Jamesy. Put you on the potatoes while I see where that damned dog's away to,' and going into his room he came out with his old coat on and the shotgun under his arm.

'Don't shoot her,' Jamesy said. 'You could give her away.'

'I'll shoot her if she's worrying the sheep. She's no damned good to anyone if we can't break her from that habit.'

He hurried out and jumped the stream, skirted the lake and quickly ascended the hill that led to the rock-heads. He put two cartridges in the breech, and on reaching the cliff top he saw below him his sheep huddled in one corner and baaing with fear. For a moment he didn't see the dog but as he rapidly descended the cliff-path and the stones bounced from him he saw her slink out from behind a rock and hobble away from him as if in pain. He called to her but she walked guiltily away in the opposite direction, stopped and looked round, and then slid into a clump of withered bracken. Behind the rock Martin saw one of his sheep with her hind leg chewed in a mess of blood. He cocked the triggers and ran to the clump of bracken, and the dog hearing him scrambled out and trailed off, her head close to the ground. Again he shouted at her. She stopped, turned her head and then as he drew nearer she lay down on her side and held up her forepaws in abject terror. Then she saw him stumble and fall against a rock and before he could drag himself to his feet she jumped up and raced for the path that led to the cliff-top. Once more she heard her name and the sharpness of it halted her with a paralysing jerk, and with her tail loose between her legs she gazed down at him as he raised the gun to his shoulder. He fired both barrels and she rolled off the path, slithered through the long grass and fell against a boulder at his feet. Rabbits streaked out from the bracken and tore past him in panic and three gulls screamed in terror and settled far out at sea. He laid the gun against the boulder and dragging the body to the edge of the sea he flung it into the tide. He washed the blood off his hands in the water and returning to the sheep he carried it home on his shoulders.

He placed her in a shed on a bundle of hay and as he came into the house Jamesy, who had changed into his old clothes, noticed the nervous shake of his hands as he broke open the breech of the gun. He plucked out the two spent cartridges, stared at the trickle of smoke that issued from them and pitched them into the fire. 'That's the end of her,' he said, 'and a damned good riddance into the bargain. I'm sorry I didn't do it long ago.'

His voice was thick and hoarse and Jamesy was suddenly afraid of him, afraid of the ugliness in it, and afraid of the quick movements as he drew off his coat and rolled back his shirt sleeves.

'Hold the sheep for me till I pour methylated spirits on her leg,' he said to Jamesy as he tore an old white shirt into strips for bandages.

Jamesy followed him out in silence and when he had doctored the sheep and was pulling down his sleeves he raised his head to the dark rafters where light was falling through a broken slate.

'How did I forget to patch that?' he shouted in spite of himself. 'Hell take it! I'm forgetting everything these days!' and he pulled forward an old box and standing on it thrust a ball of hay into the hole. 'That'll turn a shower till I get it mended. You'll not let me forget about it, lad? I can't do it tomorrow for we'll start on that field of corn if the weather lasts.'

They returned to the house and when he had carved the goose and emptied the potatoes into a basin on the table he told Jamesy to sit in for he was sure he was as hungry as a hawk. He prized off the top of a lemonade bottle and as it frothed out like a tuft of wool he laughed: 'There's a good fresh head on that fella. Don't get drunk and you after taking the pledge. And watch out for pellets when you're testing your teeth on that goose.'

He blessed himself and took a draught of stout. Jamesy lowered his head and ate without relish, and twice Martin cut more slices off the goose and forked them on to Jamesy's plate despite his sullen disapproval.

'Do you not like it? Eat it up, man, and don't shame me. Eat it while it's hot for it won't have the same flavour tomorrow. Come on, Jamesy, forget about that damned mongrel and don't let it ruin your appetite.'

'I don't want any more,' he said with petulant loneliness.

'Your friend at the other side would be glad of it wherever he is,' Martin said and refilled the mug for him with lemonade.

'He's in a good place and he has a bicycle of his own.'

'And haven't you that bicycle of mine that's out in the shed? You rode her manys a time, and tomorrow — no, the day after — you can ride her to the lighthouse and bring back a pup. What do you say to that?'

'I'm going away.'

Martin continued to eat as if he hadn't heard him. He forked another potato from the basin and when he had it peeled he offered it to Jamesy: 'There's a good floury one. All right, if you don't want it I'll take it myself.'

He drained the last of the stout and lifting the empty bottle stared at the label as if he were addressing it: 'You couldn't get fixed up now at the other side — the harvest's earlier there and they won't need new hands till the spring of the year. Is it because of the mongrel you're going?'

'No.'

'What is it then?' he said, trying to smother the vexation and impatience that troubled him.

'It's about the card,' and Jamesy looked across at him with sad looking eyes.

'What card?'

'Every fella carried his own card and handed it to the priest.'

'I'm damned but I don't see the differs. My sponsor handed mine up. Why didn't you ask me for it?'

'I was tired asking you and you didn't listen. And outside the fellas called me Martin Gallagher's baby.'

Martin put down the bottle and swayed back in his chair and laughed: 'Upon my soul that's the best ever I heard — a baby in long trousers!' And he stood up, scraped the bones off the plate into the fire and kept repeating: 'A baby in long trousers! Them fellas have no idea of size — they'd think this island was half the size of Australia. Look here, Jamesy, if they ever call you that again just you close your fist and shake it under their nose and ask them to smell it — and then ask them if they'd like to feel it. That'll baby them in fine style!'

Jamesy laughed nervously and went out but Martin didn't follow him. He sat at the fire and smoked his pipe, watching the blue dusk gather at the window and the ridge of the hills harden against the yellow sky. He was still smoking in the light of the fire when Jamesy came in again, and when the lad had seated himself on the bench under the window Martin began to talk to him of the big fish they had caught between them, of the yacht races in the lough, and of the fine mallard duck they would shoot some of these fine evenings when the stooks would be standing in the harvest fields. But all his talk and his plans failed to rouse Jamesy from the stolid dumbness that crouched and muffled him like the darkness that was hooding the hills. He knocked out his pipe on the bars of the grate, stretched himself, and lit the lamp. He thought of playing the melodeon but the withdrawn look of the boy as he leant forward with his hands drooped between his knees chilled him. He piled the dishes in the basin and as he washed them he kept up a light whistling and made an odd joke or two to which Jamesy gave no response.

'I'll drop over to Vera's for a minute or two. I've a bit of a present for Mary. I'll not be long till I'm back.' He stood with his hand on the doorlatch. 'You'll not be frightened, Jamesy?'

Jamesy shook his head and continued staring into the fire.

Martin cut down by the back of the house and saw the moon shine on the stream as it spread into the lake, and in the glimmer of a wind that stroked his face like a cobweb he heard the rustle of his corn like a fall of rain. But nothing soothed the disquiet that ravaged his soul and when he saw the light from Vera's window shine on to the white and black stones in front of her house he halted and refilled his pipe in an effort to steady himself.

He tapped at the door and lifted the latch. She was sewing at the fire and she nodded towards the closed bedroom door and pressed her finger against her lips to quell him into silence.

'Mary's asleep,' she whispered, 'she was fagged out and her face wasn't the size of your fist. It was a killing day for her. She's highly strung and she can't stand much excitement.'

He sat down opposite her, and because she had expected him to come she was wearing a new white blouse that moulded her firmly, a grey skirt, and her black hair was neatly parted in the middle and combed tightly back. There was a freshness about her that he felt rather than noticed.

'I thought you might be away at the dance tonight,' she said, whirling a piece of thread round a button she was sewing on a little frock.

'Ach, I was too tired even to think of it,' he dragged. 'I've that field of corn to cut with a scythe and I'll make a start at it in the morning.'

'You were right not to go if that's how you're fixed. Sarah's going and Jimmy Neil but you'll not miss much from what I hear.'

'I've a bit of bad news: Jamesy's leaving me,' he said abruptly.

'Jamesy! And is it that that's tired you and making you so down-in-the-mouth?' her hands rested on the frock as she looked

across at him. 'Didn't I tell you that you wouldn't hold him?
I knew from the first day I clapped an eye on him at the quay
that you wouldn't hold him. He was too mean and shifty-look-
ing. Don't worry yourself over the likes of him. And what in
the name of goodness is driving him away?'

He told her about the Confirmation card. She laughed sarcasti-
cally, checked herself and looked at Mary's door. 'You'd little
to do with your time when you hid that from him. If he knew
he was a nobody he might learn how to behave himself.'

'I'd hate to humiliate a child. That's all he is — a child. You
can't blame him for the sins of his parents.'

'I must say I thought you'd more sense. If he goes let him go
and the divil's luck go with him.'

'It's hard for me to manage a boat without him — that's the
way I look at it.'

'It's a pity Mary isn't a boy, she'd be the age now to help you.'

'If she was, Vera, you'd have other plans for her than fishing
for lobsters.'

'One never knows,' and she lifted the frock, held it out from
her and rearranged it on her lap again. He thought she was
annoyed with him and he added: 'But I must say you're doing the
right thing by Mary. The ones with the gift for the books
wouldn't stay here. They were made for something different.'

She had never heard him speak like this before and she raised
her eyes to him with pleasant curiosity. Was he speaking from
his heart or from his discontent, she wondered.

'Do you mean that, Martin?'

'Mean it! I mean every single word of it — and that's the truth.
If she takes easy to the books there's nothing here for her. The
land wouldn't hold her and married life wouldn't settle her.'

She clasped her hands on top of the frock and sat still as if
listening to her own voice or her own thoughts. She waited for
him to go on but he stared into the fire, the pipe gone dead in
his fist, and, to her discomfort, once more harped back to Jamesy.

'I looked forward to this day as I looked forward to my own Confirmation day. My own father and mother, God rest them, moved about with me. I wanted to celebrate the way they'd want but it has turned to ashes on me. The dog worried one of the sheep and I emptied the two barrels in her. Everything's gone to hell on me.'

He held the pipe loosely in his hand and stared at a crack in one of the stone flags. He felt her coming towards him but when he raised his head he saw she hadn't moved from her chair. She, herself, yearned to go over to him but instead she sat quite still and strove to stretch out to him without having to speak.

'Aye,' he sighed, 'the whole day's buckled and out of gear.'

She lifted her hand from her lap and held it out to him. He held it firmly and they both rose simultaneously. She rested her hands on his broad shoulders and raised her head to him but he gazed over her shoulder, avoiding the lonely glance she offered him.

'Listen to me,' she said. 'Put that fella out of your mind. They're all the same. They were reared with plenty of company and they'll never be content away from it.'

'I know that now.'

'You were too good to him — better than he deserved.'

'I take no thanks for that.'

She was turning from him defeated, but he caught her arm and held it tightly.

'There's something, Vera, I want to say to you,' and he spoke with a fierce earnestness that held her closer to him than the grip of his arm.

'What is it?' she said, half knowing what he was going to say.

'We'll get married at Easter.'

'Easter?'

'Aye, next Easter.'

'And Mary?'

'I'll work for her in the way you want and in the way Tom would have wanted.' He looked fixedly into her eyes as if he would pluck the answer he wanted from them. She closed her eyes to hide from the unflinching truth in his own and when she felt his arms around her and his kisses on her mouth there was no need to answer him.

'The next few months will be hard for us,' she breathed, drawing back from him and folding up the frock. 'There's Tom's people — they'll all be stiff against us.'

'The old woman won't.'

'She'll be the worst,' she said, recalling to her mind the morning of Tom's anniversary. 'Did she say anything about me when you were talking to her today?'

'No, not a grain. You needn't be afeared of her. It's Pat will take it bad.'

'Pat! — as if I care a straw what he thinks.'

Later when he was leaving she went to the door with him and they stood talking in the block of light that cleaved into the mist-filled night. The lighthouse beams were whorled with mist and the rockets were booming and rolling like barrels over the hills and trundling into the hollows of the fog. He leant against the wall, his finger picking at a flake of limewash and as it fell and turned round in the light like a moth he sighed and rested his arm on her shoulder.

'I'll give you a hand with that field tomorrow,' she said, 'and don't upset yourself any more about Jamesy — let him go if he wants to.' She leaned back against the jamb and there was a soft rustle of her arms as she chafed them with her hands to ward off the chilly air.

'I'll not think any more about him,' he said.

She stood out from the light of the door, caught his arm impulsively and squeezed it to her side. 'I love you, Martin. We've a steep road ahead of us but we'll travel it together.'

'We will,' he said.

She stood at the door as he went down the path and waved to her from the gate.

CHAPTER XII

O N leaving her he paused at the stream and beneath its trench of mist he heard it leaping over the stones on its journey to the lake. He was content, and if a wind would rise in the night and scatter the clinging mist he'd be more content for it would mean he could make an early start on his field of corn. The light in the kitchen was lowered and he knew that Jamesy had gone to bed. The whole place was strangely quiet and he missed the slow shuffling movement of his dog that usually rubbed herself against his leg on entering. He screwed up the wick in the lamp and in the brighter light saw bits of glass shining in the crevices of the hearthstone. He bent over them and then poked with a stick in the ashes below the grate and discovered the broken fragments of the ash-tray. It was gone now and he'd ask no questions about it and get no more lies — and besides there'd be no rhyme or reason in torturing the lad about it any longer. He peeped into Jamesy's room and asked in a whisper if he was asleep. Jamesy didn't answer him; he was awake but he lay still, and when the door was closed against the light from the kitchen he stared at the cross-sash of the four-paned window and at its cruciform shadow that was stretched timidly on the embrasure by the frosty light from the moon. The lighthouse opened and shut its shrunken flashes with quick precision, and Jamesy let his mind swing freely out with them over the misty fields and down below the cliff where the dog would be lying in a bloated heap in the water, its leathery lips curled back from its teeth, and the shot-torn body swaying on the waves and bumping against the rocks like a boat's fender. His mind dwelt on it with morbid pity until he heard the sheep bleat from the shed and he pulled the clothes over his head to muffle the pained sound — a sound that knotted in his mind as tightly as the bandage that bound the sheep's leg. Under the comforting dark of the clothes he felt the warm moisture of his own breath, heard Martin take off his boots and after a pause toss them under the kitchen table. He knew that if he pushed back the clothes he would see the lighthouse beams flash once, twice, three times, four times . . . and then darkness for a while except for the blurred moonlight in the window and a glistening speck in one pane like a grease drop from a candle . . . and then the shatter of the rockets, tearing through the mist and rumbling and rolling over the hills and breaking in fragments and dying far, far to seaward. . . .

Something wakened him and he sat up with a start. His heart thumped like the impatient knocking at a door, but the room was still and the air cold, and at the window was the moist yellow light of dawn and on each pane a mist like the hammock of a spider's web. The beat of his heart slackened as his courage crept back slowly, and in the stillness he heard Martin mumbling loudly from his room. He pulled on his trousers and came into the kitchen, and standing on the old sack that served as a mat he felt the cold air under the door curl round his feet like flowing water. He waited, listening, and when Martin cried out again he came into his room and saw him lying on the bed, his tattooed arm across his chest and his face gathered up as if in pain.

'Martin!' Jamesy called out, 'Martin!'

He waited, watching him stir slowly and heave himself out of his troubled sleep.

'What's wrong, Jamesy?'

'You were shouting in your sleep.'

'Me!' he said in surprise, and he rubbed his eyes and ran his fingers through his hair.

'I was dreaming, I suppose. What on earth time is it?' and he stretched out to the chair where his waistcoat hung. He looked at his watch. 'It's only four o'clock. I'll smoke for a while and go asleep again.' He swung round to the window

134

and saw the dew hanging from the eaves of the outhouses and above them the northern sky with its few fading stars. 'It'll be a good day I'm thinking, and we can make a start on that field of corn.'

'You're not cross with me for wakening you?'

'Cross! I'm heart glad. I was dreaming and I hate to dream. It's the damned goose that's upset us. Hurry back to bed like a good lad, you're shivering with cold.'

He struck a match to light his pipe and heard Jamesy plunge a mug into the crock of spring water in the kitchen. He called out to him to bring him a sup. He drank greedily, and as the water rattled into his empty stomach like the slap of water in a barrel they both laughed. 'That's the goose giving its last cackle,' Martin said and lay back on the pillow with the pipe in his mouth and his two hands under his head.

As he smoked he tried to recall his dream, patching it together from the dim pieces that floated back to him. It was about his own father and mother that he was dreaming. They had come back to him into this very room. He, himself, had returned home from his wanderings and, somehow, he was lying on his death-bed and they were clamouring round him, clutching his arms and trying to drag him back from a bottomless mist into which he was slowly sinking. He remembered how he had clung to them, endeavouring to shoulder off the burden of weariness that flowed like lead through his arms and legs and how his falling weight dragged them on top of him, adding to his paralysis and pushing him farther below the mist. And then Pat Reilly burst into the room with a long rake in his hands, and forcing himself between his mother and father he hammered the teeth of the rake against Martin's chest and shouted: 'Let him die — a bloody robber! A grabber — let him grab his seven feet of clay in the graveyard and not an inch more. Let him die — seven feet of clay is a damned sight too much for a grabber.' His father had tried to wrench the rake from his hands and his

135

mother, too, caught hold of it, and as they swung and stumbled about the room he lay powerless in the bed, his arms and body dead, and only his consciousness awake and laden with a helplessness that he couldn't throw aside. His father broke the rake, and as the three of them scrambled over the floor for the broken pieces Jamesy had wakened him.

He blew out a few smoke-rings with satisfaction and watched them widen in their ascent to the ceiling. A grabber! He hadn't thought of that when he left Vera last evening and for some reason it had thrust itself into his dream with sharp insistence. A land grabber! There was no doubt he'd have to bear that insult. Pat would fling it at him when the word about his marriage had got round, and it was what Sarah would say, and maybe it was what the old woman would think if it were hurled at her, day in and day out, by the impatient hate and haste of her own son. But whatever they'd say against him or against Vera he would not break with her to satisfy them. He'd marry her; and if they'd have children of their own he'd have something besides himself to work for, somebody to leave his place to, somebody to carry on his name and pray for him as he prayed daily for his own parents. It was true he had left the island against their wishes: they had besought him with tears to stay, and that leave-taking, he believed, had broken his mother's heart. He was young then with all the self-willed hankerings of youth, all the selfishness of self that grew from the desire to better himself. And in that hard striving his memory was always tugged towards home and he hadn't the courage or the inclination to set up a new home for himself among strange people. Lodgings, even the best of them, he found unfriendly, and then there were the miserable Sundays he had spent in the coal-ports of Cumberland or Ayr, his boat lying at the docks and nothing to remind him of home except the Mass he had attended in the mornings. Those days he remembered best because they were his worst. There was nothing natural in those ports on a Sunday, nothing except the movement of the sea or the clouds gathering on the shoulders of the hills; and there he grew to know that the more we travel the more rootless we become, and then when it's too late we've discovered that our life has passed by and we have lived with our memory only. How often had he heard the oldest men on the boats tell him that they were trapped and stunted by their shifting life, and how often had they advised him to cut the rope and clear before he became like one of themselves, satisfied and yet dissatisfied, no home life and no permanent anchorage. He was through with it and if Vera would content herself with him and with the island people he would never think back on it. He reviewed the dream again and if it hadn't been for the heavy supper he had taken he'd have believed it was a warning from his parents not to let Pat hinder or thwart him in what he had set his heart on.

He put the pipe on the chair and turned to sleep again, and when he awoke it was still early and the sun had risen. As he dressed he saw the vapour rise from the thatch on the outhouse and saw the dark blobs on the threshold where the dew had dripped from the thatch, and beside his pike of hay he saw the cat crouched near the holes where the mice were foraging. It was going to be a lovely day, and in a short while the net of mist would dissolve from the fields and leave his corn fresh for the scythe.

He came into the kitchen, took his socks from the crane above the fire and as he rubbed the grit out of the feet of them he called out to Jamesy to get up.

'Well, Jamesy,' he said when they were at their breakfast, 'we'll work till sundown and if the fry's in below the mill we'll fish from the rocks and give the boat a rest for the one night.'

'When will you get the new pup?'

Martin laughed pleasurably, aware that the lad's mood showed no trace of yesterday's strangeness.

'It'll not be till Sunday. I'll see one of the lightkeepers at Mass and I'll ask him for a black cocker.'

'I could go up on the bike now. They might all be bespoke.'

'It'd be better to leave it to me and if we can't get a cocker I'll get a good mongrel of a sheep dog from the mainland. It'd be the kind that'd suit us better. Cockers are nice to look at but they're no damned use for sheep. They'd only be good for taming them wild geese of ours.'

After the breakfast when the sun had strengthened and a slight morning breeze was blowing in from the sea he put the lame sheep in the field across the stream and taking two scythes rubbed a fine edge on each of them with the whetstone and entered his cornfield.

'Now, Jamesy, we'll make a start in God's name. When you're cutting do as I showed you at the hay. Keep the heel of the scythe close to the ground and coax it along. Swing without a jerk or force and don't take too big a swathe.'

He left him to go round the edges, and he himself standing at the head of the field that had the most sun swept into it down the slope towards the stream, his body swinging from the hips, his head lowered, and his scythe cutting like a razor. He began to sing and his singing carried over the hills and was smothered by the hum of the reaping machines in the plain of the island. By the time he had finished his song he had reached the stream and throwing down the scythe he strode back to show Jamesy how to tie the sheaves. The sun came out boldly, black beetles stumbled over the cut corn, the grazing horse looked curiously at them over the loose-stone fence, and Mary waved to them on her way to school.

At midday Vera with a red scarf round her head crossed the stream and began at once to tie sheaves, and Jamesy, who was cutting at the head, paused to watch and envy the speed of her hands. Her presence heartened Martin and on reaching her on his way down the slope he would halt to tell her he'd never be fit enough to cut as quickly as she'd tie. He would wipe the sweat from his brow or jump into the trench at the stream to daub his neck and arms with a soaked handkerchief.

'Would you not put the reaper in it — you're only killing yourself,' she advised him.

'There's too much of it lying. We're doing fine as it is. Jamesy's making a fine fist of it at the head. The reaper would miss half of it.'

His shirt was open and as she stood beside him the heat from his body flowed out so thickly she felt she could stir it with her hand. The veins bulged on his arms and the tattooed anchor looked bluer than she had ever seen it, and the specks of sweat on it glistened like glass.

'Rest yourself, Martin, for a while. I wouldn't try to cut it all in the one day.'

'I feel as fresh as the spring-well and I better make the best of it,' and he sharpened the scythe and strode up the slope again.

She turned over the sheaves with her toe, listening with growing irritation to Martin and Jamesy as they laughed together at the head of the field. In that boy she saw nothing that was lovable: his fair hair, his thin jaws that nothing could fatten, seemed to speak to her of ill-health, peevishness and bad temper. And in spite of all her warning to Martin he still saw fit to encourage him. She lifted the sheaves and arranged them stubbornly in stooks and then suddenly her arms grew tired and a dry roughness in her mouth chilled her. She went to the spring well and lifting a tin that rested on a flat stone she began to drink but seeing rust-stains at the bottom of the tin she flung it from her with disgust into the stream, and coming back to the field saw Martin standing at a stook, one hand resting on his hinch and the other on the scythe.

'That fella's leaving as much lying as he's cutting. He's only doubling your work,' she said sharply.

'He's doing fine.'

139

'He'll cut the legs off himself the way he's holding that scythe. I can't bear to look at him.'

'We all had to take the risk.'

'It'll be a dear risk if you've to boat him across to the hospital.'

Jamesy saw them staring up at him and he threw down the scythe, tied a sheaf quickly and tossed it from him with triumphant pride.

'There's country blood in him, I'm thinking,' Martin said.

'There's bastard's blood in him,' she said with a flash of spite.

'Sh-sh, he'll hear you,' Martin said.

'I don't care. He hates the sight of me. 'Tis better for him to know where he came from. He'd think nothing of giving you a swipe with that scythe as fast as he'd look at you.'

Martin smiled at her: 'You don't know him, Vera. He's as gentle a lad as I've come across in all my years.'

'If that's the case you must have spent most of it in the desert. There's a look in his eyes that frightens me and makes me afraid for Mary. I'll never rest content till you're rid of him.'

'You don't know him,' he said quietly and walked away.

On reaching the edge of the stream after his next swathe he jumped down into the trench, soused his head and neck with the water and took a drink from the tin he found floating at the grassy edge. She jumped down beside him and because they were unseen she stood close to him, her hands resting on his shoulders. 'Martin,' she said, 'it's my love for you and Mary that made me speak my mind — you know that!'

He smiled, put his arm round her, and as he kissed her she felt the cold mossy water from his lips and drew back from him in fear for herself.

'Talk to him,' he said as he helped her out of the trench. 'You don't give him as much notice as you would a stray dog.'

'You give him too much notice — that's the trouble,' she said firmly. 'I'll talk to him if it's necessary and not till then.' She lifted an armful of corn and tied it in a sheaf. 'I'll go now and make a bit of dinner for Mary.'

'It was good of you to give us a hand.'

'That's the way it should be between us,' she smiled.

He watched her unloose the red scarf from her head, cross the brown plank over the stream, and saunter past the injured sheep that was resting in the sun. 'She's hard to understand,' he said to himself, and whistling to Jamesy he went up to the house to take a tea-dinner and the remains of the cold goose.

When they returned to the field blackbirds and thrushes were hopping over the sheaves, the stooks stood in pools of shadow, and the top of the hill was grilled in a dazzle of heat. The corn at the foot of the hill was still a light green and when he had cut the patch he stooked it where it would get its fill of the ripening sun. At the head of the field Jamesy cut into it crossways and shortened each length for Martin, and by the time Vera came out to the field again they had cut half of it. Mary was with her and she kept her beside her at the foot of the field and taught her how to tie the sheaves. Suddenly Jamesy shouted excitedly as two rabbits raced out of the corn and sped up the hill. Martin, who was sharpening his scythe, raised his head to watch them but the whetstone slipped and the back of his thumb rasped against the blade. He dropped the scythe and held his wrist, watching the slow ooze of blood. Vera ran up to him and seeing the depth of the cut she made him go up to the house to wash it out, and as they left the field together he kept saying: 'It could have been worse. It's well it wasn't the front of the thumb or I couldn't grip a scythe.'

Left alone at the foot of the field Mary jumped over the sheaves and came up to Jamesy and asked him if he'd like to see where the chestnut was growing.

'Your mother wouldn't want me.'

'Come on. She'll not mind, and anyway we'll be back in a minute or two.'

She skipped down the slope, and Jamesy ran after her and jumped the stream, cartwheeled a few times on the smooth grass, walked on his hands and bouncing to his feet followed her quickly into the garden. The chestnut had a few drooping rusty leaves and he pulled one off in spite of her protest, rubbed it like tobacco between his palms, and blew the shreds into the air.

'There's the new growth,' she said, pointing to a fresh tip about two inches long. 'We'll be big by the time it's a tree.'

He had mounted the seat of the swing and wasn't listening to her, and as she pushed him he curved up towards the gable and she told him to look into the swallow's nest.

'Can you see anything?'

'I'm not big enough.'

'There might be an unhatched egg in it.'

He stood up on the seat of the swing but failed to see into it, and sitting down again he stretched out his leg and struck the nest with his toe, and as a shower of dust and grey clay rattled to the ground they crouched over the pieces, breaking them with their fingers and picking out the white feathers and dead carcasses of bees.

'I'll take one more swing and go back to the field,' he said.

'Will you indeed,' shouted Vera who had come across for iodine and had heard their voices in the garden. She ordered Mary into the house to do her lessons and approaching Jamesy she caught him roughly and shook him till his teeth rattled in his head. 'Who allowed you to come here — you bastard you!' she shouted, her face close to his. 'That's why Martin didn't show you the card — no one knows who's your father. There's the truth now!' and she made a swipe at him with her hand and he fled from her.

Back in the field he was alone, and as he lifted the scythe he repeated to himself what she had shouted at him, saw again the tight bitterness in her eyes, and decided to write to his friend in the mainland to tell him that he was leaving. The encounter with her rankled him and at the same time filled him with furious energy, and as the corn swayed and fell before his driving scythe, he found the rhythm of the work surrender itself to his concentrated vigour. He took off his coat; the sweat wriggled like live eels down his back but he didn't stop to rest, and Martin seeing the amount he had cut and that his fair hair was darkened and plastered with the sweat told him to put on his coat and rest for a while.

'We'll finish it today,' he shouted so that Vera could hear him at the foot of the field.

'He's a great wee worker,' Martin said to her. 'You'll have to admit that.'

She admitted nothing; and when all the stooks were standing like a scattered congregation round a Mass-rock Jamesy put on his coat, shouldered his scythe and left herself and Martin whispering to one another at the edge of the stream.

After supper the moon having risen it was too late to go fishing from the rocks and Martin pulling on a shirt that had aired all day on top of a bush felt refreshed and at ease and he sat down to smoke his pipe for a while before going to Vera's. Now and again he took the pipe from his mouth and shook the stem of it at Jamesy to emphasize the words of praise he had for him. 'And listen, boy, when I've that corn sold you'll have something more to add to your savings-box,' he said heartily, and standing up he began to flex his arms and crack his heels on the hearthstone before going out. And then, suddenly, Jamesy burst into tears and told him what Vera had screeched at him.

'Ach, she didn't mean it,' Martin said brusquely. 'You wouldn't heed what she says. The women's all the same — all air but no heart behind their tempers.'

'She doesn't want me. And when you marry her you'll not want me and I'll go away.'

'And who said I was going to marry her?'

'All the fellas says it.'

143

'And who'd heed what they'd say?'

He was right, Martin agreed in his own mind, and if he were married to her tomorrow the lad would have to leave. But while he had him he'd protect him from her and tonight he'd let her see that he wouldn't stand for it.

He hurried out with that resolution hardening in his mind and as he walked up the path towards her house he resolved to fling it at her at once. He knocked and pushed open the door but seeing Mary seated at the table, a book in front of her, and her eyes red with crying, the words he had framed caught in his throat and halted him in his stride.

'I'm glad you came over,' Vera said, noticing the hard look on his face. 'There's that Mary one in a sulk all evening over her sums and crying her eyes out because I wouldn't let her go over to you with her difficulties.'

'I'll have a look at them,' Martin said, coming to the table and leaning over Mary's shoulder.

It was some twenty years since he had held a school arithmetic in his hands and though he had forgotten all he had ever learnt except the fundamental rules he lifted the book and slowly studied the introduction to the circle.

'Now, Mary, what is it you don't understand?' he said with the assurance of a man conscious of his ability.

'I understand nothing about them,' she said tearfully.

'Your tears won't mend matters,' Vera put in. 'You mustn't be cross with them.'

Martin pulled a chair to the table and sat down beside her. He drew a small circle with her compass.

'Do you know what that is?' he said playfully.

'I do,' Mary said, giving a tearful laugh. 'It's a circle.'

'It's the harvest moon,' Martin said.

He drew a few more, increasing their size each time and giving them such fanciful names as: the face of the clock, the rim of a tyre, or the wheel of the mill. She pointed out the circumferences and the diameters when he asked her and then he paused, and with the air of a conjuror told her to fetch him a spool of white thread. Carefully he placed the thread round each circumference in turn, snipped the pieces off with the scissors, and placed them in a row on the paper. Vera rose from her chair and stood at the table with her arm on Martin's shoulder.

'Now, Mary,' he said, 'we'll measure the length of each thread and in that way we'll get the length of each circumference.' They did this, and then measured the diameter of each circle and divided it into its circumference. They checked their answers and found that it was always three and a bit over: 'It's always the same — three and a bit over,' Martin said. 'It never changes. It remains the same like the salt in the sea or the colour of the rainbow. And that's what they call π. They could have called it M if they liked or Q or Big Bill — but they didn't: they just baptized it with that funny letter — π.'

'I see it now,' Mary said, rubbing her palms with pleasure. 'It's very easy.'

'Aye, it's very easy,' Vera said, 'when you've a smart man like Martin to help you.'

She worked then at her sums, Martin sitting proudly beside her and looking at the bits of chestnut leaf entangled in her hair. And when she had her work finished and her school-bag buckled she went over and kissed her mother good night.

'And are you not going to give Martin one?' Vera said.

Mary smiled shyly at him, hesitated and ran to her room and from behind the open door she shouted out that she'd sing for him. They sat and heard her laughing, and then after a long pause she tried 'The Castle of Dromore' but before she had finished she burst out laughing again. 'I can't sing for laughing,' she said. 'I don't know what's wrong with me.'

'Ach, say your prayers then, and get into your bed,' Vera said, 'or you'll make yourself sick again.'

Martin lit his pipe and threw the match into the fire. What

he had come over to say he couldn't say now. She rose and made tea for him and as she handed the cup to him where he sat by the fire she said he must be a pleased man to have his corn all stooked.

'I'd great help,' he said, 'with yourself and Mary tying and Jamesy doing a man's work.'

Holding the saucer in her left hand she raised the cup to her lips, sipping slowly.

He stared in front of him: 'He's in a bad way, the poor lad, over what you said to him.'

'Is he, indeed? Well, he can get out of it without my help,' and she rattled the cup down on her saucer and closed Mary's door. 'Let me tell you I've that girl in there to think about. She's to be made a schoolteacher and I don't want any orphaned boy dragging her away from her lessons. I've enough to contend with as it is. Every one of them — her Uncle Pat, her Aunt Sarah and her granny — are trying to defeat me and turn her against my plans. But they'll not beat me, I'm telling you! They'll not — not one of them! And if your love for me can be broke by a lad like that, it isn't very deep, I must say.'

The unexpectedness of her outburst baffled him and, at that moment, he wished he'd never met her.

'It'd be right for him to know what he is when he's a bit older,' he said. 'He'd have sense enough to tackle it for himself. But to ground the life out of him before he's started to grow is — is not how I was reared. In God's name, it isn't right.'

'Hm, yourself and the old woman ought to be tied together. Upon my word the two of you'd outsermon the bishop.'

He realized now that she was a stranger and that her ways were different from his own, that her sudden slashes of anger would drive her to anything, and what she had said about the sinking of the yacht might all be true.

He threw the dregs of his tea below the grate, stood up and handed her the empty cup.

'You're not going so soon,' she said mildly.

'I want to doctor the sheep and I must get Jamesy to hold her for me before he goes to bed.'

'Martin, you were very kind to Mary. I don't know what she'd have done without you.'

'When you're older you can pick up things that puzzled you when you were young. But girls like Mary's as scarce as winter blackberries. If we couldn't do the sums at school we didn't care a straw. Indeed we broke Mrs. Reilly's heart when she was mistress in the school — she had great patience with us.'

She opened the door for him and as he stepped out into the moon-spread night she gripped his arm. 'Martin,' she said, 'don't let anything come between us!'

'I'll not,' he nodded, though his mind was entangled with doubt.

CHAPTER XIII

To make amends to Jamesy for Vera's bluntness towards
him and to erase his own dissatisfaction for his weakness
towards her, Martin cycled the following morning to the
lighthouse and brought back a black cocker pup. Its tail had
recently been docked and not having completely healed, a piece
of white cloth was tied to the tip, and when Martin planted it
down on his own kitchen floor they decided there and then to
christen it Tippy. Watching the innocent delight it afforded the
lad as it capered about the floor and tugged at the laces in his
boots he felt his own mind hardening towards Vera for the
unnecessary bitterness she was harbouring. All that week he
deliberately avoided her but on coming out of Mass on Sunday
she waited for him on the road, and sending Mary on in front to
tend the fire, they walked home together like man and wife,
and in her presence — in the lift of her head, her unroughened
skin, her neatly dressed figure — all the ill-will that had ramped
through his mind crumbled away from him. Something about
her, to which he could give no name, attracted and held him,
and when she asked him why he hadn't called over for a
whole week he made Jamesy's fear of the dark nights his only
excuse.

'You'll not be sorry when he leaves, if that's the case,' she
said, 'A lad that you've to keep beside you on a short rope is
poor comfort for anyone. You haven't much freedom with
him — have you now?'

'I suppose I haven't. But while he's with me I must look after
him the best I can.'

'A big boy like him shouldn't be afraid his lone. It's a clout
on the ear he needs.'

'You can't bully a child out of his fear. He'll grow out of it.

I'd the same fear of the dark when I was his age. But maybe the new pup I got him will help him.'

'You get him far too much. He's more like a son than a hired lad. I'd make him do my bidding if I were you.'

Two women passed them and the greeting they gave was directed more at Martin than at her.

'Hm!' Vera said with proud contempt. 'They all know what's between us and they're jealous of me.'

'Does the old woman know?'

'I'd no call to tell her. She asked me straight out and I gave her the straight answer.'

'What'd she say?'

'What'd she say! She took my two hands and squeezed them and wished me every happiness on this earth and in the next. But do you think I believed her — not a bit of me. She doesn't mean one word of it.'

'You're wrong, Vera,' he said, shaking his head. 'She means every word of it. You needn't distrust her. She's for us, if anyone is!'

'There's nobody for us, Martin. Nobody, only our own two selves. I don't trust any of them and I never did. I can feel it in the air around us.'

'And why do you trust me?' he said. 'Amn't I of the same stock, the same crop as them?'

'No, you're different. Your years away from this place changed you. I feel that but I didn't always feel it.'

'To tell you the truth I feel no change in me and I'm never content when I'm away from it. Even when I'm across for a day on the mainland I can't get back quick enough.'

'That's because you've made your home here. If you'd made a home away from it this place wouldn't trouble your memory. I often think if Tom had got away from it he wouldn't be lying now in his grave. He wasn't strong, and the damp and the hard work hastened his death.'

149

'We'll all have to go when our time comes no matter where we are. Look at his brother Pat. You can't say he doesn't thrive.'

'Pat!' she said with dry scorn. 'He's of coarser cloth than Tom and he has no feeling for anyone except himself. He changes as little as a rock because he's made of the same stuff. Pat could drown me in a puddle of water.'

'And I'm sure he could put me in the same puddle,' Martin added with a laugh.

'But it doesn't matter, Martin, what he'll say about us or what any of them say. We'll always have ourselves and little Mary,' she said and pressed his arm. 'Isn't that right?'

'It is,' he said, more to please her than to please himself, and as he left her at the gate and climbed up the hill to his own house he wondered if she would ever prevail on him to leave the island — and the more he thought of that the more unsure he felt in his love for her.

He discovered that the less he saw of her the happier he was in his own mind, and so in the evenings if the wind was too rough at his side to take out the boat he and Jamesy would set off with the rods for the sheltered rocks below the mill, and on his way along the road that was now strewn with oat-straw that had fallen from the carts he would often pause to watch the miller shovel the grain as it lay on the hot flat stones above the kiln, and amidst the steam that rose from it and burled out through the open door they would smoke a pipe together, looking down at the bay that was covered with chaff which turned to dusty gold in the setting sun. And as an evening breeze rippled in from the sea and the gulls swept channels in the floating husks the miller, his face and hair covered with meal-dust, would praise the hard-eared grain and the delight it was to handle it. Martin would listen to him with controlled impatience and then manœuvre the talk round to Vera, and with pretended unconcern seek advice from a man who was older in years and experience than himself. The miller, knowing what was between them, would praise her as a fine tidy lump of a woman — a woman that would keep a clean house, rear fine children from the right man, wouldn't squander her time in gossip or squander her purse in gallivanting across to the mainland on every boat that'd set out. Emboldened by the miller's talk Martin's indecision would weaken and he'd set off whistling down the beach, cross the hard ridges in the sand with a confident stride and join Jamesy at the point of the rock. And as there was no twilight in those harvest evenings it was late when they left the rock and returned through the fields, their feet crackling in the stubble, and the sound of their voices carrying clear and comforting over the hollows of the island. And later when the moon had risen Martin would take his gun and hiding behind a clump of stones he would shoot at the wild duck as they returned from their feeding grounds to the silvery edges of the lake. The sound of the gun would bring Vera out, and seeing her standing like a cairn of stones on top of the hill Martin would come up with a mallard duck for her or a pair of teal.

And in those evenings, the harvest saved and the potatoes pitted and covered with sedge she often heard them go off to the dances in the barns or the whist drives in the hall, and though she ate out her heart with jealousy because Mary was too young to go with her she never showed signs of it to Martin and spent her evenings sewing on the machine, preparing curtains and sheets for the new home she would set up with him. And then one day after Martin had gone to his last fair that year with a load of sheep, and after he had hauled his big boat into its winter shelter of loose-stone walls and had taken out the engine to overhaul he announced to her that they should have a dance in his house and invite a few friends. At first she held back and then agreed, and for two days she baked cake after cake of currant bread. The miller agreed to come and with him his sons and daughters, a few from the lighthouse, girls from around the quay, and Jimmy Neil and Sarah. Pat was asked but he said he wouldn't set foot next nor near it, and all that day his mother coaxed him but he shrugged his shoulders and told her to leave him at peace and not to be ferreting the soul out of him.

'And why will you not go and be agreeable?' she said as she baked bread on the griddle for Sarah to take with her.

'I'm finished with them! I've a bit of pride left in me that you've all lost,' he said. 'I'll never, so help me God, darken their doors again. It's an insult to Tom that she marry again and allow his bit of land to go with her. And it's an insult that you and Sarah instead of ignoring her only draw closer to her.'

'You shouldn't say you're finished with anyone,' the old woman chided him. 'She's free to marry again if she wants to, and let me tell you I'm glad. She has poor Mary harried to death over her books and when Martin steps in he'll bridle her chivvying ways.'

'The poor fellow doesn't know what he's marrying — that's the God's truth. You'd do right to tell him how she treats her own father and mother. She never visits them and Mary hasn't seen them since she was a baby in arms. If Martin Gallagher heard that it might save him in time.'

'Are you thinking of Martin or thinking of losing the fields?' his mother said. 'Be honest with yourself, Pat.'

'The one galls me and the other sickens me. I hate the very ground a grabber walks on.'

'And you detest a lover — is that it?' she said, turning the farls of bread on the griddle.

'They've a good friend in you — and they don't know it. But before it's too late I'll warn him of his trouble — never fear.'

'You'll run your own self into trouble the way you did over the yacht that sunk itself in the lough.'

'Herself and Martin sunk it between them — I'm sure of that now. The day she forgot to come out for Tom's anniversary should have shown us the way the wind was blowing. They were in love then, and love has only thought for itself. Thought of the dead wouldn't sweeten it I may tell you.'

'It's a great wonder with all your knowledge that you don't fall in love yourself. What'll you do when Sarah marries Jimmy Neil. And what'll you do when I'm at rest in the graveyard below. Do you ever look ahead?' she put a few twigs under the griddle and sat down in her chair.

'If I brought a young wife in here you're the girl wouldn't fancy it.'

She smiled and dusted the flour from her apron: 'Pat, my son, the day you bring her here will be a day of spring for me. It will lengthen my life; and the day Sarah gets married I'll be on my knees thanking God I lived to see it. The only brightness comes in that door is little Mary. God was good in giving us that lovely girl – she's Tom's living image.'

'We get precious little of her company if you remark.'

'Is it any wonder? She barely knows her Uncle Pat. You hardly open your mouth to her when she crosses the threshold on her way from school. You never go next nor near her house and her mother feels she isn't wanted.'

'There's no call for me to go. She has Martin Gallagher to do the work for her.'

'It's not work I mean. Why don't you drop in to see her in a neighbourly way? And why don't you show yourself at the dance tonight? If you showed friendliness, Vera would give it in return. Only I'm not fit for the hard road I'd go down oftener myself. But I've told Vera time and time again we're glad she's marrying an islandman.'

'I hope you didn't include me in that! I'm not glad and I'll never be glad till they're away like the Craigs. You've no feeling for Martin – if you had you'd tell him on the quiet the kind of her.'

'I know when to speak and when words are out of place. Decency and kindness and honesty are what I was reared to rely on. It's not out to make trouble I am. There's a strange drop in your nature wherever it came from,' she said firmly, and rising to her feet she carried the bread on a cloth and left it to cool on the window ledge. What she had said rankled him, and to annoy her he scraped out the bowl of his pipe with a penknife and though the sound put his own teeth on edge he continued at it with spiteful persistence. He allowed her to lift the heavy griddle from the fire and as she shuffled off with it into the back scullery he sat on, nourishing his discontent. At the side of the fire in a box of straw a cat lay asleep with her three kittens but on hearing a dish rattling in the scullery she hopped out of the box, the blind kittens whining from the cold air and huddling together in a ball. The old woman gave the cat her milk and it lapped it up quickly and ran back to the box, licked the kittens and stretched herself contentedly above them.

'You're not going to the dance?' she said to him as she sat down heavily on her armchair.

'I'm not!' he said sharply. 'But I'm going to say this: there's only one thought in your head about this marriage — you hope to get Mary to come to live here!'

'That's not true!' she shouted.

'You wouldn't turn her away if you were asked to take her!'

'God forgive me but you'd anger a living saint! What put that ugliness in your mind?'

'Isn't it true?'

'It's not true! It's not!' she shouted and jabbed the poker into the fire. He saw that he had aggrieved her and he hurried out and left her to herself. The house was silent; the cat licked her kittens and her movements rustled the yellow straw that cradled her.

Drawing the chair nearer to the fire the old woman began to examine his last taunt. Was it or was it not true? It wasn't — she was sure of that. She loved Mary but before God and His blessed Mother she couldn't accuse herself of such long-headed deceit as

154

to entice the child to leave her own mother. Martin would be a good stepfather — there was no need to worry on that score, no need to think for one instant that he'd bully his stepdaughter and drive her from the house. No, no, that could never be, and she couldn't wish for such cruelty in order to win Mary. What under God put that thought in Pat's head? What made him think of it? She tried to brush it from her mind, looking over at the window ledge where the steam rose from the bread and misted the window panes. It was cold outside and she hoped the frost wouldn't settle on the roads before Sarah got back from the Upper End with Jimmy Neil. Their bicycles could skid an evening like that; they could indeed, indeed they could. She tried to think of them as they'd hurry along before the cold darkness would sweep down and freeze up the roads but her thoughts soon drifted away from them and she sat up to face the taunt that eddied strongly in the well of her mind. She pondered it with scrupulous fidelity, striving to accuse herself that there was some grain of truth hidden in it and that she had only deceived herself into believing that her well-wishing for Vera and Martin was clean of all dissimulation and that out of the marriage would come a disruption that'd send Mary to live with her. 'Did I ever think of that?' she said to herself as if she were examining her conscience before entering the confessional. She hesitated before answering. No, she hadn't thought of it at any time. Was it ever present to her feelings and not in her mind? She couldn't truly say. Whatever affected Vera affected Mary — she knew that full well. She'd delve no more into these secret corners of her mind, tormenting herself with feeble scruples. Her conscience was clear; her heart was clean. She had no desire beyond the good wish and happiness for their marriage. 'That was true — before God she could say it was true,' she said aloud, and the cat pricked its ears and gazed up at her from the box. If there was nothing in what he said, then why did he cast it up to her. There was no effect without a cause —

maybe after all there was something she had said months ago that drove it into his mind.

For a moment she sat still, put some coal on the fire, and once more began to bore into her conscience, searching for some solid thought or untainted feeling that would rid her immediately from his baleful suggestion. She must have given him some cause or some hint. With pitiless actuality she pursued the past: she rehearsed the morning Vera had missed Tom's anniversary and relived what she had said afterwards to Pat and Sarah, and as that scene, as hard and definite as a soldier's foot-step, marched through her mind she could discover nothing that would support her scruples. And having unravelled that skein others advanced boldly before her but in all the conflicts she had had with him over Vera there was nothing that would stand firmly to halt the purposeful clarity that swept her heart clean. 'Thanks be to God there's nothing,' she said, and lifting her knitting before the light would leave the window she tried to rest on that final judgment. But her agitated mind throbbed and rocked, doggedly returning to the same scenes in spite of her efforts to shun them. She got up from the chair and on opening the door a rush of cold air entered the kitchen. The evening outside was grey and shrivelled, the grass in the fields without bloom, and the moss on the stone walls sharp as splashes of rust. She saw that the white road was dry, and withdrawing from the door she put on her coat and shawl, took her stick and set out into the chilly air to the chapel. In the smoke that hung in the air there lingered the smell of baking bread and as she sniffed it she stood irresolute for a minute till her dulled mind remembered that she had already tidied up the griddle and that her bread was now cooling in the window.

The holy water in the font was cold on her fingers, cold on her forehead, and as she walked up the aisle in the grey silence she was keenly aware of the rattle of her stick and the damp smell from the flaky walls. In the front of the tabernacle on the white wooden altar she swept her soul bare and asked that if any blemish lay unknownst to her in her heart God would wring it away from her or make her aware of it so that she could atone in time for her deceit. She was sorry — sorry before God if she had ever cherished any unmotherly wish about Mary. With fervour, then, she prayed that God would bless the marriage and give them their full share of happiness; she prayed for Mary, for Pat, for Sarah and Jimmy, and she prayed for the souls of all her dead and for all who had ever tramped the roads of the island.

On her way back she halted at the stream near the school and watched it run black and glossy under the road, and tumble in a frothy mass at the other side in its unchanging descent to the sea. It was here that Pat and Martin had fought, and she never passed it now without thinking of that night and without hoping that a day would come when they would draw together in that peace she wished for them. She stopped at the school where she had taught for so many years and peering through the window she saw the deserted benches with their ink-wells catching the light, and in one corner the easel with its chalky duster draped over the rung. Maybe a day would come when Mary would be in control of that room — one never knew: it was all in God's hands and all would be for the best.

On entering the house she took the confirmation photo from the mantelpiece where it rested against the clock and taking it to the light from the window she peered at it closely, at Mary's veil and joined hands, and at her own dark portrait with the eyes hidden by the shadow from her hat; her head was uplifted that day and turned away from the camera, even her hands were by her sides and not resting on Mary's shoulder; she had more thought for Martin that day than she had for Mary — anybody could see her whole attention was not given to the child. She put it back carefully against the clock and sat down, her hands on her lap, her eyes fixed on the fire banked high in the grate.

When Pat came in she was still sitting on the chair in the firelight and the bread was untouched on the window-ledge. She looked worn out and he gathered the bread on the cloth and carried it to the table for her.

'Are you asleep, mother?' he said.

'Asleep? How could I be asleep after what you said to me?'

'What did I say?'

'What did you not say!' she said solemnly.

'I said nothing I can remember,' he said with a smile.

'God forgive you! That's all I'll say — may God forgive you,' she answered with finality.

There was the sound of laughter outside, and presently Sarah and Jimmy swept into the kitchen, their faces red with cold, their movements brisk and uplifting.

'Is there no oil in the lamp that you didn't light it?' Sarah said as she unbuttoned her coat. Neither of them spoke, and sensing there was some row between them she ceased her questioning.

'We're frozen,' Jimmy said and he rubbed his hands over the fire, stamped his feet and looked down at the cat with her kittens. 'There's nothing freezes the feet off you like riding a bicycle.'

'You'd do well to walk to the dance the pair of you,' the old woman said, 'for there's a heavy frost coming — I feel it all day in the corn on my right foot.'

'I'm going down to the pub to get the proper warmth,' Pat said. 'Are you coming, Jimmy? Sarah could give you a call on her way past.'

'He's not going,' Sarah said. 'Jimmy has too much sense.'

'When you're not for the dance,' the old woman said to Pat, 'you could at least stay at home and not set the neighbours talking about us and saying what they shouldn't say.'

'Let them say whatever hell they like. I told you I'm against the marriage and I'm not going to show myself at the dance and act the hypocrite.'

'The frost has settled early on you,' Sarah said to him as she went into her room to dress herself. Her mother followed her in, and sitting on the bed she asked Sarah if she'd ever heard her say that out of Vera's marriage they might manage to get Mary to live here.

'You did not, mother. But if you did there'd be no crime or sin in it. I've often thought about that myself — often and often. Mary would always be welcome to come here.'

'She would indeed.'

'What's worrying you then?'

'Nothing at all, girl. Go and enjoy yourselves and tell Vera and Martin that we wish them well. I've a bit of bread and butter to take with you and you could slip them to Vera unknownst to anyone.'

'You'll not be staying up to wait for us?'

'Indeed, I'll not. Bed's the best place for me on a frosty night.'

Returning to the kitchen she saw Pat standing at the fire; he had the photograph in his hands but on hearing her he hurriedly put it back and it fell forward on its face on the mantelpiece and he didn't lift it again.

'You haven't changed your mind about the dance?' she begged. 'Sure you could run in for an hour or so, and when you haven't a girl to leave home you needn't stay late.'

'There'll be many a girl there that'd be glad of his company,' Jimmy said. 'Aye, many's a one.'

'He'll not always have me to keep the kettle warm for him,' his mother said. 'The island's full of men who have nothing but a dog or cat for company.'

'There's times I think it's the best company,' he said sullenly.

Sarah came from the room, her face freshly powdered, and a scarf about her head.

'Enjoy yourselves,' her mother said. 'You'll only be young once.' They went out laughing and Pat closed the door behind them.

They were alone together and the house was strangely still. She sat without moving and without looking at him. The relentless examination of her conscience had withered her strength and although she felt a longing for rest she resolved to sit up till he would return from the pub. He sat down opposite her and lit his pipe; he crossed and uncrossed his legs but didn't speak, and as he gazed at the cat he thought of his dog lying outside in the hay-shed, afraid to come in, because of the way she lept at him with her claws. That was his mother's doing, another of her fads, but he'd hold his tongue lest their bickering would again burst forth.

'You can go to bed,' he said when he saw her lift her knitting, 'for that's where I'm going. I neean't go to the pub. It's Martin I want to see and it's not likely I'd find him tonight.'

She sighed but said nothing. Her needles clicked rapidly, and seeing that she had no intention of leaving he bade her good night and went to his room. In a few minutes he heard her shuffling about the kitchen, heard the rattle of the saucer as she gave more milk to the cat, and noticing the crack of light shrink below the threshold of his door he knew she had lowered the lamp and was on her way to bed.

CHAPTER XIV

THE weather hardened into frost: ice formed in the lakes and in the streams; and along the fringes of the mill-race where it ran swift to the sea it formed in thin flakes that were bitten away during the day's sun only to reappear again under the barbed light of the stars. Under that same light the sheep sought shelter in the caves above the sea's edge, and coming forth in the morning, their breath enveloped them like smoke from a damp fire. They moved stiffly over the frosted ground and halted instinctively at the tufts of grass that were first to finger the sun, and later when the weak sun had cleared the frost from other patches they followed after it, grazing undisturbed till Martin would appear on the cliff-top with a barrow load of turnips that he tumbled down to them. And in the evenings the hills and cliffs around them resounded with the shouts of boys who came to slide on the lakes, their hob-nailed boots thundering like hooves on the frozen ground, scoring white lines on the ice and chipping sparks from the stones that projected from the margins of the lakes. Martin often accompanied Jamesy to slide with him on the lake; and in the midst of the excitement and the speed, which were too much for him, he would sneak off to Billy's for a drink, and hurry back again before the last stragglers had left the lake and had gone off singing down the road under the bright procession of stars.

On these evenings Pat always missed him at Billy's, arriving always when he had gone or maybe arriving on an evening when Martin had sat at home at his fireside reading a book. But one night as the snow was falling and Pat was standing at the door looking at the big flakes swaying in the lamplight something prompted him to go out. It was the crooked thing and the unlikely that would happen, he told himself, and if he'd go out now he'd surely meet Martin. His mother and Sarah strove to withhold him telling him that only a man without a fire would venture out on such a wild night.

'You can't expect me to stay in the house the whole damned day,' he said to them as he buttoned on his heavy coat. 'I've a mad craving for a drink and I'm going out for one.'

'Couldn't you say "No" to yourself like many another and sit and read a book?' his mother said. 'I've a few there the priest lent me and there's not a love story among the lot.'

'I've no call to read in this house,' he said, 'by and by you'll be doling out their contents to me both chapter and verse. And if I did take up a book the two of you would pelt a shower of talk at me and wouldn't be satisfied till I had closed the book and joined you. A man has no peace in a house where two women are always chattering about something.'

'If you sit down we'll promise not to open our mouths,' Sarah said.

'I wouldn't crucify you like that,' he said. 'I'm going out now and you can talk the snow out of the sky for all I care.'

A few flakes flew in as he opened the door, and as he set out muffled to the ears there wasn't the mark of a footstep or a cart-wheel to be seen in the snow. The rockets at the lighthouse boomed out intermittently and their dying roll muffled by the thick combings of snow seemed to linger on the brim of the hills before breaking in fragments in the hollows. The beam was shrunken to a yellow pallor and as it probed over the hills it seemed to emphasize the lamps in the little homes that shone out from bare windows in thin palings of light. As he passed the houses he lingered for a moment to see couples dancing to the music from a melodeon or to see a group round a table playing cards or little children undressing themselves at the fire before going to their cold rooms.

His feet were silent as he passed, his coat was plastered with snow and he could see nothing only the black rims of the buttons and the dark wrinkles in his sleeves. He shook the snow off himself, beat his cap against the wall of the pub and stumbled up the dark passage that led to the bar. Martin was there leaning against the end of the counter, his hand nursing a glass of porter, and blobs of water at his feet. Other men, their legs relaxed in front of them, were seated on a form arranged against the wall, and the barman with his sleeves rolled up was resting his hands on the handle of a cork-puller, trying to show interest in the different groups at the same time.

'That's a cold drink you're having, Martin. Have a snap of whisky,' Pat said to him as he opened his coat and shook off the remaining fragments of snow.

'I daren't mix the drinks,' Martin said. 'The old stomach would declare war.'

'War or no war finish that and have something warm,' Pat coaxed and nodded for two whiskies.

They talked of the hard spell of weather and of the miserable state the mallard were in. 'I shot four the other evening and they were only a ball of feathers.'

'There's damn all for them to eat in the Lower End,' Pat said with a cute smile. 'Jimmy Neil shot a few in his moss and he tells me they were as fat as geese.'

'You couldn't heed Jimmy. It's tame duck he has shot in mistake. There's no feeding for them in the whole island — everything's frozen hard. I'll warrant he didn't offer you one.'

'He did not.'

'He didn't want to lose Sarah,' Martin said and lifted his glass: 'Here's to their health anyway!' He called for two more whiskies: 'This will be my last. I'd a few bottles in me before you arrived.'

'A man can hold a good load on a cold night,' Pat said, noticing that Martin's eyes were heavy and his voice thickening. 'Here's to your own big day!' he added and raised his glass. 'When is it to be?'

'At Easter. God knows what'll happen before that.'

Pat put his arm on Martin's shoulder: 'That's one thing won't trouble me — marriage. I'll be my own boss always. I'm better off as I am.'

'You've the old woman and Sarah to keep you company.'

'By the way things is shaping I won't have Sarah long.'

'And you'll not always have your mother — God spare her health for many a day.'

Pat paused and lowered his voice: 'In a place like this you can never be sure of your span of life. Look at your own father and mother — they lasted no time at all.'

'God be good to them but my going away didn't lengthen their days. I often think of that.'

'Vera's father and mother are both hale and hearty at the other side?'

'I don't know. I never hear her talk of them.'

'That's a queer way for any daughter to get on.'

Martin shook his head and stared at the rings of froth on an empty glass of porter on the counter. He counted them beginning at the top and counted them from the bottom while his mind staggered back to the evening he had measured the circumferences of circles for Mary.

'Mary's a fine wee girl,' he said, 'and a right clever wee girl into the bargain.'

'You never heard her talk of her grandmother and granda at the other side.'

'No, I did not,' Martin said, 'I did not indeed.'

'It's an unnatural way to rear a child. Not for eight years or more was she brought to see them. It's unnatural.'

'It is, it is indeed,' Martin admitted drowsily, and from the haze of his memory that was falling and lifting like a wave he dragged forward his last meeting with his own father and mother and how they had besought him for the love of God not to leave them. He sighed and muttered something that Pat couldn't hear.

'It's unnatural, Pat,' he said.

'They don't have much luck.'

'It could all be,' Martin said. 'It could all be,' and he leaned on the counter and rubbed his face with his hand, and in the silence that was as deep as the snow outside he recalled how he couldn't get back in time to see either his father or mother before they died. 'A shadow follows them, Pat,' he said, as if answering some question that was put to him.

Pat ordered more drinks but Billy looked at Martin who was leaning across the counter, his head resting on his outstretched arms: 'He's had enough. He was drinking before you came in,' Billy said, and went to the other end to tidy up.

'Vera should bring wee Mary to see them,' Pat said as Martin raised his head from the counter.

'It's unnatural. You'd not find the like among us. Amn't I right in what I'm saying, Pat? I'll talk to her some of these fine days.'

'Everybody knows the way of it,' Pat said. 'Any of the men here could tell you. It's no secret. But it's none of my damned business what she does now.'

'It's mine,' he said and put a hand on Pat's shoulder. 'She'll change all that — never fear,' and he stumbled, his cap falling on to the counter. He screwed it on to his head, and with his finger made squiggles in a patch of mist his breath had made on the counter. They were alone. They hadn't heard the others go out. Pat threw a beseeching look at Billy but he ignored him, and after sweeping up the corks from the back of the counter he lowered the lamp above their heads — the signal for them to go.

Outside the snow was still falling, the moulds of footsteps filling up again, and the rockets still thundering through the thickness of the sky. Martin staggered against a barrel and gazed stupidly at a crate of empty bottles whose tops were ringed with snow. 'Circles and circumferences everywhere,' he said, scooping the snow from the barrel top, and with a kick sent a jingle among the bottles.

He shook hands with Pat and parted from him. Then he stopped, hailed him again, and once more shook his hand. 'You'll be at the wedding,' he said. 'You'll come and sing for us. We'll have good drink that morning for all who want it. And whisper,' he went on, leaning on Pat's shoulder and talking into his ear: 'The wee yacht — she's sunk but you know I'd no hand in it.' He brushed the snow off Pat's shoulder: 'None of the Reillys hold spite. Isn't that right. Damn the spite one of them holds! And your mother the best woman that ever tramped the roads of this island! Good night to you,' and he raised his cap like a farewell and went off singing to himself through the snow.

Around him the hills were white and no sound in the air except the shuddering sound of rockets and a boat blowing somewhere out at sea. Lights had gone out in the cottages, and the windows were black and cold except where a red lamp burned before a picture of the Sacred Heart. He passed the Craigs' cottage where there was a hole in the thatch big enough to swallow a bag of meal, and coming to the hill that led into the Lower End he halted to rest himself for the steep climb. Beside him the mill-stream, black and glossy as glass, rode unhampered by the snow; and as he saw the flakes fall into it and disappear, some lines from Burns drove unconnectedly through his mind. He plunged up the hill, repeating lines and phrases to himself till his effort resolved itself into what he sought, and having found them he shouted them aloud with pleasurable satisfaction:

Pleasures are like poppies spread,
You seize the flower, its bloom is shed;
Or like the snow falls in the river,
A moment white — then melts for ever.

166

'And gone for ever, and gone for ever,' he laughed as he reached the top of the hill. His cap fell off but as he stooped to lift it he fell forward into the snow-covered heather at the side of the road. He dozed, and it was Jamesy who found him half an hour later. He had sat up waiting for him but on seeing the light go out from Vera's window fright drove him on to the road and he ran with the dog ahead of him.

Jamesy shook him and helped him to his feet, and resting one arm on Jamesy's shoulder he sang scraps of songs and fumbled in his pocket for sweets he had bought for him.

'You're a fine boy, Jamesy. A fine boy though everything's unnatural this unholy night:

> Come, my love, and let us roam
> Through the towns and across the foam.
> East and west we'll travel together,
> Bracelets and silver and fine new leather —
> Oh — roh — oh roh — oh — roo
> I'm the man to buckle your shoe.

It's an unnatural way to find me but I'm not drunk, Jamesy boy, indeed I'm not drunk. I'm not so foolish. No!'

In the house he sat on a chair at the fire, scraped the snow from his cap with his fingers and flung it on the floor. He stretched out his feet and as Jamesy unlaced his boots for him, using a fork to unloose the knots that had hardened with the snow, he kept patting the boy's head and telling him he was the best lad in the whole island. With his coat off and his stockinged feet on the warm hearthstone he sat forward, his head drooped on his chest, and the steam rising from the legs of his trousers. Jamesy, waiting for him to go to bed, and afraid that he might fall into the fire or upset the lamp on the wall, began to eat the sweets to keep himself awake. He shuddered, but not in terror, as the window-frames shook in the boom from the rockets and an odd snowflake flew against the pane like a moth, leaving a glistening drop of water behind it.

The dog's paw-marks dried on the floor, the fire sank in the grate, and Martin sitting up with a start rubbed his eyes and stared at the clock: 'It's time we were in bed, son,' he said and looked round for his candlestick. Jamesy got it for him, lit it with a twist of paper and put it in his hand.

'You're a fine boy — a fine boy,' he said drowsily and shuffled to his room, and after he had groaned out his prayers like an old woman and had blown out his candle Jamesy quenched the lamp in the kitchen and went to his own room.

In the morning, seeing the window panes muffled with snow, he lay in the warmth of his bed waiting for Martin's familiar sounds from the kitchen. But Martin hadn't risen and going in to waken him he was greeted with a thick, hoarse voice that was barely recognizable.

'You'll have to fend and fodder for yourself today,' he said. 'I've a weight of cold on me that would sink a ship and I'll stay in bed till it shifts.' He had filled his pipe but after lighting it he pushed it away with disgust: 'The pipe's a great doctor — you're not up to the mark if a smoke gives you no pleasure.'

'Will I get the nurse to run up?'

'You'll get no nurse for me! You'll go down to Billy's after your breakfast and fetch me two good glasses of whisky and that'll lift it before the day's half out. And listen — not a murmur to anyone that I'm in bed for I don't intend to be long in it. It'll be a long time — a hell of a long time before you find me pelootered and stupid like last night. Never start the drink — you might be one of the fellas that can't call a halt: it's either in your blood or not in it but you needn't start to find out.'

When he was ready for the road Jamesy came into the room and asked was it two glasses he wanted or one.

'I think I said two and we'll let it lie at that — it's a bad thing to go back on your word. Two glasses but not more for it

168

wouldn't do to let the precious drink go to waste. And listen: Billy has no paper so you better bring a bit to wrap round the bottle.'

He hurried out with the dog through the snow and hurried back again, meeting no one on the way and seeing no footmarks in the snow around Vera's gate.

'Nobody saw me coming or going,' he said, 'and I'm thinking that Mary's not at school for there's no footmarks round her gate.'

'Nobody saw you,' Martin said huskily. 'Aye, there isn't a house between this and Billy's that didn't see you. They all saw you and they know damned well what your errand was. Every house here has eyes in the front of its head and at the back of its head — they'll know you weren't going for a pocketful of corks on a day like this.'

He emptied the whisky into a bowl, scalded it with boiling water and sweetened it with sugar, and rolling himself in the blankets like a chrysalis he told Jamesy to stay on guard round the house till he'd waken from his winter sleep.

After he had given hay to the horse and the cows, Jamesy began to make a snowman at the back of the house but on seeing Vera come down the white field and across the plank bridge to the well he hid himself in the byre till she was gone. He cocked a rusty basin on the head of the snowman, pushed stones into its stomach, and hung a piece of sacking round its neck for a muffler. He began to pelt it with snowballs, and the dog, running to retrieve them ran up the leg of the snowman, gripped the bit of sack in its teeth but the head came off and rolled down the hill. Jamesy's volley of abuse wakened Martin and he tapped the window and signalled to him to come in. His voice was still hoarse, the pipe still lay untouched on the table, and the small of his back ached as if girded with a hoop of iron.

'You're for the road again, Jamesy. I'm as stiff as a dead gurnet and you'll have to get me a bottle of Sloan's liniment. If that doesn't supple me you'll have to ask the miller to step up and measure me for the graveyard,' he said with a pained smile.

It was on his way out from the shop and while he was staring at the label on the bottle that he dunted into Vera as she came forward with a basket in her hand. She noticed the bottle at once and asked if it was for Martin.

'It is,' he muttered, and was turning away when she called him back sharply.

'Is he sick?' she said, her eyes gliding over his unwashed face and his long coat trailing in the snow.

He didn't answer her or flinch from her, and returned her hard penetrating stare with a look of secret and proud confidence.

'Is he in bed sick?' she said and gripped his arm.

'I don't know,' he said gruffly.

'You don't know? What way is that to talk to anyone? Was he in bed when he sent you for the liniment?' she said with cold anger, and her grip sent a flash of pain through his arm.

'It's none of your damned business,' he answered with a boldness that brought a flush to her cheeks. He wrenched himself free and stepped away from her.

'Why didn't you come and tell me he was sick, you pup?'

'He told me not to tell anyone,' he said with cool defiance. The colour left her cheeks, and the reflected light from the snowy road heightened her pallor.

'We'll see,' she said and withdrew to the shop.

Driven by a rush of strength from his encounter he began to whistle as he hurried through the snow. The sun came out strong; the stone fences were robbed of snow, and the rocks on the hill-tops shone like tin-foil. 'I'm not afraid of her,' he said aloud, flinging a snowball at a gatepost along the way.

'I'm damned but they'll have the nurse with me before you can wink,' Martin said, after Jamesy told him he had met Vera. 'Give me that bottle quick,' and he pulled the cork out with his teeth, lifted up his shirt, and poured half the bottle on the small of his back. 'Now, Jamesy, pummel me as if I were a bag of meal. And don't give up even if I bawl like a bull.' He gritted his teeth and clenched the rail of the bed as Jamesy rubbed him but finding the pain unbearable he twisted away from the boy's hands and lay on his back, smiling in spite of himself, and closing his eyes until the pain receded.

'That'll do for the first round,' he breathed out. 'I don't know what in hell is the matter with me. I'm like an Upper End and a Lower End and no road between them . . . Put on a good fire and I'll get up and sit at it. When you've the spirit to do it you can do anything.'

Vera came in and found him huddled over the fire. She had come straight from the shop, and with her basket resting on her lap she noticed immediately his pale face and unshaven chin. But it was the unswept floor and the crumbs on the table that told her more about his condition than he did himself. The sharp smell of liniment made her cough.

'You had a right to send for me, Martin.'

'Ach, I didn't want to alarm you. I thought I'd shake it off in an hour or two.'

'If you take my advice you'll fight it off in bed and send for the nurse. The Lower End doesn't trouble her much at any time. Indeed, I'd nurse you myself only you know how they'd talk. And there's that Jamesy fellow out there and I wouldn't trust him as far as I could throw him. His ears are always out on stilts and you never know what news he spreads.'

'Leave him out of it. He does his best and does what I tell him. A word of praise and he's ready to leap the lake for you.'

'Maybe he would and maybe he wouldn't,' she said with a knowledgeable air, and despite his protests she took off her coat and tidied the kitchen. The sun, strong and bright, shone through the window in a smoky beam of light, and from outside there sounded a rapid drip of water from the eaves.

171

'There's a fine touch of heat in that sun,' she said, dusting the ledge of the window.

'The cold's gone. The spring will come with a rush and I'll do the ploughing after the ground dries.'

'Easter will be on top of us before we know where we are.'

'It will. But it's well we've everything ready. I've asked Pat to the wedding and he's coming.'

'What's changed him, I wonder? He's not doing it for any love he bears us.'

'Love or no love he's coming, and with one or two of your own besides your father and mother we'll have a tidy group for Mrs. McKinley to feed that morning.'

'I'd rather there was nobody there except ourselves — Sarah and Mary and the old woman and the priest.'

'And what under God would your people think you were marrying? I might look like the scrapings of a scarecrow at the moment. But I'll be spruce and tidy that morning. Your father and mother will have to come.'

'There's plenty of time to arrange fiddle-faddles of that nature. It's best to do things quietly for I'm not the one for a big noise and fuss. When we go away we'll only stay a few days in Belfast. Poor Mary would fret her heart out after I'm away.'

'While we're there we'll seek out the Craigs. I'm dying to see the old man and I mightn't get another chance to see him.'

'The Craigs never cost me a thought. I'd rather we'd seek out some good bargains in the shops.'

'We can do that too,' he said, 'but it'd be unfriendly not to visit the old man. He'd be glad to see us and give us his blessing.'

She was standing now with her back to him, gazing out at the webbed shadow the ornamental gate stretched on the snow, no longer paying heed to what he was saying about the Craigs. She saw Jamesy carrying a piece of rusty corrugated iron under his arm, climb the hill and sleigh on the snow with a shout of delight.

172

'Will you get back to bed, Martin, and I'll send your lad for the nurse?' she said with quick urgency. 'It's better not to let that cold get a grip on you.' He nodded and she hurried across the road to Jamesy.

'Go for the nurse at once,' she said to him.

'Who says I'm to go for the nurse?'

'I say it!'

'I'll not do what you tell me.'

'Martin says you're to go for the nurse — at once!' He slouched past her and she gave him a push and told him not to doddle like an old man. 'It's not much you think of him — not much you care. You wouldn't care a straw if he were at death's door this instant,' she added. Jamesy went into the house.

'It'd be better to get her, Jamesy,' Martin said to him. 'But she'll not have me long under her eye. I'll be up tomorrow — never fear.'

Martin was alone again; he shuffled into his room and as he undressed he saw the drip from the eaves drilling tiny holes in the snow, and the perched snowman gradually growing smaller as streams of water swirled from its skirts down the hill.

'The spring's coming!' he sighed and glanced at his pipe wondering if he could enjoy a smoke. 'Ach, I'll wait till I hear what she says. I suppose she'll try to frighten me by putting some fancy name on my ailment.'

Vera waited for Jamesy's return outside her gate.

'Is she coming?' she challenged him as he came along the road. He hadn't expected to see her and he started and stared at her in silence. Her spiteful look no longer baffled him and he stiffened himself and shouted: 'She might and she mightn't!' and he swaggered past her finding a revengeful satisfaction in his double answer.

'You're getting too big for your boots, my boyo. It'll not be long now till I put an end to your tantrums,' she called after him.

And later when the nurse was leaving and Vera was talking

to her at the door she raised her voice so that Jamesy could hear her: 'You may be sure, nurse, that I'll do my best for him. That lad he has is not much good for anything. He can't even wash himself.'

Jamesy hated her and wished he had the power to hurt her but the consciousness of his weakness and the upsetting disturbance of these two women moving freely through the house made him think of the free life his red-haired friend was having on the mainland and he decided to leave on the lighthouse boat in the morning and seek him out. With that intention he rose early, packed his case and made his bed as he had always made it since his arrival. Standing at the table to take his breakfast he watched Vera fill her bucket at the well and the water sway over the brim as she planted it on the ground. He thought she would have turned home but on seeing her arrange her hair and pull down her sleeves he fled into the seclusion of his room. She lifted the latch without knocking, and observing the steam rising from the cup on the table she knew she had disturbed him. She went into Martin's room and closed the door behind her.

He tiptoed across the floor with his case, and going to the well he emptied her bucket over the stones and threw it into the stream. For a moment he watched it swing round on the current under the plank-bridge and jog towards the lake. He ran off and on reaching the first hill noticed that the dog was following him. 'Go home!' he shouted, 'Go home!' and as he threw a stone that bounced on the road over the dog's head the dog picked it up and dropped it at his feet. He clouted it on the head but it still followed him. He took the back road that edged the sea and as he saw the mill-race, fat and sleek from the melting snow, tumble its brown froth into the sea he began to cry for the first time. 'Go on home!' he shouted angrily at the dog and flung a fistful of gravel at it. The spaniel stopped but as Jamesy ran to get away from it it raced after him. Near the quay geese hissed at it with outstretched necks and two curs gathered round it, sniffing and raising the hair on their backs. The dog followed him no farther and after the boat had pulled out from the quay he saw it ramble home along the white road near the mill. For a long time he gazed at it with moist eyes and followed it in imagination up the long hill he knew so well. The helmsman eyed him with puzzled curiosity, and Jamesy lowered his head and fumbled with the clasp on his case.

CHAPTER XV

THE impatient scratching of the dog at the door wakened
Martin and he raised himself from the pillow and listened
to the emptiness and quietness of the house. He called out
to Jamesy but getting no answer he went to the window and
called out from there. He went back to bed but the dog continued to whimper and he rose and let it in. The fire was dead
out, and Jamesy's cup of tea with a scum of milk on it lay on the
table. The dog bounded into the lad's room and sniffed and
ran round with distressed attention. Martin followed it. The
bed was made as usual but the nails behind the door no longer
held his clothes and nothing hung from them except a piece of
knotted cord. The case, which had lain beneath a small table
since the first day of his arrival, was gone.

'He's left me!' Martin said to himself. 'I knew it would
come to this but he had the right to tell me. He had the right
to wait till I was on my feet and not leave me in the lurch.'

He returned to the kitchen and threw paper and sticks into
the grate. 'I'll stay up now even if it kills me,' he said, gazing at
the blueness of the tattooed anchor against the pallor of his
flesh. 'He was a good lad and I don't blame him for going — I
blame him for the way he took of doing it.'

He put some water in a saucepan and when it was boiled he
began to shave and dress himself. His legs were numb, and a
certain heaviness about his chest cramped his desire to move
briskly. He wouldn't count the things he had done for him;
he had done nothing but what the lad deserved and deserved
well. He had worked hard and he had earned every shilling
he gave him and every shoe that shod him and every shirt that
covered his back.

He sat at the fire and lit his pipe; the tobacco tasted sweeter but he only took a few pulls at it and pushed it from him. He tried to read a book but his mind wandered from it and the print dazzled his eyes. He pulled on his heavy coat and went out. Everything seemed queer and distant; the cold breath from the snow had gone but the blue sky was frozen and streaked with strings of cloud. In a heap at the back of the house were all the decorations of Jamesy's snowman: the rusty basin, a rag of damp sacking and a fistful of stones. He threw the basin into the ash-pit and was returning to the house when he heard Vera call to him from the side of her hill. He pretended not to hear her. He bolted the door, hesitated, and unbolted it again. He wanted to be alone but in a few minutes he saw her pass the window.

'Jamesy's left me,' he said before she could blame him for getting out of bed. 'Left without a word or even a whisper that he was going.'

'Are you sure he's gone?'

'His room's as bare as the day I fixed it up for him.'

'I always knew he was a weakling,' she said, trying to disguise her pleasure, and realizing that they were free at last to talk to one another without interruption. Her hidden love for him sprung up unimpeded and unhampered by any prying eye and she longed for the opportunity to show it.

'Don't worry about him, Martin, he'll get fixed up at the other side. You'll only do yourself harm,' she said and sat on the floor at his feet, her head resting against his knees. She stroked his hand and traced the anchor with her finger. 'You were far too good to him,' she said.

'I'll miss him. I was used to hearing him move about the house — there was some comfort in that.'

'It won't be long till we are both together,' she sighed, 'and living under the one roof and in a room of our own. I'll make you happy, Martin. I know I will,' and she closed her eyes in an effort to restrain the rush of love that possessed her. But Martin felt no strength or desire to respond to her. He had never

177

seen her like this before and he himself had never felt so cold towards her. He had no energy and no inclination for pretence, and allowed himself to submit to his mood of listless immobility. She raised her eyes to him but he wasn't looking at her, and she got to her feet and stood beside him for a moment running her fingers through his hair: 'Martin, Martin,' she said, 'don't think about him. He didn't think much for you when he left you like this.'

He sat quite still with his open hands on his knees. With Jamesy he had been content, and it was only since she came into his life that discontent had come with it. Had he passed the age for marrying? — he'd never say that to her: he'd abide by his pledged word to her and implore God's guidance. At this moment she filled him with a mild repulsion and he wished she'd go out and leave him to himself. He resented the things she was doing for him: the cleaning up of the dishes and the making of his bed. His freedom was being pilfered from him bit by bit and he could no longer call the house his own.

'I've turned your mattress for you and you'll find it a bit more comfortable,' she said, standing at the open door of his room.

'I'm not going back to bed for anyone. I'll fight off the dregs on my feet,' he said and turned round to the fire.

'You might do yourself harm, Martin, by getting up too soon.'

'Did he say anything to you about leaving?'

'Jamesy — is it? Hm, he never spoke a word to me and since you took sick I could never get a civil answer out of him. Indeed I'd have complained to you but I didn't want to upset you. You'd find out for yourself time enough.' For a moment she thought of telling him about the bucket he had pitched into the stream but, for some reason, checked herself. She sat down opposite him. He wished she'd go and leave him to himself. Her presence and her voice were annoying him, and it was with difficulty he smothered the impulse to shout at her to leave him in peace.

'You're very kind to me,' he managed to say, 'very kind and I'll not forget you for it.'

The distant formality of his voice baffled her and she regarded him with puzzled astonishment, her usual pride squeezed into a dry servility by the strangeness of his manner. She didn't know him; it's his sickness that has changed him, she thought. She must have patience and not vex him.

'Do you feel cold, Martin?'

He shook his head.

'Would you like something to eat? It wouldn't take me long boiling up the kettle for you.'

'I don't want anything.' When would she go! He closed his eyes and thought of Jamesy, wondering what he'd do on reaching the other side.

'He'll get fixed up all right — there'll be no fear of that,' he said, half to himself.

She pretended not to hear him as she stood at the window and saw the lake blue with spring and a few patches of snow that magpied the hills. A single fly crawled on the window-sash, struggling out of its winter sleep, its wings dusted with lime-wash.

'I heard the larks singing on my way to the well this morning.'

'They're at it early,' he said after a pause. 'He'll be able to tell them that he can plough — that'll stand to him. I could have given him a letter if only he'd told me.'

She tore a corner off a piece of paper, crushed it down on the fly, and threw it in the fire. How can he feel so strongly for an orphan like that! What on earth did he see in him that she didn't see! She had never known a minute's peace while he was skulking about the hills and the road — and Mary on her way from school. Her mind would be at ease now.

She stood with her back to the fire, her hands loosely by her

179

sides. What she yearned to possess he was giving to another. The limp and lonely droop of his head drew her nearer to him; she touched his shoulder lightly:

'Martin,' she said, 'some day you'll have a boy of your own blood.'

He smiled with his lips closed and stretched out his hand to her.

'Yes, Martin, that will come. Every bit of me wants that! I'll live for it! Do you hear me, Martin?'

'We'll live and work for that, please God!'

She knelt on the floor at his feet and rested her head on his knees. She felt the pressure of his hand on her shoulder, the stroke of his fingers on her hair, and knew if she had raised her head she'd have seen his eyes filled with tears.

CHAPTER XVI

WITHIN a week he got a letter from a mainland farmer inquiring about Jamesy's character. He replied to it at once, praising the lad's willingness to work and expressing a regret that the island couldn't hold him. He missed him, now that he had to do his spring ploughing, and he missed him most of all when he had refitted the engine in the boat and was out morning and evening on the sea tending his lobster-pots. He failed to get a man to partner him because the Lower End suited none of them, and most of them were already joined up with boats that had more convenient harbourage at the quay. But these disappointments hung loose about him, for night after night when his work was done himself and Vera were together, preparing everything for the wedding. Mary, bent over her exercise at the kitchen table, would listen to them, sharing with exultant silence in their plans, and the next day retell all that she had heard to her granny and with round-eyed delight describe in detail her mother's wedding-clothes.

But a few days before the wedding the three of them set out one evening to pay a visit to the old woman, and as they passed slowly along with the low sun showing up the little bumps and hollows on the road the people, gazing furtively at them from the windows, said in their own minds that they would be happy, that Martin looked happy and that even Vera Reilly was losing her flinty look. And when they had passed the last two cottages the doors opened simultaneously and two women came out to collect the clothes that had been drying on the bushes, and saying to one another that they just had them in in time before the dew would fall they paused with the bundles of clothes in their hands and looked up the road at the receding figures: 'Well?' one said.

'It'd be hard to tell,' the other answered.

'They look well together.'

'It takes more than looks.'

'Do you think would she . . . ?'

'There's nothing to ail her having three or four.'

'She's still fresh.'

'She is just.'

'And Martin's no weakling. He's as broad as the gable-end of that house.'

'Poor Tom . . . He was the colour of that sheet you have in your hand.'

'But he was kind. Young Mary's the dead spit of him.'

'Vera's hard.'

'This might soften her. It might indeed . . . There's a cold snap in that air.'

'I think I'll go in with these clothes. The dew could fall on them even you're holding them in your warm arms.'

'It could indeed. I'll take in my own . . . I can't see the pair of them any more. I suppose they're away to visit the old woman. They didn't turn off the road to the lighthouse, for I kept my eye on them while I was gathering the clothes.'

'I see Pat ploughing out on the side of the hill . . . I heard it said he was against the marriage.'

'Och, sure he's against everything — he'd take offence at the grass growing!'

Even after the sun had set they were still holding their bundles of clothes in their hands, gossiping, and glancing at Pat as he ploughed below the slope of the hill. They saw Sarah go up to him, and they saw him stop his horses for a minute and then drive them forward again, with Sarah following him for half the length of the field.

The two women had guessed right: Pat was against the marriage and though Sarah had pleaded with him to come into the house he shrugged his shoulders and damned her for meddling with him and interrupting his work. He wouldn't go next or near the house while they were there, he told her. And he wouldn't go to the wedding! He'd have no hand or part in it! He wouldn't insult Tom's memory!

'You'd think they were committing some crime,' his mother said to him that night after Vera and Martin had gone. 'What under God will they think of you at all, at all?'

'I don't give a damn what they think!'

'There's no call to swear... Would you not go to the wedding even to keep people from talking and putting a twist on what you do?'

'I'll not be missed. It's her own people the neighbours will miss — her own father and mother, her own brothers and sister. Why should I go? What does she want me to go for?'

'It's me that wants you to go,' his mother entreated. 'For my sake and for Sarah's you should go. We never hold spite. Poor Tom knows that she's doing what is right and natural. She's still young!'

'That's the trouble — she's too young!' he said and looked away from her where she sat in the glow of the fire. He waited for her to say something but as she remained wrapped in silence he turned to her again: 'Do you see now why I'm dead against it?'

She shook her head with slow sorrow.

'If she had children by Martin,' he said after a pause, 'people won't think much of our stock.'

'I never knew you had so much bad pride in you! And to think that you'd wish ill-luck to another to satisfy your pride!' She shook her head: 'May God forgive you, Pat — that's all I can say to you.'

'It's Tom I'm thinking of,' he said with a rush.

'Keep his name out of it. He has gone where no tongue or thought can hurt him. He knows that Vera is in the right and you are in the wrong. And Mary — it'll be nice example for her if you ignore her mother's wedding.'

'Mary! — there's a lot behind that that you hide!'

'Pat, son, don't bring that up again. For the love of God don't.'

'I will!' he said. 'Why don't you say straight out what plan you have in your mind for Tom's child? Vera knows what it is — that's why she's getting Sarah to stay in the Lower End with Mary till they come back from Belfast. Why didn't she make arrangements for the child to stay here for the few days? Vera's too clever! She's making a fool of you and Sarah but she'll not have me on the same rope.'

'It's not the time or the place to quarrel with you. A wedding's a time for rejoicing — it's the place where the first miracle was wrought . . . Anyway you told Martin you were going.'

'I must have been drunk if I told him that. Don't bother me any more about it. I'm not going! he shouted. 'Damn the foot will I stir from this house to go.'

He kept his word, and on the morning of the wedding he stayed in his bed listening to Sarah and his mother fussing about in the kitchen to get out in time. His mother came to him again and asked him to change his mind but he shook his head and turned his back on her, and later he sat up in his bed and heard the cheers at the chapel gates as the couple came out, heard the shotguns go off and two trap-loads of laughing people sally past his window. He lay on till the road was empty of people and getting up he tiptoed about the kitchen for fear of making noise. The fire was unlit and he knew they must have gone to Holy Communion at the Mass.

'You'd think there was nobody else in the house but the two of them,' he said, raking out the ashes. He stopped and threw the poker on to the hob: 'It can stay out — I'm not going to light it for them!' and he sat at the table and took a breakfast of cold milk and bread, and when he had finished he slipped out by the back of the house and concealing himself behind a loose-stone wall he gazed down at the armful of houses at the quay and at the empty boat flashing its bunting of colours in the sun. His head throbbed, and time and again he looked round him like a fugitive. He saw the stream of people trickle from one of the houses, saw a puff of smoke from a shotgun, then the report and a cheer from the crowd. He crouched lower behind the wall and crept unseen to the back of the house.

No one had seen him and no one on the quay was thinking about him His mother in the excitement and in her joy had forgotten about him and as she stood holding Mary's hand and looking at Vera dusting the confetti from Martin's shoulders she suddenly thought of Tom's wedding and began to weep, and in the silence of her mind prayed God to spare her until Sarah was married.

'Be a good girl, Mary,' Vera shouted up to them from the boat. 'Take good care of Sarah till we come back. I'll have something nice for you.'

The boat moved out from the quay; three shots were fired into the air, and as the people cheered Martin stood up and waved his hat to them, and as he sat down he recalled old Craig's leave-taking, and he whispered to Vera that they mustn't forget to call to see him. She nodded but on reaching Belfast he mentioned the old man's name again and she told him to give her head peace about the Craigs and let her enjoy her first visit to the city.

He didn't refer to it again until their last morning in the small hotel near the docks. She was brushing her hair at the mirror in their room and smiling at him as he knelt on the lid of her suitcase in order to close it.

'You've half the town in that case,' he said.

'I've only a few bits of frock material for Mary,' she said and bent back her head laughing. He kissed her, lifted her in his arms and swung round with her on the floor.

'You'll toss my hair again,' she said, 'and keep us late for the train.'

'We'll take the next one and that'll give us an hour or two to visit the Craigs. You'll come, Vera — won't you?' and he coaxed her with playful kisses till she agreed.

But later, as he led her down the parallel streets of small red-brick houses in his search for Turn Street she began to lament her decision and to complain of the heat of the day and the tiredness of her feet. They passed weaving factories and through the open windows saw revolving wheels and trembling leather belts and smelt the oily smell of unwashed air spilling out through the fluffed ventilators. The throbbing and chattering of the machines and the dizzy height of the buildings made her grip his arm and implore him to turn back. 'We're not far from it now,' he said. 'We'd have no luck if we didn't see it through.' He hurried on, and she trailed two steps behind him, down one street where old women with lemon-coloured faces sat on their door-steps in the sun, down another where big boys played with a rag-ball between the lamp-posts, and then they reached Turn Street, and as she moved along looking from one side to the other she noticed the dusty pigeons feeding on crusts flung on the street and two kittens jumping in and out between the spokes of a handcart.

'Do you know the number of the house?' she whispered.

'I don't but we can ask somebody,' he said, standing and looking about him with shy bewilderment.

'Don't keep me standing here and everybody gaping at us,' she said crossly.

'Wait now, wait now! I see somebody we both know,' he said and walked forward confidently. Old Craig was seated on a chair in the sun, his waistcoat open, his stick upright between his legs, and above him hanging on a nail was a caged thrush.

Martin and Vera stopped in front of him and he raised his head and stared at them without speaking.

'Do you not know me, Michael John?' Martin said, stretching out his hand.

The old man looked from one to the other, then spat on his hand and gripped Martin's.

186

'Sweet God in Heaven this is a day!' he said, rising stiffly from his chair, leading them into the small kitchen and calling out to his daughter: 'Where are you, Kate? Where are you? For the love of God come quick till you see.'

His daughter who was hanging out clothes in the yard rushed in shouting: 'What the divil's wrong with you now?' and on seeing the strangers in the kitchen she dropped her voice and stood twisting her hands in her apron. She recognized them at once, and into her mind rushed her last meeting with Martin as he stood in his cart and his horse shieing from Danny's painted ball. She sat opposite them, fiddling at the buttons on her black blouse and pushing back a strand of hair that had fallen over her forehead. The untidiness of the kitchen, the pear-shaped hole in the curtain at the window and the wet floor of the scullery confused and silenced her, as she glanced at Vera in her new wedding suit and the glossy handbag on her lap. With a faint smile she heard them speak of their marriage, heard her father give them his blessing, and then launch into the familiar litany of his leave-taking; she did not stop him but slipped away to change her clothes and tidy her hair. In a few minutes she was back in the kitchen again and now she was in full control of herself, wishing them every happiness and pleading with her father to stop talking till she'd hear the sound of her own voice. She bustled from the kitchen to the scullery, spread a cloth on the table and laid down her best cups and saucers for the tea. Her father paid no heed to her as he inquired about the old house and the thatch on the roof, and, in his anxiety not to forget anything, he scarcely waited for Martin to answer him. His mind ranged over the whole island from north to south, east and west, picking out each house in his mind's eye, crossing hills and roads swifter than a swallow, till he had inquired about every family on the island. Then his voice slowed as he asked about the crops, the fishing, the boats, and if anything had been done yet to deepen the pier at Ballycastle.

187

'Nothing has been done,' Vera said, 'and nothing will be done till they make their voices heard . . . Indeed when I used to work on the mainland I saw an island boat trying to land and a wave breaking over it and the heads of the crew above the water like birds on a plank.'

'It'll always be the same hardships,' Kate put in. 'Nobody with a grain of sense would live there. Here we've every comfort: water on a tap inside your house, gas to cook on and coal delivered on your doorstep.'

The old man spat in the fire and turned his stick between his palms: 'There's nothing here only rush and noise. The houses sit shoulder to shoulder in front of you and at the back there's only a rotten entry that never tastes the sun. Raise your head anywhere and there's only a narrow space of sky. Space to move in and breathe in is a great thing. Blessed God but I'd give one of my eyes to see the hills again and feel the space opening out like a fresh wind. Space is a grand thing. Look at this box of a kitchen — you couldn't turn a wheelbarrow in it without chipping the walls. Space, I tell you, is as wholesome as a clean wind. It's a great thing is space!'

'Comfort and ease is a great thing,' the daughter put in.

'I know what made me and what's killing me. My eyes were accustomed to look out on width. My breath was made for a wind with a sting in it. What interest have I in coal carts or breadmen's carts or in men that sing round the doors for a few halfpence? I live here but my mind doesn't.'

'Don't heed him, friends. He's always cross and never contented. There's a handful of old people in the street and ye'd never hear a word of complaint from them.'

'I'll never rest in this place,' he boomed out. 'Let them who were reared in it take their fill of it. My memory's wide and their's is as thin as a thread. Let me get back where the streams night and day run sweet to the sea.'

'Sit in to the table and take this drop of tea. You can't leave till you see wee Danny. He's at school and he'll be in for his lunch any minute now.'

'Till you see wee Danny!' scorned the old man. 'You'll not know the poor lad — he's as thin as that stick of mine. This is no place to rear a country child.'

'He's growing, da.'

'He's growing brazen like the rest of them. I tell you, Martin, I couldn't sit out at that door but they insult me. I take the air when they're at school. And Danny — he's as bad and worse than any of them.'

'Is it any wonder? You're too crabbed and if they play near you you chase them away . . . Take this cup of tea and stop lamenting sometime.'

When they were nearly finished Danny burst in with a lad chasing after him. He was laughing and out of breath, and he stood up abashed, and wiping his nose on his cuff stared at the visitors.

'Danny,' said his mother, 'shake hands with these people they'll not take a bite out of you.'

'Would you look at the cut of him?' said the old man staring at his bare legs that were thrust into canvas slippers. 'There's as much ink on his legs as'd write a history of Ireland.'

'They're washed for him every night in a bucket,' his mother said, smoothing Danny's hair with her hand.

'In a bucket,' mocked the old man. 'Ah, when I was young we'd a whole field of wet grass to wash them in, and if it wasn't wet we had the dew on it. Every night before bedtime we ran through the grass to wash our legs . . . Ah, Danny, this man here could tell you about it,' he added, pointing to Martin. 'Every day he passes the house where you were born and if you'd give him one of your pigeons in a paper bag he'd let it off for you from the very doorstep. Wouldn't you do that for him, Martin?'

'I would and welcome,' Martin said.

189

'And you'd tie a bit of thatch on its leg for him?'

'I'd tie the whole house on its leg for him,' Martin smiled.

'It might lose itself,' Danny said.

'It'll be back this evening before your bed-time,' his granda said. 'Every bird returns to where it was reared. Your pigeon will have something to coo about when it comes back! Man alive it'll keep the others awake all night with its talk.'

When they were leaving, Martin carried the pigeon in a cardboard box punctured with air-holes. The old man went out with them, and although his daughter told him to go no farther than the head of the street he walked with them to the tram-stop, and all the time he kept saying to them that he wished to God he was going the whole way with them. At the tram-stop they couldn't get away from him: as tram after tram passed he coaxed them to wait for the next but at the end they had to drag themselves away from him and to their embarrassment as they boarded the tram they heard him shout: 'May God send you children that'll love their calf-ground.'

In the train going home Martin stood at the open window looking back at the city with its tall factory chimneys shaking their whips of black smoke above the greyness that eternally smothered the houses. The train ran along the edge of the lough, and he saw with detachment a few sooty gulls perched on the broken sea-wall and below them the unwashed waves with its floating papers and orange skins. The train whistled into a tunnel and out again into the clean sunlit air, the white smoke from the engine lassoing the trees, bulging into the telegraph wires and caterpillaring its shadow across the fields. He stretched himself contentedly and turned from the window: 'Well, Vera, it's great to be going home again. You're happy, Vera?'

Sitting opposite him she smiled but didn't speak. She saw him stretch himself full length on the seat with a newspaper under his feet; he smiled and closed his eyes, and closing her own to the jogging rhythm of the train she wondered if she'd ever be happy. The air whorled in through the open window and flicked the dangling labels on their cases on the rack. She opened her eyes. The pigeon scuffled in its box and the leather belt of the window tapped against the door. On her right she saw the suburban houses on the hill and to her left, amidst the breaking fragments of the engine's smoke, she caught a glimpse of the sea. They were hurrying home but her memory and desire were tugged back to the few days she had spent among the shops and excitement of the city. She sighed, took off her hat and twirled it round on the point of her finger before placing it on the seat beside her. She closed her eyes again and let her hands lie limp on her lap. The wheels thumped and rumbled, restless as the tossing thoughts of her mind. She shook her head in answer to her own questions. No, she could never bury herself for ever on the island — that could never be! There was nothing on the island for anyone — nothing. What chance has Mary in a place like that? — a child like her with a mind and grace for better things. She was her mother and she'd see to it that the child would not waste her life as she had wasted hers. In another few years she'd be ready for the training college. There'd be the expense of the travelling — they could never meet it if they were stuck out there like a lighthouse on a rock! They couldn't stay on there without her. It'd be madness. No, no, they couldn't. Martin would have to change! If he'd do that they could make ends meet. They could all be contented together. He could take a job on a boat again and they could get a little house on the outskirts of the city and she could have him home at the week-ends. They might even get a house overlooking the lough where he could see them through a telescope on his passage in or out. She smiled sweetly and glanced over at him. Oh, if he'd only stir and open his eyes she'd tell him what she was thinking, for after all it was better in the long run to be honest and straight with him.

She leant forward to touch him, but the pigeon scuffled in its box and she sat back again and heard the hurried throb of her own heart. The bird's pink claw appeared at one of the holes, then a ray of sunlight fell on the box and the pigeon moved frantically and poked its head out of one hole and then another. She took the box on her lap, lifted the lid gently and peered in at the grey-blue hunch of feathers. It stretched its neck under the caressing stroke of her finger, and then suddenly it fluttered its wings and in an instant shot out through the window. With a cry she jumped to her feet, saw it disappear into the white smoke, entangle itself in the telegraph wires and fall like a stone to the ground. The commotion wakened Martin.

'The pigeon's gone!' she said breathlessly. He looked out of the window but saw nothing only the empty sky. She tried to tell him what happened but her distracted mind jumbled her telling of it, for nothing was clear to her mind only the last sight of it as it fell through the wires — and that part she withheld from him.

'It'll be home in about ten minutes. What on earth will the old man think of me at all?' he said, standing with the box in his hand. 'To hell with it,' and he flung the box out of the window. 'He had his mind set on a bit of thatch.'

She gave a nervous laugh and smiled up at him: 'Couldn't you send him a bag of thatch if it came to that?'

'You needn't joke about it, for when I'm given a thing to do I like to see it through. Anybody could see he was dying to talk of the island; the old pigeon would have given him something more to talk about.'

'He talked too much about the island for my taste,' she said, taking out a small mirror and arranging her hat on her head. 'I'm sure he has that daughter of his worried to death with his talk.' She powdered her face and swept the dust from her lap with a quick movement. 'Indeed if I were out of it tomorrow its name wouldn't sweeten my tongue.'

'You only imagine that, Vera. I had the same notion when I

left it but somehow I was always drawn back to it. My father and mother held me as much as the place itself. Your own parents have the same grip on you and you wouldn't know it till you're far away from them.'

'Don't I? They live next door to me, you may say, and I seldom want to see them.'

'But we'll see them today — won't we?'

She shook her head and turned her face to the window. He sat beside her and put his arm round her.

'Why do you not want me to see them, Vera? Since they couldn't come to the wedding we better go to them.'

'I told you lies about them, Martin. I told you they didn't like travelling on the water. It was all lies. I didn't ask them and I told them nothing about it. There's the truth out now!'

She took a handkerchief from her bag and began to cry, and he toyed with the leather strap of the window and slapped it against his hand as she began to describe her home and the life she had led there before her first marriage.

'I had to keep them at arm's length — the whole lot of them. I worked hard when I was at home. I wasn't lazy but they are. I dread meeting them. It's money they ask me for all the time — Money! And where do they think I could get it — me and Tom that had to look at every penny twice before parting with it. No, Martin, they don't hold me the way you were held. There's something different in us that I can't explain.'

He stroked her hand: 'All the same, Vera, it'd be better to call for a minute or two before the boat leaves. We needn't stay long. They'll have heard about the wedding by this time and I'd be happier in my mind if we called.'

'We won't call — never!'

'Never? — you can't say that because you nor me can't stand by it always. Whatever else they are they're your own flesh and blood. And anyway they can't take much from us because

193

we've nothing to give them only a bit of our company now and then — that wouldn't cost us much, would it?'

By the time they had reached Ballycastle he had failed to win her round to him, and when they were walking slowly out of the station he once more stopped and pleaded with her.

'We'll miss the boat,' she said.

'We'll not miss it.'

'Come on and don't stand there as if we were quarrelling. Everybody's gaping at us.' She forced a smile and lifted one of the cases, and he had to hurry to keep up with her. Suddenly he stopped and put down his suitcase again.

'I'll not be content, Vera, till we call on them — that's all.'

She gazed guiltily round her at the familiar houses and at the heeled-up farm carts arranged round the Square. Two women, whom she knew, bowed to her, and seeing them stand at a nearby shop and pretend to interest themselves in the bales of cloth stacked at the door she gripped Martin's arm in a spurt of temper: 'Lift the cases and come on! . . . We'll come back some day soon and bring Mary with us — they'd love to see her.'

Without murmuring he lifted the cases and hurried after her, and on reaching the sea he heard her sigh freely. The island-boat was at the point of the quay laden with boxes of groceries and a few barrels of stout. None of the crew was around and they sat down to rest on an empty box in the sun. The tide was going out, and around them was the smell of tarred ropes and the smell of salt from the drying pools in the uneven stones of the quay. Martin opened his waistcoat, soaked his handkerchief in one of the pools and wiped his face and neck.

'Ah, Vera, there's great freshness in that air,' he said and breathed in loudly. 'Great freshness! There's something in what old Craig says — there's space here and a cleanness.that lifts the heart.'

She didn't answer him. She saw a few empty rowboats

194

tilted on the sand by the outgoing tide and heard the sizzle of the seaweed as it dried in the sun. She closed her eyes.

'You're tired, Vera. You'll be glad to get your head down tonight.'

She nodded, and by thinking of Mary and the welcome she'd have for them she managed to lift the heaviness from her heart.

CHAPTER XVII

ABOUT a fortnight later old Craig followed them back to the island. Martin was transferring the ornamental gate with the ship's wheel from the house on the hill when he saw the old man trudging towards him on the road. As he drew nearer he recognized him at once and placing the gate against the stone fence of the field he hurried to meet him.

'You're not your lone, Michael John?' he asked with happy surprise and squeezed his hand. He noticed the tired face wrinkled like a dry shammy, the tie-knot hanging loose from the collar, and the black coat with the tattered button-holes. The old man was out of breath.

'I've come back, Martin,' he said, 'and you'll help me. The rubbishy life has me bate.'

'You're more than welcome to anything we have. Come up to the house. Did anyone come with you?'

'Not a one. They don't know where I am. I got the longing and I made my way alone.'

Martin drew a chair up to the fire and bade him rest himself till he'd get Vera.

She was in the fowl-house and he came to meet her laughing and rubbing his hands.

'I don't see what there is to laugh at,' she said after he had laughed out his tale. 'I'll not take hand or part in it. It's too soon for us to get mixed up in other people's troubles. Why didn't he go to other houses? That's what you get for calling on them — you knew I was dead set against it from the start. This will be a lock that'll be difficult to open. What'd you say to him?'

'I brought him into the house.'

'You'd little else to do with your time. Why didn't you stay at your gate and leave me to deal with him!' She closed the fowl-house door with a snap. 'And where is he going to stay the night — we've no room for him. He's going out of this and let whoever likes look after him — I'm not!' The cold unfriendliness of her voice roused him.

'You better let him stay till we find out the ins and outs of the whole business.'

'Out on the road he's going this very instant!'

'He's not going out if I know anything. You're not going to bring ill-luck on the house by turning out an old man.'

'I'm telling you he's going right now!' she brushed past him but he gripped her arm.

'Let go that arm!'

'I'll let it go when you listen to what I've to say for once. He's not going. He's not fit to go and you can't turn him away without a bite to eat.'

'They'll not have it to say that I encouraged him.' She broke away from him and he followed her.

'This is a nice carry on,' she said at the threshold but the old man was dozing over the fire and he didn't hear her.

'He's done out,' Martin said quietly, and lifted the old man's stick from the floor and rested it against the wall. 'Lay the table and I'll boil up the kettle,' and as he raked the fire the old man stirred and opened his eyes.

'I'm back, Vera.'

'So I see,' she said, standing in the middle of the floor with her arms folded.

'I'm a sore trouble to you,' he said, turning his head away from her and gazing at the flitter of twigs under the kettle.

'You're no trouble at all,' she said with dry scorn. 'Martin will run you across in the boat and see you off on the evening train.'

'Surely you're not thinking of going back this evening?' Martin exclaimed with feigned surprise.

'I am not — nor tomorrow night, nor the day after, nor the day after that!' he said emotionally.

197

'Any friend of my father's is welcome to what I have,' Martin said.

Vera spread a cloth on the table, and going into her room she signalled to Martin to follow her. He ignored her and she came back again and began to upbraid the old man for leaving his good home and the worry he'd cause his daughter.

'I'll cause them no worry. I know when I'm not wanted. That's the God's truth I'm telling you.'

'You don't need to be told when you're not wanted,' Martin put in, 'it's a thing you feel — you'd feel it in the air as you'd feel the end of summer. Vera will make you a good cup of tea and I'll fix up a bed for you in the house on the hill.'

From the window Vera watched him stride down the field, across the plank bridge and up to the old house. In a few minutes he was carrying out a mattress and leaving it to air in the sun, and before she had wet the tea smoke was rising above the roof and some burling through the open door because the chimney was damp, and after merging above the ash trees it was carried down into the hollow by the light wind. Looking out again she saw him spread out the blankets on the rocks — blankets that had belonged to Jamesy and which she wished to burn — and saw the spaniel career up and down the hill and race in and out of the house like a mad thing. He can sweep it and tidy it as much as he likes but she'd not partner him in this pantomime.

'Sit over to the table, Mister Craig,' she said, 'I'm sure you're hungry.'

'You're a kind girl, Vera Reilly,' he said, her old name coming naturally to his lips. 'A kind girl and I'm more than thankful to ye. More than thankful. God in heaven it's grand to see a bit of butter and the freshness sweating out of it.'

Vera Reilly, Vera Reilly, she repeated to herself — and the strangeness of it drew and knotted her mind. Vera Reilly, Tom Reilly, Pat Reilly! Her name had changed but Mary's hadn't. She was still Mary Reilly — and as she turned it over and over again in her mind it seemed for the moment she was thinking of a daughter of Pat's and not of her own child.

'You'd hardly know Mary if you saw her,' she said aloud, sitting down at the table and buttering bread for him. 'She's grown into a big girl.'

'And why wouldn't I know her? Indeed if I saw her in a crowded church in the town I'd know her. I would indeed,' he answered warmly. 'She's the dead spit of her own father. Ah, God rest Tom Reilly!'

'I think she'll be made monitress in the school very soon.'

'And why wouldn't she? The Reillys were all a heady lot. The old woman turned out many's a good scholar in her day. And do you know? — a day will come when your own daughter will be mistress in the same school. That'll be a fine day for you to see! She'll be among her own all her days!'

With her finger she toyed with a knife on the table, spinning it round on its joint, pursuing her own thoughts and not daring to mention Mary's name again. She couldn't understand how or why she should be discussing Mary with an old man whose mind was rooted as firmly as Martin's in this hole-and-corner of an island. She would never be one of them; she would never understand them and they'd never understand her.

She didn't hear Martin come in until he spoke. 'The house is ready for you, Michael John, and there's a bed in it fit for a king.'

'I'll not trouble you for very long for as soon as I get the roof mended on my own home I'll go there. I'm used to every corner of it and could find my way about it blindfolded.'

'You can stay on the hill as long as you like. It'll keep the house in good health.'

'I know I'm welcome, Martin. Ah, it's a fine thing to have friends who don't count the cost and it's a fine thing for a friend not to add to cost. It's only when you're away in a strange place and among strangers that you know what you've lost.'

'Your poor daughter will be at a loss this moment Vera,' interrupted. 'She'll be at a loss to know where you are.'

'Divil the bit of her! Do you know what she told me last night? She told me it didn't matter where a man was buried — he'd be dead and the clay he lay in wouldn't give him a headache. There's what the change done to her — it broke her respect for me and for my people. It was that that settled me. And this morning I made the excuse to go to the shop for tobacco and on my way up the street wee Danny and his playboys shouted names at me — and that finished me.'

Martin handed him his stick and went out with him, and at the stream that raced under the road the old man faced east and then west, and at the sight of the yellow marigolds swaying in the black drifting water all the stress of the day slunk away from him like a shadow of cloud. They sauntered up to the house: the windows were all open, a fresh wind blowing through it and a bright fire blazing in the grate. The concrete floor was swept clean, and the bareness of the kitchen with only a table, a chair and a small chest gave it a spaciousness that overjoyed him. He stared at the circles of brightness on the wall where lids of pots used to hang, at the long smoky wedge from the oil-lamp, and at the pine-timbered ceiling that hadn't lost its gloss.

'It's too good for the likes of me, Martin. But I'll not overstay my time.'

'Nonsense, it's dying for somebody to put fire and wind through it.'

They went into his bedroom where the canvas that covered the wire mattress revealed a netted pattern of rust and where the empty wardrobe with its doors lying open echoed their voices.

'It's vacant looking,' Martin excused, 'but it'll look better when I've the bed made.'

'It'll taste better when I put the smell of the old pipe through it. There's nothing like tobacco for taking the chill off a room.'

There was nothing in Jamesy's old room except the smell of fresh planed boards, two model yachts, new ropes, lobster-pots, a vice and other carpenter's tools. They were in a disorderly array and the old man guessed at once that they had been swept out of the kitchen to make room for him. He laid a hand on Martin's shoulder but overcome by the feelings he could not express he shook his head and sat down on the chair by the fire.

'Fill up the pipe, Michael John, and smoke yer fill and I'll sing "The Prodigal's Return",' Martin said, noticing the droop in the old shoulders.

'Come here to me, Martin. I've a thing to say to you: I've a few pounds put by and I've my pension book. I'll be buried here — won't you see to that?'

'Of course I will,' Martin said, 'but you'll see many of us down before you go.'

'I'll not. I've had my day and I'm content. A man's time has come when he yearns for the place that reared him — did you ever hear that?'

'I did but I don't believe it. I came back but I've no notion of dying yet.'

'God grant it'll find us ready when it does come. And if it does I'll be content to die here. I'll not complain and in the next world I hope I'll get a corner near your own father and some of the boys — man dear, we could have great crack together!'

'That's the spirit, Michael John!'

'Be God I hope the spirit will last till tomorrow. I'll need every drop of it to face my daughter when she comes rampaging on that doorstep. But you leave her to me, Martin. I'll handle her. She'll follow me like fish after fry.'

It happened as he had expected, for the following morning his daughter accompanied by little Danny arrived to take him home, and as soon as the mail boat put in at the quay they stepped off it and on discovering the whereabouts of the old man they did not take time to break their hunger but set off immediately for Martin's. She did not pause to chat with a neighbour, and she did not rest by the roadside to appease the whining complaints of her tired son — she had come for one purpose and she would not rest nor eat till she had seen it through. Near Vera's Danny whimpered from a stitch in his side and she bade him rest himself till she'd come back. She swept up the path and into the house without knocking the door. Both Martin and Vera were in the house and though they had observed her furious haste up the path they strove to put on a surprised air. She didn't give them time to welcome her.

'Well!' she shot at Martin. 'Where is he?'

Martin was unloosing the tangle in a fishing line and he bit at a knot with his teeth to excuse himself for not answering.

'Go on, Martin,' Vera said in a meek, polite voice, 'speak up. You know I'd nothing to do with this business.'

'He's in the house on the hill. You didn't expect me to let him lie out on the hills with the sheep,' Martin excused.

'He's coming home right now.'

'Won't you sit down for a minute and rest yourself?' Vera invited timidly.

'I'll not rest a foot till I have him back with me,' she exclaimed and wheeled out of the house. At one of the lakes near the road she found Danny throwing stones at the coots and she called to him sharply and walked on. Her father, standing at the gable-end, saw them coming and he immediately disappeared into the house and shot the bar in the door. She rapped the door smartly with her knuckles, waited a few seconds and rapped again. Getting no answer she went to the window and glared in at him where he stood in the middle of the floor.

'Open the door, granda. You're coming back with me. A nice thing to do on your own daughter,' she cried. 'I'm the one to take care of you properly.'

'You can go home without me, daughter,' he shouted back.

'Open the door a minute till I speak to you. I've brought wee Danny with me.'

'I'll not open the door — not for one minute nor two minutes nor for half a second. I'm staying here where I belong and where I've friends that want me.'

'I'll get the priest to talk to you!' she flashed.

'You can get a row of bishops and the British Navy! I'm not budging one foot. Do you hear me, Katie Colligan?'

She dropped the harshness in her voice, pulled out a handkerchief and spoke again: 'You've me worried silly and I don't know what I'm doing. Wee Danny cried his eyes out since you left.'

'Put them in again if he has. If he yelled his tongue out it'd be far better for him. He has the manners of a cross dog.'

She beckoned Danny with her finger, and lifting him under the arms till his head appeared above the window-sill she whispered to him to cry. But Danny couldn't see into the house because his face was too far from the pane and instead of crying he felt her hands were tickly and he squirmed and laughed till she let him go. She returned to the door and this time rapped with urgent gentleness.

'Who's there?' he called out.

'It's me. It's your own daughter,' she said penitently.

'Go on home like a good girl or you'll miss your boat.'

'We can't live without your pension money,' she cried.

'If I was under the sod you'd have to live without it. I'll die here and I'll be buried here.' He paused for a moment and then added: 'Go on home, girl, to your husband — he needs you but I don't.'

She walked round the house and peered in at each window in turn. Then Danny lifted a disabled toy yacht from a heap of rubbish and she snatched it from him and flung it over the roof of the outhouses. 'I was mad to bring you,' she scolded. 'I want you to be sad-looking and you look as if you were on your holidays.'

She sat down on an upturned box under one of the ash trees, drew Danny towards her and waited with taut silence. There was no sound of the door being opened, and she clicked her tongue and hastened back to the window. She pressed her face to the pane and with tears in her eyes besought him to come home with her. She dabbed her eyes with her handkerchief, knocked once more at the door and whispered something to Danny. He rounded his mouth to the keyhole and called out: 'Granda, come on home, please.' She prompted him again: 'Granda let me stay with you for a few days.' The boy took his mouth from the keyhole and put his eye to it. He saw his granda push back his chair and shuffle to the door. She stood back and waited. She could hear him breathing loudly. She raised the latch but found that the door was still barred.

'Is that you again, Katie?' he shouted. 'Are you going to stand there all day and miss the boat? I'm not going back with you — do you hear me? Go home at once to your husband and do what I bid you.'

'You'll rue this day let me tell you! I'll make Martin Gallagher pay for it—never you fear. It's his interference done this on me.'

'He'd nothing to do with it, I tell you. You broke your promise to me. It'd be too much expense for you to bring my remains here but I'll see that you'll not be out one penny piece the day I die. I've friends here that'll do what I bid them do.'

'Will you open the door — even to shake hands with me and wee Danny?'

'I'll open the window.'

'Stay, stay, stay! You'll not have luck for this!'

She pulled Danny by the arm and turned away, and on reaching Vera's gateway she looked back and saw him out on the hill. She sent Danny on in front to the quay and approached Vera's, mumbling to herself in an agony of enraged bitterness. The door stood wide open, for they were afraid to close it in case she'd hurl a stone through the window. At the threshold she drew up, and without taking time for breath she hurled a gale of abuse into the kitchen: she cursed Martin for interfering between a father and daughter; and she shook her arms in a mad frenzy and screamed out that it was a thousand pities he didn't break his miserable neck the day his horse shied from Danny's painted ball. Oh, but it was a sorry day for her that he didn't stay away from the island once he was out of it. There was a blight on everything he touched and sooner or later there'd be a blight on the girl he married. She paused for breath, wiped the spittle from her mouth and braced herself for another spate. But her store of damnation was exhausted, her voice thinned out to a thread and broke in a hoarse shatter of incoherence. Finally she pinned him with her eyes and wished with all her might that he'd never live to dandle a child of his own on his knee.

They sat in silence, allowing her storm of words to blow itself out without their help or hindrance. She almost ran down the path and as she wrenched open the ornamental gate they heard it creak on its strained hinges.

Vera heaved out her breath in one sigh: 'I'm that weak you could knock me down with a feather.'

'The air's nicely disinfected,' Martin smiled calmly. 'It's well Mary's at school — the language of Turn Street would be a nice addition to *The Merchant of Venice*.'

'I knew from the first it would bode no good,' she said as he handed her a drink of spring water.

'What in hell's name had I to do with it?'

'If you remark nobody else bothered about him.'

'It was to me he came. I couldn't do anything else but what I did. Any of the neighbours would do the same for him.'

'They would not. They tack away from trouble as they would from the first-of-ebb. You'll find they'll not stir hand or foot to help him — he'll be the baby you'll dandle on your knee.'

She was wrong. That night the quiet road in the Lower End echoed to the footfalls of the men who came to see him and

Martin's dog, unaccustomed to the noise, barked himself hoarse. They crowded into the kitchen and sat on the concrete floor, and over and over again as they heard how he had barricaded himself in the house they enlarged it in their own imaginations and declared that from now on one of their usual dances should be rechristened 'The Siege of Rathlin'. He regaled them with his life in the city and exclaimed that though he was far from the island he had never left it. How could he marry another place at his time of day? — he could not and he did not. He was far lonelier among the throngs of the city than he was among the bare roads of the land that reared him.

They sent two lads for a case of stout and Martin played his melodeon. It was late when they broke up, and Martin was the last to leave after he had seen the old man into bed. He was contented with himself, for it seemed in some mysterious way that by sharing his own house he was attending his own father and doing something for him that he was incapable of doing for himself. 'God have mercy on my father and mother!' he breathed out into the night air. They'd have done the same and wouldn't have searched for thanks. He passed through the bare posts that once had swung his gate and descended into the hollow. The stars sparkled like frost among the young leaves of the ash trees, sat brightly on the backbone of the hills and dipped their silver swords in the lake. The dog stirred at the sound of the lonely footfall and began once more to bark. There was no light in the window except an odd flicker of the fire, and he knew that Vera had gone to bed.

He tiptoed into the room and she gave a wide awake cough.

'You've brought sweet peace to the Lower End,' she mocked. 'How's Mary to settle at her work if that traffic's to continue night after night? She'll not be appointed monitress if that hullaballoo goes on for long. And there's that senseless dog out there barking like a demon.'

'He's after telling me he's not for staying long on the hill. It's

206

too far from the chapel for one thing, and it's too far from the pub for another.'

'That's a sensible notion — I hope you didn't rob him of it.'

'If he wants to return to his old house I'll not hold him against his pleasure. I have often thought the house above would suit Sarah and Jimmy.'

'I don't want any neighbours — Sarah or Jimmy or anybody else. We're content as we are.'

'If Jimmy were here we could make a good haul together at the lobsters. I find it hard work since Jamesy left me — lad and all as he was.'

She didn't answer him: she realized that that partnership would lengthen and strengthen his reason for staying on in the island when she'd be ready to leave. She coughed, and cleared her throat.

'I hope you didn't mention that to Sarah.'

'I didn't but it's been on my mind for some time.'

'There's a lot in that mind of yours that I know nothing of. Are you going to be like the rest of them and treat me like a stranger?'

'Nobody that I see treats you as a stranger. It's your ownself that does it. Why don't you give yourself to the island and to everybody in it? If you did that you'd have less to complain of. You'd be content in your own mind and you'd make young Mary content in hers.'

'Give myself! I've given too much of myself already,' she said and turned her back to him.

'We'll go to sleep on that,' he sighed, sensing that she was poised for a night's quarrel. 'Good night now, Vera.'

'Oh, good night,' she said with dry irony. The dog gave out a muffled growl. 'Listen to the contentment of him! Oh, yes, but we mustn't think of that. We must give ourselves!' She gave a sigh of hopeless resignation and closed her eyes from the stars that stared in brazenly at the window.

CHAPTER XVIII

In the house on the hill the old man contented himself for some weeks. He rejoiced in the strengthening of the sun, watching it toss its pages of light upon the lake and in the evenings spread its quilts of shadow upon the fields. Swallows with their navy-blue wings streeled low across the hills, clipped round the corners of the house and sped across the lake to dip in their own reflections. With slow, patient pleasure he sucked at his pipe, sometimes pondering on the life he had led in the city or thinking of the letters he had recently received from his three married daughters — daughters who had all married light-keepers and scattered from him. And those letters were all written to the same prearranged pattern — commanding him to stop his nonsense and go back at once to Katie who was so kind and so willing to look after him. Hm! he grunted and spat out with free satisfaction. A son wouldn't ask the like of that — a son would understand. It's a pity God hadn't given him a son, or a couple of sons, instead of selfish daughters: daughters who didn't give a straw for you after they were married. Not that he cared a cloth button for the airs and graces they put on whenever they visited him years back. Let them give their advice to their husbands and children — that's their job; and they should leave him alone and let him live his last few years in the way he wanted to. He'd not listen to them! Divil the foot would he budge for any of them. He had burnt their letters — and now that they were burnt he'd also burn all thought of them.

And so during the day Martin could see him seated on a box at the white gable, his plump shadow moving on the wall with the movement of the sun. And often when Martin sailed up to the house to collect his fishing gear before going to the boat he would see him smoking at his ease, his old coat spotted with sunlight that slanted through the ash trees, and his withered eyes searching the road for the miller or someone of his own age to trudge up and talk with him. Sometimes, if no one arrived, Martin would delay longer than he should and instead of going out in the boat before the sun had set they would enter the house and talk in the firelight, and always Martin would manoeuvre the conversation round to his own father and mother.

'Tell me straight, Michael John,' he asked one evening, 'did my father talk much about me after I left?'

'Wouldn't he be the queer sort of a father if he didn't.'

'Did he take it bad — my leaving them?'

'He never spoke of it to me — never. Wherever you went his blessing went with you. Your name was always in his mouth but he never faulted you. But, times, he used to wonder what under God drove you away. You'd no brothers, and the place here and everything in it was yours after their day.'

'Did he fret much, do you think? My mother did — I know that from the letters she used to write me. I could feel it in them though she never said it barefaced: "Don't worry about us the both of us is doing well" — that's the way she ended every letter. But isn't it strange, Michael John, I could never get back in time for any of their funerals? That often worried me.'

'I suppose, in a way, that was your punishment.'

'Punishment for what?'

'Ach, punishment for leaving them when you'd no call to be leaving them.' But noticing the struck expression on Martin's face he added brusquely: 'But you've done well since you come home — there's no two ways about that. And if your father stepped in that door he'd tell you he was proud of you. Proud of the way you fenced and drained and added to his place. He would indeed. I hope to God you'll have a son or two to follow after you. A son can understand a father but a daughter can't. When a son's content he's content but a daughter's only content when she's making changes. I hope you'll have a few sons.'

'I hope we will — there's plenty of time for that.'

'There's nothing like striking early. You've a good healthy wife and Mary's a fine lump of a wee girl. But tell me, why does she not run up to see me — Mary, I mean? She hasn't crossed that door since I came back. She has not.'

'She's busy. She's always at her books, for she's expecting the school inspector any of these days and he'll make her a monitress if she answers up well. But she'll have plenty of time to gallivant after that. You'll be tired looking at her.'

'It'll not be up here she'll be coming. She'll be dropping in to see me in the old house on her way from school.' He paused and tapped his pipe on the heel of his hand. 'If you're not too busy you could knock a bit of sheeting over the hole in the roof. Would you do that?'

'I'll do that any day. But mind you we'd rather you stay here.'

'I know, I know that rightly, Martin. But now that the warm days is here I'd like to get settled in where I belong. A fire or two and the doors wide open to the sun would soon sweat the dampness out of the walls.'

Martin sensed what the trouble was; and that night he spoke of it to Vera and accused her of not being warm with the old man or even allowing Mary to run up now and again to brush out the floor for him. 'And now he's going back to an old house where he might get his death,' he added.

'You're too soft in your ways. Isn't that the proper place for him? Since he returned you can't put your nose outside that door but there's somebody either going or coming on the road. You'd think there was a regatta in the lough every day with all that traffic.'

'It's strange, Vera, that you loved the crowds in the city; and here you can't bear to have a caller and want to see that road stripped of every footfall.'

'The city was made for crowds and the crowds mind their own business and allow you to mind yours. But here — they're always poking their eyes out to see if you've anything new on your back. Upon my word you couldn't nurse a sick hen but they'd know about it!'

'And help you to cure it!'

'Be glad if it died. They're only content to see you discontented.'

'To hell with that for talk,' Martin said, losing his patience. 'It's a pity you wouldn't straighten out the twist in you. You only give the people here the scrapings of your kindness and think the worst of everyone. It's not the way I was reared.'

And so they wrangled, and as he struggled with himself how best to avoid scenes that both wearied him and wearied her he sought release in an unnatural silence or by helping Mary with her homework in the evenings after the old man had left the hill. For this help Vera rebuked him, for she believed he was ruining her child and that she'd make a poor show at answering the school inspector when left on her own. But after the inspector's visit to the island and Mary was appointed monitress her mother's commanding sternness vanished. She was overjoyed. She called often with the grandmother after Mass on Sunday; and the grandmother, now that she had persuaded Pat to recondition an old wheelless trap that had lain for years under the hayshed, would get Sarah to drive her down in the warm evenings to the Lower End, and in those visits she brought for Mary armfuls of books that she had accumulated during her years teaching in the school. Pat still kept his distance and the only thing that pleased him was that Vera showed no signs of having children. To celebrate Mary's appointment Vera brought her to Belfast for a short holiday, and during their absence Martin and Jimmy Neil boated sheep across for the autumn fairs, and on one of those journeys Vera's brother who was standing idly at the quay asked to be employed in driving the sheep to the market square. It was only when Martin was paying him that he discovered who he was, and going into a pub then for a few drinks he chatted with forced friendliness, feeling ill at ease that he couldn't speak openly with him and ask him across for a couple of days to the island. For a few days he concealed this meeting from Vera, and then one evening finding her in a light-hearted mood he mentioned it casually.

'What'd you employ him for? — of all people,' she said. 'I hope you didn't do it to slight me.'

'I didn't know who he was from Adam and I didn't find out till I was paying him the few shillings. I stood him a couple of drinks after that. He seemed a decent fellow and I'd employ him again if I'd need.'

'If you invited him to your boarding house on the hill,' she mocked, 'you wouldn't get rid of him as easily as old Craig. Did he talk about me?'

'Not much — he just hoped you were well,' he went on, with pleasant banter. 'I'll go up home with him next time. I will indeed.'

'Please yourself,' she said with dry contempt. 'Please yourself, Mister Martin Gallagher. Aren't we sailing along quite well without them? Let me tell you if you give them an inch they'll take a span.'

'You've peculiar ways of dealing with your own flesh and blood. It'll come against you some day, if you're not careful.'

'If it does I'll not blame you. Let the lazy fend for themselves is my belief. Why doesn't he and his brother take a spade in their hands and work decently for some farmer instead of hanging round hotels and scrounging round the golf course looking for jobs that a lad out of school could do? They'd my heart broke when I was working in the shop at the quay. But I'll say no more.'

With the coming of the harvest and the falling off in his catch of lobsters his visits to the mainland were less frequent and he didn't meet with him again. The fry were in, and he was out every good evening in the small boat getting big hauls of fish and salting them for the winter. And in one of these evenings, the sunlight lying flat and gold upon the fields, she allowed Mary to accompany him, and as in the old days when she used to go out with her father Vera wrapped her up warmly, tied a scarf round her head and gave her an oilskin to spread on her knees. They tried to get her to come, too, but she laughed and said she was getting too old and too stiff for climbing in and out of boats. 'And I'm too big to be carried,' she smiled with a shy glance at Martin, 'and anyway you and Martin are becoming great pals and I'd only spoil the company.'

'Come on with us, Vera,' Martin coaxed in an unusual way, 'and we'll make a night of it. There'll be a full moon rising on the water.'

'I'll not,' she sighed. 'Go on the pair of you and we'll make a night of it when you come back. I'll have a nice supper waiting for you.'

She heard them singing as they marched off, and when they waved to her from the top of a hill she stood at the gate and waved back to them. They cut off the road and descended the path to the shore, and as the dog raced after rabbits they forgot about him and as they pushed out the boat he plunged in and swam after them. They hoisted him aboard but he stood on one of the seats and shook himself and as they laughed and bent from his flying spray of water they shouted at him and pushed him up to the bow. He sat there, his front paws shivering on the gunwale, his eyes fixed on the other boats that fished farther out from the shore. Mary leaned back in the stern. The sea was as smooth as a lake, and in the transparent water she could see brown tangles of weed and the apple green of the bottom when they passed over patches of sand. It was too soon yet to throw out the lines and she trailed her hand in the water and gazed around her at the hushed quiet of the autumn evening. Far out black steamers seemed to be sitting above the level of the sea and she could hear the engines throbbing as clearly as the pound of the oars in her own boat. On the green slopes of the shore the sheep lay at rest and below them among the rusty decaying bracken she knew the rabbits would be lying eating the moist grass. Martin told her to unroll the lines, and as he rowed up under the cliffs of the lighthouse she shivered in the humps of cold shadow they stretched out upon the sea. The lamp was being lighted and she saw the revolving lens like a huge green marble and its feeble light like the slit in a cat's eye. But on their way back the light thickened suddenly, the dusk set in and the mast-lights on the steamers twinkled timidly.

'Look out, Mary, you'll be busy in a minute,' Martin said, and scarcely had he spoken when the three lines were plucking simultaneously, and as quickly as he unhooked the fish for her and shot the boat forward with a jerk at the oars than the lines were flipping again. She laughed gleefully, and in her excitement the oilskin slipped from her lap and the salt water smarted her knees. Her arms were tired, her head was dizzy with turning from one side to the other and the dog, disturbed by the flapping of the fish, began to bark and was answered by another dog somewhere in the dusk of the shore. The men in the other boats hearing the laughter and seeing the white bellies of the fish as Mary swung them in, rowed across hurriedly and followed Martin's strip of sea. And now for the space of half an hour all the boats were busy, swinging in the fish and flinging out the lines, and then as suddenly as they had begun the fish ceased biting, the darkness crouched into the hollows of the land, matches glowed on the red faces of the men as they lit their pipes and above the rim of the sea the moon rolled up like a huge orange. Handfuls of phosphorescence dripped from the oars like sequins, Mary told herself, or like gold specks in oil; and then suddenly as she heard the wooden rollock of oars from all the boats she thought of passages in *Moby Dick* that Martin used to read to her. The dog came down from the bow, sliding over the fish as he snuggled in at her feet. The boat was heading

214

for home. The rocks stretched their paws into the path of moonlight and she saw the thin ebbing tide lipping in pebbles of light
round the stones of the shore. Her bare knees were scalded with
the water; her hands were numb and as she sucked them she
spat out the taste of salt and the oily taste of fish. Then through
the saturated grass they climbed; unseen cobwebs clung to her
face like disarranged hair and as she brushed them away she
hugged Martin's arm and listened to the dog as he panted madly
after the crowded scent of rabbits. They came on to the road
and saw the moon shuffle its cards of light on the round top of a
lake. They began to sing 'The Castle of Dromore':

> October winds lament around the Castle of Dromore,
> But peace is in her lofty halls, my dearest treasure store;
> Though autumn leaves may droop and die
> A bud of spring are you.
> Sing hushaby loo-la-loo-loo-lan
> Sing hushaby loo-la-loo.

Mary left off at the first verse and he had to finish it himself
and at the end of it saw that her eyes were moist with unshed
tears.

'What's wrong, Mary?' he asked her.

'I don't know. I feel I want to cry and laugh at the same
time.'

'Laugh then,' he said and began to sing 'The Rachery Man',
and as they rollicked along he swung her arm and let his voice
rise over the hills till it drowned the echo of their footsteps and
dispelled the solid look of shadow that a hill hunched over the
road. Vera met them on the road, and when they entered the
kitchen she had the table spread, and there was the smell of
apples from an apple cake she had just taken from the oven.

CHAPTER XIX

SOME weeks later Vera discovered she was pregnant. She didn't tell Martin but resolved to conceal it from him as long as she could. She relapsed into her former mood of selfish independence. She wanted no one. She was short with Sarah when she came down to the Lower End on Sunday evenings, and that coldness and stiffness made the calls less frequent. She resented Martin's going out to the whist drives or to the dances in the hall. She wouldn't go with him if she were asked and she wouldn't allow Mary to go. She didn't want her little girl to grow into a gadabout — as it was she was nearly as wild as Jamesy Rainey, and what was more she was growing into a big girl and she didn't want her head turned.

'A whist drive would do her good,' Martin defended vexatiously, 'and as for a dance — she could sit and look on and we'd leave early. She could oblige the company with a song or two. She has a sweet voice and it's a pity nobody gets a chance of hearing it.'

'She'll sing at her books if I'm any judge. You'd soon have her as bad a runner as yourself.'

'Do you want me to sit at home in the evenings?'

'You can go or stay for all the comfort you are to me. You can go and live in the house on the hill for that matter.'

'Ach, Vera, what's wrong with you at all? What's come over you of late?'

'Nothing! I'm sure Pat Reilly could tell you what's wrong with me.'

He gave her a comprehending look. Noticing that he had understood she lowered her eyes from the earnestness of his gaze and shrugged her shoulders: 'You've a nice way of treating your child I must say.'

'Why didn't you tell me, Vera, before this?'

'Haven't you your eyes in your head as well as another. You've no kindness. You're as hard as Pat Reilly.'

He tried to put his arms round her but she pushed him away: 'You can go off now to your dance and enjoy yourself at my expense.'

'It's the best bit of news since Michael John's return,' he said and lit up his pipe with furious haste. 'You're the best wee woman in this island — I mean that!'

'That's not much of a compliment — nor much consolation. If you had to have the carrying of one you wouldn't be so sprightly.'

'Did you tell Mrs. Reilly?'

'She does more than pray on a Sunday. I mightn't have any need to tell her.'

'Heaven's above — she'll be delighted. Let me tell her.'

'Don't make an old woman of yourself. I'll tell her next Sunday or the Sunday after, and maybe I'll not tell her at all.'

'When I was at the other side a month ago I saw some lovely boards that'd have made a fine cradle. If I'd only known!'

'I wasn't sure a month ago,' she answered, her needles darting quickly as she knitted a warm jacket for Mary.

He took the pipe from his mouth: 'Then in the name of God how did you expect me to know — answer me that?'

Baulked by his questions, discomfited and entangled by her wrath and her failure to hurt him, she raised her voice and beseeched him, if he had any manliness, not to be cross-examining her like a cold judge in a witness box. She had enough to bear as it was. She didn't know what she was saying or what she was doing! She'd never be able to bring it into the world. She didn't want it — that was all.

His voice became quiet with slow reminiscence: 'Do you remember the day Jamesy left me? Do you remember, Vera, you said you'd live for this?'

'I don't remember and I don't want to remember. I don't want it I tell you!'

'You better tell that to the priest in the confessional. There's many a woman has six or seven and are glad to have them.'

'It's easy for you to sit up there and talk. You know nothing of the pain of it.'

'Have you no trust in the God that made you?'

'I have and this is how I'm rewarded!'

He ceased his questions; he wished to be kind but found himself floundering in the mesh and tangle of her sinful conversation. There was something in her nature he'd never fathom. He knocked out his pipe and stretched himself languidly. He only hoped that she would tell the Reillys soon — for they went out of their way to help at the wedding and always wished them well.

The following Sunday after first Mass she decided to tell the old woman, and when she opened the door she found that she was alone at the fire and combing her grey hair in preparation for second Mass. She hurriedly took the hairpins from her mouth and poked up the fire.

'It's a brave morning, Vera,' she greeted. 'It's good to see somebody rising early. Pat's out at first but Sarah and myself are going to second. I'm glad to see you but you'll excuse me for finding me like this — combing my hair at the fire. The room inside is chilly at this time of the year. You'll take a cup of hot tea in your hand?'

'No, thank you, I wasn't fasting.'

'Was Mary out with you?'

'She was — she's away on home with Martin.'

Afraid that Pat would bounce in on her or that Sarah would appear she decided to say what she had to say at once. But for a moment she toyed with her black kid gloves on her lap, smoothing out the wrinkles, and folding one glove on top of the other. She lifted them in her hand, glanced round at the window, and listened to the people outside on their way home from Mass. She cleared her throat and then in a level voice she said:

'You'll be glad to hear I'm expecting again.'

The old woman halted the sweep of the comb to her hair and stared at her with her mouth open.

'Glad — oh, thanks be to the good God for that! Ah, Martin will be the proud and happy man.' Slowly her eyes travelled over Vera and she rose from her chair and stretching out her two arms bent and kissed her on each cheek.

'Of course it'll not be for a very long time yet,' Vera said, discerning that the old woman had noticed her thinness.

'Martin knows?' the old woman said in a whisper.

'You don't think I'd keep him from the secret?' Vera smiled drily.

'Of course not! What am I babbling about! And what am I standing here for! Wait now, wait now.' She went into her room and Vera could hear the chink of a bottle. She was on her feet and ready to leave when the old woman called her into the room.

'You'll take a glass of wine. I got two bottles in for the Christmas but we'll open one now and drink the health of the new child.'

Vera tried to desist but the old woman had already closed the door behind her and was pushing her into a wicker armchair at the window. She began to pierce the cork with the cork-screw but not having the strength to pull it out she asked Vera to help her. She filled up two wine glasses, placed them on the table and closed the window because the air was cold. The old woman began to give her advice — not to be stretching or over-working, and above all to wear warm clothing in this hard weather. But Vera wasn't listening to her; above the old woman's head she saw a little frame containing three snapshots: one of Mary and the old woman taken on Confirmation day, one of Mary in her First Communion frock and veil, and the other of Tom holding a large fish in each hand. She couldn't remember where the one of Tom was taken, and from where she sat she couldn't note the blurred background.

'Well, Vera girl,' sighed the old woman, lifting the glass to her lips, 'here's to your health and to the health of the little one. Please God, everything will go well with you.' She sipped at the wine, one hand on the glass and one resting on Vera's hand that lay on the table. 'It's great news, and later if you want any rest Mary could stay here for a while.'

'I'm afraid she'll be needed to help her own mother,' Vera said coolly.

'That's true — what am I rambling about this blessed morning,' the old woman said, sensing immediately that she had blundered; her trembling fingers jabbled the wine on to the table, and scarcely knowing what she was saying she spoke on, endeavouring to bury her unconscious mistake under a load of words: 'Of course you'll need her. She's no longer a child. She's a big monitress now and she'll be of great help to you. Great help when you need her most. It'd be no trouble for her to make Martin his dinner. Martin for that matter could make his own — he could indeed, poor Martin.'

Vera drained her glass: 'I never let Martin do that,' and she patted her lips with her handkerchief. 'He never cooked a meal since we were married — never.'

'Sure I know that rightly, Vera. But I was only saying he could if he had to. But, thank God, he never has to do that. There's our Pat and he couldn't boil an egg for himself. He's no good around the fire — no good. I hope he's lucky to get a wife as good as yourself.'

Sarah's step sounded in the kitchen, then the back door was opened, and they could hear her calling the hens for their feed. 'I'm keeping you late for Mass,' Vera said and got to her feet.

'We've plenty of time. The bell hasn't gone,' the old woman said, glancing at Vera and then at her own half-full glass. But

Vera made no move to sit down again, and the old woman hoisted herself to her feet by resting her hands on the table. 'I'll not drink any more of it. It goes to my head and makes my tongue as loose as a bell. I hope I haven't talked any nonsense.' She smiled and put her two hands on Vera's shoulders; Vera lowered her eyes to pull on her gloves.

'We'll remember you in our prayers, Vera. Take good care of yourself.' Her hands felt the thin fabric of Vera's coat. 'Keep yourself warm, girl, and don't do anything foolish.'

Vera breathed with relief as she descended the path to the road.

She was glad she hadn't met Pat and she was glad she hadn't to retell her story to Sarah. She could feel the effects of the wine and she walked slowly, resting now and again on the breast-high wall, and gazing down at the angle of houses above the quay or across the sea to the hills of the mainland. Her breath hung round her like smoke, and in the cold air there was the melancholy sound of the breaking waves and the sharp clang of a bucket from one of the houses. Her health was good, she told herself, despite the warnings and prying eyes of the old woman. She had no sickness in the mornings, and there was nothing wrong with her except a certain peevishness and shortness of temper that was natural to one in her condition. Everyone would be delighted except the one who should be! But they'd never know her reason: if they did they'd nag the soul out of her with their unwanted advice. What under God would take you away to the city? they'd say to her: you with a strong husband, a fine slated house with a new range and a daughter well-set on the road to be mistress in the school; and tell me, what kind of a job would Martin get in the city? — a job in a boat: you'd be as well not married at all in that case! She smiled with contempt and shrugged her shoulders. She thought of the new baby: if it'd be a boy nothing would lift Martin out of this place — that was certain! But if she couldn't get him to leave she'd go away herself and take Mary with her — she had all her plans set. And the new child! She began to calculate: it'd be two years old by the time she'd be ready to leave for the city. But then who could she get to mind it when she'd be out working at some job to keep the new home together. She'd never get a satisfactory answer to that! She clicked her tongue and hastened her step. How did she ever get herself into this condition? — wouldn't anyone have thought she was finished with child-bearing and child-rearing. It was like a chain tether—no matter where she turned it held her. But she'd break it—in some way she'd break it but she didn't know how!

Her mood hardened. Each week she saw that she was filling out, and she was conscious that everyone was noticing her. Her black hair lost its customary gloss and her face grew pale. With Martin she had no patience. She nagged at him, argued and disagreed with him, and snatching at his simplest remarks would dissect them before him to prove that he was being deliberately cruel to her. He found himself thrown into a silence that was even worse than a clash of words. He didn't speak of his trouble to others — not even to Michael John. And knowing his own nature he kept clear of the pub — she would never have that to pitch against him. Often in the long dark evenings it was the presence of Mary quietly doing her homework at the kitchen table that gave him his moments of peace, and after she had packed her books in her bag and gone to bed he would stand at the door smoking his pipe and looking at the flashes from the lighthouse striding brilliantly through the hard darkness of the night. Vera would be seated at the fire knitting a tiny woollen jacket and he would say to her over his shoulder: 'It's a lovely night' or 'Rain is not far off' or 'I must rise early and cart up more sea-weed for the fields' but to these remarks he would get no answer. He would withdraw from the door, then, and taking off his boots would place them carefully at the side of the fire and saying 'Good night, Vera,' would steal off to his room. Then, sometimes, he would hear her rattling the brushes

222

or even filling up a bucket of water to scrub the floor, and he'd wish to God that her time had come. For days she would scarcely speak a word to him. She often attacked Mary for biting her nails or fingering her hair and when he would intervene with a calm word she would set upon him and tell him to mind his own business and not interfere in the rearing of a child that wasn't his.

'She's like a child of mine — I feel that about her,' he affirmed.

'She calls you "father" now, but it's against my wishes and my training.'

She warned Mary not to speak outside of what went on in the house, and she warned her, now that the darkness fell early, to hurry home from school and not be arriving after the lighthouse had been lit. She always took a walk as far as the mill hill to meet her, and the bleak stillness of those evenings with the first stars appearing in the sky filled her with an impatient dread that made her want to cry out against the forces that crippled her. Seeing Mary's dark outline on the white road she would hasten forward, hold her cold hand in her own and walk slowly home. But one day Mary was late. Old Michael John had asked her into the house to thread a needle for him and when she had it done she smiled at the clumsy way he prodded the needle into the coat he was patching and taking it from him commenced to do it for him. It was quite dark when she left and she began to run, her schoolbag bumping on her back. Her mother was standing on top of the hill, and without waiting for an explanation she began to beat her. Mary struggled away from her, and sobbing bitterly ran back along the road to her granny's.

Passing the shop she saw the door open and in the box of light two women moving out with baskets in their hands. She ceased her crying, wiped her tears with her sleeve and hurried on ahead of the gossiping women.

Sarah and Pat and her granny were seated at the table and all

223

three turned their heads as the door opened. She stared at them for a moment, looked at the bright lamp on the wall and finding that her lips would not obey her she sobbed afresh. The old woman sat with her on the sofa, her arm tightly round her and her hand stroking her hair that had lost its ribbon. Between her sobs and the scraps of answers she made to their questions they managed to piece together what had happened.

'All along I was right,' Pat said sternly, 'and maybe now you'll see she's not fit to rear Tom's child!'

His mother raised her head and tried to silence him with her eyes.

He ignored her reproachful look and went on in his own way: 'You'll stay here with us — in this house that reared your father. He'd not stand for the like of this! He'd not put up with it for half a day.'

'Quiet, Pat!' his mother said. 'Manys a time I had the same trouble with you all. Vera has enough on her mind without you adding to it. You needn't make a mountain out of a molehill. Poor Vera has a hard time in front of her. . . .'

'I'm sure Mary has put a hard time behind her if we knew all that goes on,' he said.

'Sarah, make a nice cup of tea for Mary and when she has that taken we'll all go down in the trap. Your mother didn't mean it, Mary. She'll be worrying about you but she'll know where you are.'

'There'll be no trap yoked by my hands at this time of the day,' Pat shouted.

'You'll leave this to me, son,' his mother answered, and placing her fingers under Mary's chin she made her look up at her. 'Smile now, Mary. That's better!' and as she smiled — a smile that was half a cry — some expression on her face reminded her of Tom, and to hide her emotion she got up and busied herself about the table. In a few minutes she was back again; and brushing back Mary's disordered hair she took a hairpin from her own and affixed it to the child's.

'You mustn't blame your mother — you mustn't do that. She'll be bringing you a little companion soon and it's that that worries her and makes her vexed. But there'll be a lovely time coming and you'll be wheeling the new baby up to see us on a Sunday. Your mother will be the happy lady then and she'll not be cross with you any more.'

'Don't come down with me. I'll be able to go myself,' Mary said gallantly. 'I'm not afraid of the dark.'

'There's no need to take out the trap,' Sarah said. 'I have to go to the shop in any case and I'll walk on down with her.'

Pat put on his coat and went out, and as Mary took her tea the old woman leafed through the books in her schoolbag and kept up a continual chat with Mary about the subjects she liked and disliked and questioned her about the load of books she had already given her; and by the time she was ready for the road the incident had lost its edge and as she set off with Sarah they talked about the day that her father's boat had sunk in the lough and about a young kestrel that Jimmy Neil had got stuffed and was now sitting in a glass case in his kitchen along with a stuffed owl.

Sarah went into the shop and bought her sweets, and on the road near Michael John's they met Martin coming to look for her. Himself and Sarah whispered together for a while and presently Sarah left them and they continued the journey together. At the top of the mill hill she found her ribbon on the road and smoothing it out with her fingers tied a bow in her hair.

'You shouldn't have stayed so late at your granny's,' her mother said to her as she took her coat from her and put it on a hanger behind the door of her room. None of them spoke of the row, and that night Vera went back to sleep with Martin.

CHAPTER XX

FOR a long time afterwards Mary was seldom late. Her granny used to wait for her at the end of schooltime, speak to her for a few minutes and warn her not to dally on the road home. But one day when Mary arrived from school she struggled out of the shoulder-straps of her schoolbag and let it fall on the wooden sofa behind her. She lay down beside it without saying a word. Her face was flushed and her mother stood over her and accused her of running to make up for the time she had overstayed at her granny's. Mary sat up and shook her head, and when her mother took the dinner from the oven, one plate over the other to keep it warm, she dragged herself to the table. She lifted the fork and, pushing the plate away from her with limp distaste, rested her head on her spread out arms.

'Have you eaten too many dainties at your granny's that you can't take your good dinner? Is the food your own mother makes for you no longer to your liking?'

'I took nothing at my granny's only a drink of fresh buttermilk.'

'Don't you know by this time that buttermilk destroys your appetite. Eat up your dinner and none of your nonsense. You're getting too thin of late and everybody's remarking it.'

She forced herself to eat, but the food seemed to have a nauseous papery taste, and at every mouthful she expected to be sick.

'I can't take it, mother. It'll only make me sick.'

'Away and scrape it to the hens then. They'll gobble it up and humiliate you. You know it's a sin to waste good food. Go on at once — take it out to the fowl when you're told.'

She rose reluctantly and took the spoon her mother thrust into her hand.

'Maybe I could eat it tomorrow,' she entreated and held back.

'You'll do what you're told. Throw it to the hens — I'm not going to do it for you. Some day, my lady, you'll be glad of it. You're spoiled — spoiled by your granny and your Aunt Sarah. Buttermilk, indeed!'

From the window her mother watched the hens racing from all corners of the field as Mary went out with the plate. She noticed that she was crying and she was sorry she hadn't branded her humiliation deeper by ordering her to scrape it into the fire — in future that's the way she'd deal with her if she showed any more of her fads.

Martin came in and seeing Mary seated dejectedly on the sofa he sat beside her and asked what was wrong with his little girl.

'She's getting notions now about her food, if you please,' Vera said impatiently. 'Didoes and fiddle-faddles she wants: biscuits and lemonade, sweets and chocolate — and turns up her nose at the nice dinner I kept warm for her.'

'Maybe she's out of sorts. Isn't that it, girlie?' he said and patted her knee.

'If she is it is an incurable disease with her. I've had my eye on her for a long time and she's getting as close and silent as her own father used to be.'

Martin put his arm round her and she snuggled close to him and buried her head on his breast.

'That's right — pet her up and turn her against her own mother. I used to have some control over her but since you crossed my path I've none. And what with her granny and the rest of them, my rearing of her is like weaving the wind.'

'Her poor head's as hot as a red coal,' he said gently.

'Hot with sulks and bad temper! Coddle her now and make her think she is sick. She has the makings of a fine play-actor if you heed me.'

She went out and entered the garden, and with a trowel

began to prepare the soil for a few packets of lettuce and onion seeds that she had bought. She didn't stay long, and coming back she saw a steaming cup of milk on the table and Martin filling a hot-jar from the kettle.

'I think, Vera, she's sickening for something.'

'She's sickening for a good smack I owe her for a long time.'

He lowered his voice as he heard Mary get into bed: 'Can't you let her grow up with all the ailments that a child must have? I remember when I was young . . .'

'You needn't tell me about when you were young. Wasn't I the eldest of four and helped to nurse them through the measles and be kept awake night after night with the whoop of them from the whooping-cough.'

'And who had to listen to you when you had it? — your own mother and father I suppose.'

'I don't think I'd any ailments.'

'No, you wouldn't!' he said, and turned his back on her and wiped the splashed jar with a cloth.

'Give that to me — if she's sick her own mother's the one to look after her . . . If you'd deepen that stream and rid the damp from the foot of the field it'd answer you better. A time will come when we'll need stilts to get near the spring. But I suppose you'll wait till the horse sinks and breaks it's back in it before you'll move a finger.' He said nothing but followed her into the room. Mary was lying back, her ribbon still in her hair; her face was red and swollen, her breathing quick. Vera unloosed the ribbon, rolled it up and put it in a cardboard-box on the table.

'Do you think we should get the priest?' Martin said.

'You're Job's comforter I must say. Wouldn't it be better to get the nurse's opinion first?'

'I'll throw my leg over the bicycle and go for her.'

'You'll throw the spade into your hand and deepen that stream so that a body can get a bucket of water without having to wade through muck and slush — I'm never done scraping the clabber off my boots.'

'Will I go for the nurse or will I not?'

Mary whimpered, opened her eyes and gazed round her feverishly: 'Could I have a drink, mother? My throat's scorching.'

'I have it here for you,' Martin said, and as he lifted the cup of milk there was a thin wrinkled skin floating on top and he skimmed it off with the spoon and threw it on the floor. He put his arm under her back and held the cup to her lips. She sipped it twice, shook her head and lay back exhausted on the pillow.

'I'll give her a spoonful of castor oil and she'll be all right in the morning,' Vera said. 'We can't be tormenting the nurse at every turn of the clock like some people. Where are you sick, child?' she said, leaning over the bed and smoothing Mary's forehead.

'It's my stomach, mother. There's like a red hot knife sticking in me.'

'I wish her granny had more sense. Imagine a drink of buttermilk to a child on an empty stomach. She has a touch of colic and nothing more. I'll be able to doctor her myself.'

'All right,' Martin said, 'you know more about these things than I do.'

He went outside and took his spade. He widened and deepened the stream where it entered the lake, resting for a minute or two to wipe the sweat from his brow, or to look at the yellow whins that were a spawn of colour on the hills, or to glance up at the house in case Vera needed him. His land was ploughed, the soil cracked and dry, but the air was cold and no sign of a leaf on the ash trees above at his old house. Time and again he blew on his hands to warm them while behind him the withered reeds rattled like hailstones in the breeze and the muddied water from the stream chafed the chilly look from the lake. He hoped

Vera would think of lighting a fire in Mary's room, but when he looked up at the chimney in the gable-end it was as cold-looking as a tombstone. He quit the work early and hurried back to the house.

'How is she?' he said in a hushed voice.

'Don't talk so low, Martin, or you'll frighten me.' Vera said. 'She's sleeping if she's let alone. Now, don't go near her.'

'It's bitter cold. Maybe we should give her a bit of a fire.'

'She's as warm as toast. I gave her another blanket when I saw the mist on the window.'

'Is there much sickness among the school-children, did you hear?'

'Now how would I hear that? You know I don't spend my time gossiping with the neighbours. You've more traffickings with the people than I have.'

'I thought, maybe, Mary would tell you.'

'Mary doesn't talk much to her mother. Her granny has her well brought up — this is only a lodging house for Mary as far as they're concerned.'

'Ach, Vera, don't be bitter for the love of God. The child's sick and we mustn't be snapping at one another and she lying awake listening to us.'

'I'm glad you've some interest in somebody without me having to tell you.'

'The stream's widened if that's what you mean. I'd have done it long ago only for the ploughing, and anyway it'd have dried out itself in a week or two.'

'The clothes dry as stiff as a board these days but I never saw much signs of that slush following suit.'

He lit the lamp on the wall and sat down, and when she asked him if he wasn't going out for a gossip with old Craig he shook his head. He took his copy of *Moby Dick* from the shelf, filled his pipe but put it back in his pocket without lighting it. She wondered he wasn't sick to death of reading that book; she

230

wouldn't mind if he kept it to himself but he was always reading bits of it out to Mary as if she'd be interested in a mad ship with a mad captain chasing after a mad whale!

He pulled his chair under the lamp and opened the book. In a few minutes, he thought, he'd be wrapped round with the quietness that that book afforded him: he hoped to hear the thump of Ahab's ivory leg on the bare boards of the deck, the hiss of the pipe that was flung into the sea, the tug and twist of the wind as it brushed round the corners of the deck or tore itself like streaming paper among the rigging. But he felt nothing of these things and saw nothing only the small fine print on the pages in front of him. He closed the book and laid it on his lap. He heard the wind rising outside and he glanced across at Vera as she stared into the fire and took the clips from her hair. He searched his mind for something to say that would ease the stress between them.

'I'll sleep with Mary tonight, Vera. It'd be better that you get your rest. You'll need it all with the condition you're in.'

'If you were worrying about my condition you'd have deepened that stream long ago.'

'It's done now and I hope well done,' he said and tapped his fingers on the back of the book.

She held the hair-pins in her mouth and brushed her hair vigorously. He'd have loved to tell her how black and thick it was but his fear withheld him: any remark he'd make now would be twisted and thrown back at him, forcing him to believe he was deliberately cruel to her. She got up, and taking a cup of cold water from the crock she went into Mary's room and closed the door.

He was alone now, alone with the heaviness that sickness brought upon a house, alone with the weariness of his wife's misunderstanding. But things could be worse — much worse. She had great health and he was thankful to God for that. She was a good wife and a good mother. She kept the place spotless

231

and she was thrifty and had money saved. It wasn't all her fault. He was awkward — awkward in his silence, in his speech, and, he supposed, awkward too in showing kindness. There was a way in being kind — his own father and mother had it, old Mrs. Reilly had it and old Michael John. His own journeyings had robbed him of it and he was sure it was that clumsiness that drove Jamesy from him. He'd try his best to understand her. She was harsh and rough at times but it was her condition that was the cause of it. He'd have to allow for that and forgive her everything because of it. When Mary's better and their own child is rolling about the floor all this roughness between them would be made smooth.

He lowered the wick in the lamp and knelt down to say his prayers. He prayed for patience, for kindness, and for the strength to work his fields; he prayed for Mary and for his own child that was forming in his wife's womb; he prayed for wisdom to know himself with all his faults; and he prayed for the dead.

He quenched the lamp and going into his room he left the door open so that he would hear her if she called and needed him. He lay on his back and listened to the wind. It raked round the eaves of the house and hummed in the loose-stone walls of the fields. His mind followed it over the cold dry clay, where maybe a bird would be sheltering under a turned furrow, through the dry stiff rods of the lake and down to the sea where the waves broke in a coggle of froth on the rough rocks. He was asleep in a few minutes.

A cry from Mary wakened him and he got up at once, lit a candle and pulled on his trousers. She was retching into a basin that her mother held for her but on seeing the candle she cried out that it was burning her. She lay back, tossed from side to side, and tried to throw off the weight of blankets that seemed to crush her. She began to talk in a strange polite voice that bewildered them . . . Four ducks in a pond and a green whale beyond . . . Now, girls and boys, good handwriting: the girls slope their letters north and the boys east . . . don't let Jamesy touch the chestnut tree . . . up the airy mountain and down the rushy glen . . . for fear of Ahab and his wooden leg . . . a moon shines bright on such a night as this . . . granny has a mole on her chin. . . .

Vera shuddered and Martin drew her close to him. 'Oh,' she sighed, 'her poor little mind's astray with all that trash you read out to her.'

'Is she very hot?'

'Her heart's fluttering like a little bird's.'

'What is it, do you think?'

'I don't know; she can't bear me to touch her. You've her all ruined on me. I'm not allowed to rear my own child.' She suddenly broke down. He hurried from the room, and in a few minutes the front door opened and the wind whined through the house. He wheeled out the bicycle and set off into the windy darkness with nothing but the beams of the lighthouse lighting up the road. He pedalled down the hill to the flat road of the island. The pebbles bounced from under his tyres and the unhindered wind was salty on his lips. He rapped at the nurse's window and she pulled a coat round her nightdress and listened to him. She'd be all right she assured him; there was no fever about and there was no cause to worry or send for the priest. Her stomach was upset — that was all. She gave him two tablets to give her. She'd run down to have a look at her first thing in the morning.

The tablets soothed her, and when she was settled he sat at the table in the room and prevailed on Vera to lie for a while on his bed. He rested his head on his hands and dozed. A burst of hailstones against the window roused him; he watched them melt on the pane and the primrose light of dawn brim up on the brow of the hill. On the table the glass of water with its level as thin as a watch glass turned yellow in the light and began to tremble as he tiptoed across the floorboards in the room.

Before the fire in the range had reddened in the draught from the storm the nurse was at the door. She took Mary's temperature, pressed her tongue down with a spoon and examined her throat. 'The pain is here, nurse,' Mary said, pressing her two hands against her side, but screamed aloud when the nurse touched her.

'Do you think she is very bad?' Vera said helplessly.

'If that wind falls away you should take her across. I'd be happy in my mind if the doctor saw her.' She went into the kitchen; she mixed a plaster of mustard and cornflour and whispered to Martin that she'd tell the priest to call on her way home.

'Let Martin look after her, Vera. You're not fit. You'll have to think of other things,' the nurse advised her.

'That's what I tell her,' Martin exclaimed.

'It must be serious if a mother can't look after her own child.'

'Mary's a strong girl. She'll get over it all right.'

'Why did you frighten me then about the doctor, and the wind outside blowing half a gale.'

'I want to take every precaution.'

Martin walked with her to the gate and drew from her what it was she feared.

'It's a bad case of appendicitis,' she explained. 'You stay with her and I'll tell the priest.'

'You better tell the Reillys. I'll need Pat's help with the boat.'

Vera was crying. He tried to comfort her: 'It's God's will and you must look at it that way.'

'Oh, everything's blamed on God. The same was said when Tom died. The same will be said if anything happens Mary.' She wiped her eyes and flung her arms wide in despair: 'Listen to me, Martin. Listen to me! We'll go away. There's no doctor here and what does a storm care about sickness! Will you leave with me, Martin? We'll go away where there's some comfort. I can't stay here any longer! It's wearing me down. I can't bear it!'

234

'Quiet now. I'll do anything for you.'

'I couldn't rear another child here, Martin. Give me your word that you'll quit this place.'

'She'll be all right. We'll get her across. That wind will die away.'

'No matter what happens we'll leave. Promise me that, Martin. Promise me!' she begged.

'I will!' he said. 'I'll go away with you if you want.'

The news of Mary's sickness travelled fast. From the houses on the main road they had seen the nurse set out in the early morning, later the priest pass on his bicycle, and then the Reillys in their trap. It wasn't a time for idle gossip, and those of the neighbours who had no young children to look after set off to help, and once more Vera found her kitchen crowded as it was during Tom's illness and death. The strain was too much for her and at the nurse's bidding she stole off and lay down for a while. Though the room door was closed she could hear the shuffling of the people's feet and the low tone of their voices as they talked of the wind and the bad run on the shores at the other side. The boat could never land, she told herself. How could it land in a gale like that! She knew full well the shallowness of the mainland quay. Hadn't she often watched the scenes from the window of the shop where she worked: the waves racing in as sharp as a scythe-blade and breaking in front of the quay in a fizz of froth like suds in a washtub — froth that couldn't float a stick! There was no depth of water there: she had spoke about it often — dear knows she had, but her shouts were like pieces of paper scattered and lost in a wind. If Mary was once over this they'd clear out of it all. He'd have to leave. How could he expect her to bring his child into the world in a place with no doctor? God never meant that for any woman. And what did the mainland people care about them or their boats? — not a straw: the island people were a botheration to them. No, she was wrong there — she who once worked in a shop should know

235

she was wrong. The cattle dealers loved them — they could strike a good bargain on sheep and cattle that were always a trouble to ship across. And the publicans loved them — they could earn a wheen of shillings from them on a fair day. No, an island that has no landing place on the other side is fit only for a jail. 'A jail,' she said aloud, 'a jail! But it'll hold me no longer. I've done my term and served my sentence.' She sat up. A bramble bush outside was scraping its thorny briars against the wall of the garden and she saw them bend and rise in the wind like a fishing rod. *She lay back and wondered what time of day it was. But she couldn't think with her senses numbed and dredged by the distraught voices in the kitchen. What was happening to her at all, at all? All these people whom she had carefully avoided were gathering round her and clinging to her house like the limewash on the wall. No matter what she had said or hadn't done they were round her at every turn — friends who were strangers and strangers becoming friends. She had no foothold anywhere — neither inside her mind nor outside it. Everything she had fought against and thrown aside like old rags were swept into her kitchen against her will. You cannot live alone in a lonely place: what you flee from clings to you like wet clay to your shoes. She sat up again and listened to their annoying whisperings and to the unknown meaning of their shuffling footsteps. What were they saying and where were they going? She must see to it and not lie here any longer. She came into the kitchen.

'They're ready to go,' the old woman said to her.

Vera gave her a pained, reproachful look: 'It's a pity you gave her that buttermilk yesterday.'

'That didn't do it,' the nurse said firmly. 'A drink was better for her than solid food. I'm sure of that . . . Sit down, Vera, on this chair. Don't worry — Martin will make a landing all right and I'll send a telegram and there'll be an ambulance on the quay to meet them.'

'I'll go with them,' Vera said.

'You can't, Vera!' the old woman said and patted her on the shoulder. 'You daren't go, child. You'll lose everything if you go.'

'I'll lose everything if I don't. What more is there to lose if Mary's taken from me?'

'We know nothing of what is for our good. Have faith in God's mercy. I lost one child and I lost my husband and we both lost Tom. Mary won't be taken from us.'

With a dazed look she watched Martin take his oilskins from the back of the door and Pat and Jimmy Neil go out, each carrying a tin of petrol. Sarah and the nurse came from the room.

'Sarah will mind her and shield her like a mother,' the old woman said.

It was that that settled it. Vera got to her feet: 'No one will take that child but myself. Her own mother is the one to go with her.'

Through the open door a sudden shower of hailstones could be seen bouncing on the dry road and filling up the cart-ruts. They waited for it to pass before setting out after the men. Sarah carried Mary wrapped in blankets; Vera and the nurse walked beside her, and neighbour women bunched round them and shielded them from the wind that fled cold across the hail-stoned fields. On the brow of the hills the wind moulded the clothes to their bodies and their breath hung like a frosty halo about their heads. The sky was a solid grey without hint or light of sun.

They cut off the road and descended the path that led to Martin's boat. They were sheltered here; a skylark was singing, and on the grassy slopes sheep with their young lambs were hurrying away from them with urgent cries. Around the rocks on the shore the water was calm but out from the land where the water met the wind it was twisted and crinkled in scattering patches of darkness.

Sarah and Vera were placed in the boat, their backs to the wind and away from the engine's exhaust so that its flying spray wouldn't sting their faces. Mary lay on their laps. A brown sail was wrapped round their backs and tied about their feet; their hands were hidden and save for the paleness of their faces and the moist glitter of their eyes they looked like a strange cargo of old bales. Pat took the tiller and Martin cranked up the engine, and as they moved out their eyes scanned the mainland where the breaking waves spouted white against the cliffs. No floating thing was to be seen — no tramp steamer, no collier, nothing that would give them a sense of safety on their width of sea. They rounded the island's point and came full blast into the cowardly blow from the west wind. The boat rocked and lurched; its beams creaked and shuddered in the troughs of the waves, and the water under the floorboards slapped like a half empty barrel.

'It's not as bad as I thought,' Martin shouted. 'It's only in squalls. Sit tight now all of you, there's another shower coming up.' In the gap of sky to the west he saw a moving cliff of hailstones hurrying forward, and he prepared himself to meet it. He wasn't afraid of it; his grief had stiffened his courage and turned away fear. A few stray hailstones bounced on the deck before the advancing squall: then it broke over them without mercy, rattling on the canvas like pellets and tearing into the sea like a shaking sieve. The women sat still; they closed their eyes under the battery of the squall, and when it had passed they saw the dry hailstones lying like snow on the floor, on the seats and on the wrinkles in the men's boots. One side of Pat's face was red and as he rubbed it with his frozen hand to draw the warmth back to it he stole a glance at Vera. She was gazing at him with mild eyes but her pale skin had the look of the dead. He thought he had hated her, but now he was swept with sudden tenderness for her, and in their exchange of looks he felt all his bitterness peel away from him. He remembered words his mother had often said to him: 'A man sinks low when he finds a revengeful satisfaction in another's pain.' A shower of spray splashed over the bow and made him pay heed to the throbbing tiller in his hand.

'We'll make it all right!' he said aloud. 'We'll land — even if we've to beach her!'

Another wave struck her and washed the hailstones from the bow. She rose high on a wave and their eyes searched the mainland shore. They could hear the boom of the waves breaking against the rocks and see tails of sand being carried inland from the beach. The bay was deserted; the golf course deserted; and as they drew within sight of the quay they saw nothing only the white flying masses of breaking water running like a waterfall down its concrete sides. Martin eased the engine and counted the waves: after every fourth wave that broke over the quay there was a short spell before they broke again. To run in on the lull and turn her bow outwards was their only chance. They saw the ambulance now at the foot of the quay and a few men moving towards it from the lee of the boat-house.

'Land us and head off again before the waves break,' Martin shouted to Pat; Jimmy Neil threw out the old motor tyres that served as fenders and lifted a coil of rope in readiness to fling it on to the quay. Martin shot her forward but as they ran in they saw the seaweed and limpits growing on the sides of the quay and he turned out again. 'She'll ground,' he said, 'the backdraught leaves no depth of water! Keep her near the point, Pat. It's our only hope.' He once more counted the waves and crouched over the engine; the boat rushed in, curved and ran alongside the point of the quay; the thrown rope was caught, turned once round a bollard and held fast as the stern of the boat sunk low in the bodiless froth. In a few moments the women were helped up the wet steps, and as Jimmy and Pat headed out with the boat the last glimpse they saw of them was the ambulance doors swing open and a brown canvas stretcher being draw from the inside.

CHAPTER XXI

SINCE there was no room in the ambulance for the three of them Martin had to walk from the quay, up through the sleepy town and up the windy hill to the hospital. When he reached it the door was ajar and he pushed it open without ringing the bell and tiptoed along a wide corridor. A nurse hurried past him with rolled up sleeves and he was conscious of the stir of air in her wake and the smell of methylated spirit. He glanced shyly into the small wards at each side, and on reaching the end of the corridor where a flight of stairs led to another storey he stood gazing uncomfortably around him with his cap in his hand. He was ready to ascend the stairs when he saw Sarah lean over the banisters with a handkerchief in her hand. She ran down to him and burst out crying.

'I thought you'd never come,' she cried.

'What's wrong, Sarah? Where's Vera?'

'Ah, God help you!' she said and her lower lip trembled. She made an upward gesture with her eyes, and as they mounted the steps together she sobbed: 'It's Vera . . . Oh, I can't tell anything . . . My mind's astray on me. . . .'

'Is she all right?'

'I don't know . . . It all happened sudden. . . .'

Two nurses were whispering together outside a glass-panelled door and he approached them and told him what he wanted.

'You're her husband,' one said and cast him a look of studied sympathy. 'The doctor's with her at the moment. Take a seat in the corridor till he's finished.'

'She shouldn't have ventured across,' Sarah said to him as he sat down beside her. 'We were all against it. And the doctor scolded me as if I was to blame.'

'You've done your best and I am more than thankful to you. Under God I don't know what I'd have done without you and Jimmy and Pat.'

In front of them the grey-skied windows shuddered in the wind and hard hailstones rattled against the pane without wetting it. A nurse passed, put her hand on one of the radiators and disappeared into one of the wards. Martin got up and stood at the window, tapping at the sash with his fingers and gazing down at a heap of coal covered with hailstones. On the grey skyline three bare trees were windblown like witches broomsticks, and below him he watched the white vapour from the ambulance as it passed out through the gate. A movement in the corridor made him turn, and a nurse came forward screwing on the top of her fountain pen.

'You may come in now. But you mustn't stop long. Your wife needs complete rest.'

There were five beds at each side of the ward and Vera's was at the far end with a screen of pale green cloth around it.

Her face was the colour of death and he smelt brandy from her lips as he bent over to kiss her. Her forehead was damp with sweat but her eyes were bright and her arms lying limp on top of the white quilt.

'You'll be all right,' he said awkwardly. 'Lie quiet and you'll be all right. All the nurses say you'll be all right and they know what they're talking about.'

She closed her eyes and shook her head slowly: 'No, Martin, I've no strength left in me. If anything happens to Mary I can't live . . . And if anything happens her, bury her with her father and . . .'

'She'll be all right. We got her across in good time. You'll see she'll be all right. Don't be fretting like that.'

'And if anything happens me bury me beside them. . . .'

He bit his lip and fought back his tears. He put his cap on the bed and smoothed back the damp hair from her brow.

241

'Tell my father and mother.'

'I will, Vera; I will. And when you're better we'll leave the island.'

'I've no spirit left for anything now, Martin. They should have a deep pier at this side. No one would listen to me.'

'We'll leave it all behind us! You'll have no call to worry any more.'

'It's too late.'

'It's not, it's not! Don't give in like that for the love of God!' He lifted her hand and pressed it with tender courage. The pained expression on his face hurt her and she closed her eyes as he said:

'You'll be all right and so will Mary. There'll be great times coming — never fear. We'll go away the three of us wherever you want. Remember that — won't you!' A nurse tapped him on the shoulder and told him he must go. He smiled timidly at Vera and lifted his cap: 'I'll not be far away. I'll be back soon. Lie quiet now and don't be fretting.'

Signing to Sarah where she sat on her chair in the corridor they went together into Mary's ward. There was no screen round her bed and she was fast asleep, her cheeks a glossy red.

'You'd think to look at her that nothing ailed her,' Sarah whispered to him. But he didn't answer her at once, for he was conscious of the other patients staring at him.

'Let her sleep — it's best not to disturb her,' he said, plucking Sarah's sleeve and hurrying from the ward. He pulled on his cap and walked down the corridor and out to the raw, cold air, where they stood irresolute, debating with one another what was best to do, and finally deciding that they'd arrange first where they should stay for the night and leave the call on Vera's father and mother until later. She needs rest, the doctor had said, and it would be better not to tell them immediately.

On his way to the house near the quay — a house owned by an island woman who had settled on the mainland — he bought

242

a cheap razor and some soap, and with Sarah still crying and accusing herself for not having persuaded Vera to stay at home he begged her not to speak of that again.

'You did your best. Everyone did and there's no use blaming anyone or anybody. Nothing happens by chance, and if she had stayed something worse might have befallen her. She has doctors here and every attention — you must look at it that way, Sarah.'

The house overlooked the sea and in the small room with a fire in the grate they saw the darkness press tight against the window and the dark pane reflect the oil-lamp on the tea-table. The wind was falling but the sea outside was loud and fretful, booming into the small room like distant thunder. They took their meal in heavy silence, and as soon as they were finished they didn't rest but set out again to the back of the town where Vera's people lived.

Sarah, who knew the house, led him up a cobbled one-way street where the lighted blinds in the windows held the shadows of a plant in a pot or hunched bird in a cage. It was the mother who opened the door and she brought them at once into the red-painted kitchen. Vera's father was bent over the fire in his shirt sleeves reading a newspaper, and because he was hard of hearing his wife had to raise her voice to make herself understood: 'This is Vera's husband I'm telling you. The islandman she married second time.'

'You're welcome,' he said, putting a rough-edged magnifying glass in his waistcoat pocket. 'She didn't come herself?'

His wife had to shout again, and shook her head at Sarah as much as to say that's the way I'm bothered.

'Oh, she's in hospital,' he said, 'that's bad — that's bad news. And what be the matter with her?' he added, putting away his paper and buttoning his waistcoat.

'Her little girl's in the hospital too. The both of them's in the hospital,' the mother said.

'Is it fever?' he asked, and he looked up at his wife and then at Martin and Sarah seated on the sofa. Martin nudged Sarah to explain it to them.

'Well I never heard the like of that!' the mother answered. 'But she was always headstrong — always wanting her own way. Could you not have slipped off without her?'

'Nothing would do her but come with Mary,' Sarah said.

'And what good could she do to a child with an appendix! She's got herself in a nice fix now. The seldom time she comes across she could have stayed where she was for this once. She'll be a wiser girl when she's over this. Did she tell yez to call here?'

'She did. She was to come over to see you and bring Mary but she never got the chance,' Martin said and felt his face reddening.

'Although I'm her mother I'll say she had always an odd way with her. She was never a great caller at any time. But she should have told us about her marriage,' the mother went on, combing her hair at a small mirror on the wall. The father got up from his chair and she handed him his coat that was hanging on a nail on the back of the door. 'We'll run up for a minute or two, Jack,' she said, 'and these people will come with us.'

The door of the hospital was closed and through the opaque glass panels there shone a greenish light. Martin rang the bell and heard it sound down the corridor. Sarah shuddered audibly with the cold and he rang again, and presently there was a jingle of keys and the door was opened slightly by the porter.

'Oh, you're the people from the island. Step in a minute till I see if anything can be done,' he said, opening the door wide.

It was warm inside, the windows covered with mist, and brass pots with green plants in them arranged outside each ward. After the porter had gone off, the stillness and quietness of the corridor quelled their inclination to talk, and they stood bunched together round the door they had entered. A nurse came towards them and none of them moved forward to meet her.

'She's sleeping now and you better come back tomorrow,' the nurse said to them.

'Could we not look at her just for a wee minute?' the mother pleaded.

'I'm sorry. The patients are all settled down for the night. Come back early in the morning. She's sleeping and you might disturb her.'

'And the little girl — how's she?' Martin asked.

The nurse hesitated: 'She's being operated on at once. But you needn't worry — we've plenty of cases like that every week. You could leave me your address in town. We always like to have it just in case of emergency.'

Outside in the street the mother offered to put them up for the night: 'We haven't a great deal of room. But you could sleep on the sofa and the lady could sleep with my other daughter. You'd be very welcome.'

Martin thanked her and explained that they had already settled up in a house at the quay. 'But we'll call to see you before we go back to the island . . . And when Vera's better you'll come across some day soon to see us.'

'We're not great sailors but maybe we'll manage that,' she said, as she linked her husband by the arm and bade them good night.

'They're quiet inoffensive people,' Martin said to Sarah as they went up to the church on the hill. 'For some reason Vera didn't get on well with them.'

'That used to worry my mother in the old days, and she was never done picking at Tom to do something about it. He did nothing and then one day she tackled Vera and was told quite sharply to mind her own business. She ceased talking about it after that.'

'It's all very strange,' Martin said, recalling his own weary efforts.

The church inside was dark except for the red sanctuary lamp

245

suspended from the ceiling and the wavering lights from the candelabra round Our Lady's altar. He knelt in a seat near the back and Sarah moved up the aisle to the altar rails. He sat quite still, drooped his arms over the seat and stared in front of him, trying to concentrate on his few simple prayers. But his mind was empty, dazed by the sleepless night and the journey on the boat, and as he found himself swaying and tilting into a hollow well of thoughtless space he jerked himself awake and listened to a squall of wind thumping against the windows and heaving against the granite walls of the church. He closed his eyes and thanked God for their safe landing at the quay, but as he strove to pray for their quick recovery the thoughts of the hospital held fast his mind, and the forlorn rattle of pennies that Sarah dropped in an offering box drew his attention. He watched her light two candles, affix them in the pronged sockets of the brass candelabra, kneel erect at the altar rails and cross herself with slow, fervent concentration. He sat up to wait for her, shut his eyes from the reflection of candlelight on the varnished seats and folded his arms. He wakened when she touched him on the shoulder, and lifting his cap he genuflected and went out with her.

'I can't pray and I can't think,' he said, 'and I don't believe I can feel. It seems days ago that we landed at the quay.'

'You're wore out and you need sleep. We should be thankful to God we came the time we did. Another hour, I heard them say in the house, and we couldn't have landed. When this is over we'll have to see about getting that quay deepened. Vera was never done talking about it.'

'It'll not be her worry any more. We're going away. It's only when you're hurt yourself by some fault outside your control you begin to look for a remedy. She knew the danger there was at this side and that's why she came out with us.'

'Ah, Martin, after your trouble is over you'll see things brighter and you'll not leave—you needn't think things like that.'

They reached the end of the road and turned left where the

houses faced the mouth of the sea. Shop windows were lighted, and on the red blinds of the public houses could be seen the shadow of whisky bottles. He told her to go on to the house and he'd follow later, as the sleep had gone off him. She gripped his arm and besought him not to take any drink.

'I just want to walk round and tire myself before turning in,' he said.

'You'll not touch the drink, Martin?'

'I won't!' he said and buttoned up his coat. 'I won't — that's my solemn word. I'll not be long after you.' He rubbed his hands, looked up at the drift of stars among the pathways of the clouds, and hurried away past the warm windows of the pubs.

He passed the deserted seats that overlooked the tennis courts and crossed the wooden bridge where its wet planks gleamed in the starlight and trembled in the flood of mountain water that burled under it on its way to the sea. Its wire supports hummed in the wind and drowned the noise of the trees around the golf course, and coming on to the sand he gazed seawards across the jabbling water that strangled the light from the stars. Out in front of him was the black mound of the island with its white cliffs at one end and above them a solitary light from a house, and it seemed to him as if he were looking at a big black whale. The backbone of the hills stood out against the flashes of light from the East lighthouse and he sensed among the permanence of the flashes the coming break with his own home. He'd go away — he'd hold tight to his word; and maybe if Mary would live and his own child would live they'd be able to make a better home away from it.

He trudged on over the extent of sand, his feet crackling in the limpet shells, and the taste of salt on his mouth. A spot of rain against his cheek made him turn and he was surprised to see how far he had wandered from the bunched lights of the town. He put up the collar of his coat and hurried back through the rain. Sarah was standing at the door looking out for him and as she stepped into the light from the hallway she felt the shoulders of his coat, took it from him and draped it over a chair at the kitchen range.

In bed he fell asleep at once, but wakened quite fresh and was surprised to hear the clock below him strike the hour of two. It was dark in the room but outside the wind had fallen and the sea breathed easily. He was about to light his pipe when he heard a knock at the front door and looking out of the window saw a policeman, the lamp of his bicycle shining on the wet pavement.

'Is it a message from the hospital?' Martin asked.

'It is. Are you Martin Gallagher? They'd like you to come up – your child is very sick,' the policeman said.

He hurried downstairs, and Sarah who had slept in a room on the ground floor was already dressed.

'I just lay on top of the bed,' she said. 'Something told me we'd be needed. I didn't like the way the nurse took the address.'

Ahead of them on the deserted road they saw the swaying light of the policeman's bicycle, and on reaching the hospital the porter seated beside a radiator in the corridor was awaiting them. In Mary's ward there was a screen round her bed and some of the other patients were propped against their pillows and praying with rosary beads in their hands. A nurse was holding a lighted candle in Mary's hand and as Martin and Sarah knelt down at the bedside she leaned forward and closed the already sightless eyes. The nurse nodded her head sadly towards them and blew out the candle.

'If she'd been here a day sooner she would have got over it,' the nurse said to them.

'Ah, God, it would have been better if we had stayed on the island,' Sarah cried. 'She would have died at home. We'd all have been with her – her mother and grandmother and Pat and myself and everybody. . . .'

In the corridor they whispered together with the nurse, wondering if it would be wise to tell her mother.

'The priest will be on his rounds early and I'll leave it in his hands,' the nurse said kindly. 'I'll explain everything to him.'

'Let him leave it as late as possible,' Martin said. 'The longer we wait the better.'

'He'll know what's best himself,' Sarah put in.

Outside they walked in the middle of the road through the dark silent streets of the town.

'Poor Mary,' he said, 'I loved that child as if she were my very own. God be good to her!' and his lips quivered, and in the darkness his tears flowed freely. They walked slowly, each of them gathering some bleak consolation from the noise and movement of their own footsteps.

'This will kill Vera,' he sighed. 'She lived for her; she made her own life move round her — God knows she did.'

'My own mother will take it badly,' Sarah said. 'She'll grieve and fret over it but she has a way of accepting these things that is beyond me. I'll never be like my own mother — never. Everyone in the island is a child of hers — everyone. But somehow Mary was her pet, and after his death it was Mary she talked of most and not Tom — I thought that strange. But old people have queer ways and see things differently from us.'

'If we'd taken her across a day sooner she'd have been all right, the nurse said to me. But she never complained of any pain until the day before yesterday. And our own nurse lost no time after she examined her.'

'Somehow, Martin, it was all to be. It's God's will.'

The greyness was now lifting from the sea, and over the hills of the island stretched the yellow scarf of the dawn. Since they had so much to arrange there'd be no sense in going to bed and so they sat in the small parlour until the early sun glittered forth and the first milk van roused the street. An alarm clock buzzed in the room above them and the landlady rose and made them their breakfast.

Martin wired to Pat to come across with the boat, and when he had that off his hands he arranged with an undertaker about the coffin and once more climbed the hill to the hospital. The screen was still round Vera's bed but she didn't hear him enter, for her eyes were closed, her hands loose upon the quilt and the gold wedding ring bright upon her finger.

She had had a long night, and during her wide awakefullness her thoughts ran free and, against her will, the past lurched forward and packed itself tight before her without gap or chink, and she was forced to abandon herself to it and follow it into the repellent places it had led her: she had lived for the future, for herself and for Mary, and all that she had hoped and lived for was breaking up like a spent wave at her feet. She had done nothing for anyone; she had turned her back on her own people; she had broken Tom's heart, and out of some viciousness in her nature she had sunk the little yacht which was his pride. There was nothing in her soul but sourness — the sourness of an unwashed churn. She had placed faith in nothing only her own self and her own strong will — and now that, too, was breaking up. How could anyone have loved her? What had she done to make Martin love her? — she didn't know. And now his child that lay in her womb no longer stirred. She'd deserve to lose it — to lose everything. God — if she could live it again! Her body had shuddered as if from an icy wind but her feet touching the hot jar drew her mind to the bed she lay on and to a dim light that reflected on the grey ceiling above her. Her head had heaved as if she was on the boat again, and time and again she had felt the urge to cry out but controlled herself. To lie still, to lie still — maybe if she'd do that she'd feel once more the tremorings of her unborn child and live to see Mary nurse it for her and take it out to the swing in the garden. She had dozed then but somehow the movements and quick pad of feet out in the corridor had sharpened her senses with dread for Mary. And that morning when the ward had wakened to the sound of cutlery being rattled down on trays a nurse had hurried to her with a thermometer, took her temperature, and to the simple question Vera had put to her she had evaded it by saying she was only on duty and would find out. And later when a priest had come slowly to the inside of the screen she had already guessed what it was he had to tell her. She had wept silently and made her confession, and when he had told her that we are all in God's hands and that we are not the measure of all things she had remembered that the same had been said to her after Tom's death. With her eyes closed she was still pondering on these words when Martin touched her hand.

She grasped his hand with her two hands and looked at him steadily: 'I've been told all, Martin,' and she shook her head upon her black hair that was loose upon the pillow. 'I wish I were on my feet and could help you. You've done all you could do and nobody, not even her own father, could have done better. She didn't suffer. Ah, Martin, I've had a long night and I sensed that this would happen. I didn't deserve to have her. I wasn't good to her.'

'No, Vera, you mustn't say that.'

'I turned her against all that her father loved. And now I am having my reward!'

'You did your very best for her.'

She shook her head and sobbed. He had no handkerchief and he lifted the corner of the quilt and wiped her tears.

'I was spoiled. I was bitter and heartless, but if God allows me to live a while I'll try to undo it all. My father and mother called a short while ago. They were kind to me and I don't deserve it. I want to live, and yet I haven't strength to raise myself on the pillow. I lived for what was to come and in my foolishness didn't know that this was it. No, Martin, we must live each day as best we can and not wait for the great days to come. The days are here but we do not live them because they're not the kind we want. We cry out against them, and before long the years are upon us and we are still preparing to live. We must do our best, enjoy our bit of home and our bit of life now. To live for the future is to live for the fog. Now's the time — now!'

'We'll go away, Vera, the two of us . . . We'll go away.'

'We can't, Martin; we take it all with us . . . We can't run away from our own selves . . . Bury her with her own father . . . Maybe I'll be allowed to live and . . .' Her voice suddenly broke and her lips trembled.

He looked round and seeing nothing but the screen behind him he lifted her hand and pressed it to his lips: 'You'll get well, Vera, and we'll have our child. I know we will! I'll not leave you and I'll be back again this evening. I'll cross in the morning for the funeral, but I'll come back here after it. I'll not leave this town until you're leaving with me. Do you hear me, Vera? We'll be leaving it together — the two of us.'

That afternoon the boat came for Mary, and that night the coffin lay in the island chapel. In the morning, after Mass, they buried her beside her own father.

Martin returned to the mainland, and each day he called at the hospital, and after each visit he thought he saw some improvement in her. She pleaded with him to go back home until she was ready to leave. She had her mother and father, her brothers and sister to keep her company, she told him, and he had nothing but the cold idleness of a strange town. He didn't heed her, and each day he brought her fruit, despite her protests that she had to give it away, and piled it on the small table beside her bed.

But one morning when he arrived and saw the white-capped heads of three nurses above the bed-screen he sensed that something was wrong and he halted in the middle of the ward, clutching his bag of oranges. The staring patients in the ward discomfited him and he turned away and stood about in the

252

corridor, awaiting the departure of the nurses. His face reddened when one of them approached, advising him to make his visit as short as possible this morning. He scarcely heard what she was saying to him, but once he was securely hidden behind the bed-screen he breathed easily, and Vera noticing the heightened colour in his cheeks told him he shouldn't be hurrying for she wouldn't leave without him or, for that matter, run off with the young doctor. Her little jokes made him feel that her health was improving; but, when he left the bag of fruit on the table, the weary lift of her hand and the slow reproving shake of her head wrested that feeling from his mind.

To keep him from asking the question she did not want to hear and did not want to answer, she gathered her strength and plied him with questions on how he spent his time about the town. He stayed mostly with the boatmen around the quay, he explained, or with the islandmen whenever they were across, and on fair days mixed amongst the farmers, trying to spot Jamesy or find out where he was now hired.

'And have you found out yet?' she asked, and closed her eyes.

'He had to leave the place he was in. Himself and another fellow pinched a bicycle.'

With her eyes closed she shook her head slowly, and her lack of strength and interest prevented her from saying what was in her mind — that there never was any good in the same Jamesy!

'And where is he now?' she forced herself to say, and heard his voice dwindling far away from her.

'I heard he was somewhere in Tyrone. But he'll grow up all right if the other playboy isn't near him,' and he stopped speaking and remembered the stolen ashtray and the bits of it he had discovered in the dunghill when forking dung out to the fields.

Vera seemed to be sleeping. He stared at her with pained pity; her face was colourless, her eye-lids a dark brown, and

253

her black hair combed back from her forehead. His lips quivered
and he touched her hand. She opened her eyes slightly and
closed them again.

'You're wore out, Vera girl. I'll go and let you sleep. Keep
well, Vera. Everything all right?'

She nodded a yes and a no, and as he tiptoed away from the
bed her tears flowed freely: she hadn't to tell him what she already
knew — that there was no hope for their unborn child.

At the head of the ward a nurse met him: 'I was just going
for you, Mister Gallagher. Your wife needs complete rest.
There may be a slight operation. But she'll pull through all
right. Don't worry now — you'll have her home with you in a
week or two.'

'I wasn't told about an operation. Will it be today?'

'I don't know. Perhaps, there mightn't be one at all. It's
the doctors that decide these things. But don't worry now like
a good man.'

They were hiding something from him — he was sure of
that! Ah, God in Heaven, why didn't they speak out straight
and tell him the truth! Over and over again he repeated that
to himself as he walked away from the hospital and wandered
on a strange road that led into the hills at the back of the town.
Whatever else he would do he would keep away from the drink.
He spoke to farmers, noted the fine healthy land, and found
himself in the district where Jamesy used to be hired. One or two
remembered the lad but no one knew for certain where he had
gone.

Returning to the town Martin saw his landlady standing at the
door; she had been on the look-out for him — there was an
urgent message for him from the hospital.

'It's the end!' he said as he hurried away from her. At the
hospital gate he met Vera's mother and father on their way
out. The mother looked at him and cried: 'You're too late, son,
and so were we.'

'It was wrong done to let her come across with you,' the father said.

'Don't talk like that, Jack,' the mother spoke aloud. 'Vera had a will of her own. Once her mind was made up, no one could turn her — I know that well. I don't blame you, son, or blame anyone. . . .'

The following morning the boat came for them. Jimmy Neil was there, and Pat, and they helped Martin and her father and her two brothers to carry the coffin over the uneven stones of the mainland quay. The boat moved out into the bright sunshine. The sea was calm. The island hills were topped with light and skirted with shadow. It seemed quite close to them, and as they entered the bay the reflections of the white cliffs in the water bent like rubber in the widening ripples from the boat. The bleating of the lambs waded across the noiseless water. Martin could see the people moving out from the white houses down to the pier and he suddenly thought of the day the Craigs were leaving and how the island people had mourned them.

He stretched his hand into the water and dabbed his forehead. Jimmy Neil put the tyre-fenders athwart the gunwale and began to coil the dry mooring rope.

'You'll stay with me tonight, Jimmy?' Martin said to him.

'I will surely, Martin.'

'Tomorrow I'll move up to the house on the hill again. The house in the hollow is yours and Sarah's any time you want to move into it. You'll not forget that!'

The boat's engine stopped and she glided in. Jimmy threw the rope to those on the quay; it was caught, slipped through an iron ring and held fast.